LOVE AND DUTY AT BLACKBERRY FARM

BLACKBERRY FARM SERIES - BOOK THREE

ROSIE CLARKE

Boldwood

First published in Great Britain in 2023 by Boldwood Books Ltd.

Copyright © Rosie Clarke, 2023

Cover Design by Colin Thomas

Cover Photography: Colin Thomas and Alamy

A CIP catalogue record for this book is available from the British Library.

Paperback ISBN 978-1-80415-752-7

Large Print ISBN 978-1-80415-753-4

Hardback ISBN 978-1-80415-751-0

Ebook ISBN 978-1-80415-755-8

Kindle ISBN 978-1-80415-754-1

Audio CD ISBN 978-1-80415-746-6

MP3 CD ISBN 978-1-80415-747-3

Digital audio download ISBN 978-1-80415-748-0

Boldwood Books Ltd
23 Bowerdean Street
London SW6 3TN
www.boldwoodbooks.com

1

Artie Talbot stood looking across the flat sweep of low-lying land, covered just now in heavy snow. Cold and crisp, it clung to trees, hedges, and bushes – a blanket of undulating white on the rich dark earth beneath. There would be no work in the fields for a while now after the big snow storm of the previous day and night. It was January 1942 and like the snow, the terrible war had taken a grip on them all. In December the previous year, Japan had bombed Pearl Harbour, which meant that America had now entered the war. Everyone said it would help to stem the tide of German advances, but as yet nothing much had happened to make Artie think the war was coming to an end. Bombs had recently inflicted death and injury in Liverpool and the conflict was still raging elsewhere; as far as he could see, it was likely to drag on for years yet.

Cupping his winter-reddened hands to light a cigarette, Artie reflected on the past months of trauma his family had endured. First, Tom Gilbert, his elder half-brother, was reported missing and then injured, now thankfully he was recovered and back at work in the army as a training instructor, and then John, his younger brother... For a time, they'd all thought he was lost for good, but he was found in a military hospital in Portsmouth, badly injured, both physically and mentally, as far as they could tell from the telegram they'd received. He'd been hurt when his plane went down over Europe, in German-held territory, but was thankfully alive and recovering at last after months of uncertainty.

Artie frowned as he thought of the other tragedy, the murder of John's girlfriend – Faith Goodjohn. The murderer was unknown but believed to be her uncle, a man Artie had never trusted or liked. If what seemed likely had happened, Ralph had attacked Faith brutally, causing her to give birth to John's son alone and in awful pain, only to die of her injuries before anyone could reach her.

It was that terrible death that had cast a shadow over the family, though his poor mother, Pam, had done her best to give them a good Christmas. It hadn't been easy for her, but, somehow, they'd had a big cockerel for dinner, followed by a suet pudding with treacle and tinned fruit from his father's secret hoard in the attics of the ancient farmhouse. His mother had taken charge of the baby, delighting in her new grandchild, and helped by Artie's younger sister, Susan, and Lizzie, Tom's wife. It was the joy of the baby's survival that had brought them through a time of grief. Lizzie was pregnant herself and said it was good practice for when her child was born, which wouldn't be long now.

Artie frowned as he thought about John's child. He'd ragged his brother unmercifully about being a virgin, but now he was a father – and the father of a motherless child. What would that do to his brother? Artie could only imagine the pain it would cause when they told him about Faith's terrible death. His father had declared that John should not be told for the time being.

'Give him time to recover from his wounds first,' Arthur Talbot had instructed them when they'd discussed it. 'When we do tell him, it has to be the truth, so keep it to yourselves if you write to him. If Faith had given birth in the normal way and lived, the news of his son would have given him an incentive to get better – but how do you tell a man that the woman he loves was murdered?'

They'd all shaken their heads over it, none of them having the answer. Yet Artie was uneasy with keeping the secret from John. In his shoes, he'd want to know he had a son – or at least, he thought he would. God, he couldn't think what he'd do if something like that had happened to Jeanie Salmons.

Jeanie was one of their land girls, a vivacious, pretty girl with flame-red hair. She had been with them from the start of the war, when Tom first went off to join the army. They'd had a couple of other land girls since, but they hadn't stayed long. A new girl was arriving any day now, though at this time of the year, with weather this bad, there wasn't much for them to do. The animals had to be tended, of course, but he and Jeanie managed the milking between them. It was only when the real work of ploughing, planting and then harvesting began that they needed another pair of hands.

The land demanded attention if it was to produce the food the nation needed; it was hard, slogging work at times and men who tended it were often tied to it for life by both duty and a kind of love. At the moment, Artie had a love/hate relationship with the land; he felt it his duty to make sure his father's farm didn't suffer because Tom was away serving in the army, and yet there was something within him that made him resent the duty that bound him and he could not quite suppress a feeling of bitterness that he couldn't join his brothers in the fight to keep the country safe.

Shaking off his mood of depression, Artie turned back towards his tractor. No way was he going to work on the land today, but the huge tyres on the tractor were better on ungritted roads than his father's car. He'd come down to the low-lying fen land in Sutton to check on some pigs that were kept well away from the farm and, having fed and watered them, he could go home for breakfast and a warm by the fire. Since even the ditches were frozen, he would ask his mother what jobs she needed doing in the house. It was on days like this that door hinges got repaired and ceilings were whitewashed.

Throwing his cigarette into the snow – the third of the morning; he was smoking too much – and squaring his shoulders, he trudged back to the tractor and started it, the thought of hot fried potatoes with an egg, or perhaps some streaky bacon if he was lucky, warming him already.

His tractor chugged steadily up the steep lane, so thick with ice it would have been impossible for a car, reaching the top in time to see a car go sliding across the road into the hedge and the ditch on the far side. Artie drove the tractor across the road; it was like a sheet of glass beneath the top coating of white. He saw the woman at the wheel looking shocked and pale, and dismounted, going to peer down at her.

'Don't worry, I'll get you out,' he said and slid down the steep side of the ditch on his bottom. Luckily, the car looked almost undamaged, apart from a few scratches, and the side door opened easily to his wiry strength. The woman was young and looked upset as he reached in and grabbed her, lifting her clear and pulling her out. He helped her to gain the top of the slippery ditch and then rescued her bag from the passenger seat, before scrambling out after her. His trousers were wet through but his waxed jacket had kept his top half dry. 'That was a bit of luck; that ditch is very deep, but the snow must have stopped the car sinking to the bottom. You're not hurt, are you?'

'Just shaken,' she said. 'I drove over from Cambridge, but it was a terrible journey. The main roads were not too bad, but these country ones are different. Besides, I learned to drive in the summer and I'm not used to icy roads. I'm looking for a farm near here somewhere, but I got a bit lost; it was foggy back there...'

'You're in Sutton, at the top of Painter's Lane. Where did you want to go?'

'Blackberry Farm in Mepal,' she said. 'I must have missed the turning somewhere.'

'I can take you on the tractor. I'm Artie Talbot – my father is Arthur Talbot—'

'Really?' She looked at him incredulously, as if she wasn't sure whether to believe him. 'I'm Annie Salmons – Jeanie's sister. I got an unexpected home leave and I've been seconded to Addenbrooke's Hospital in Cambridge for a while, so I thought I would grab the chance to visit her, before I start back to work.'

'Good grief!' Artie was astonished. He stared at her in disbelief. 'You don't look a bit like her.'

Annie laughed. 'I know. Jeanie is different to the rest of us – Mum says she's a throwback to her granny, who was a redhead. I look more like my dad, so they say.'

'Can you climb up on the tractor?' Artie asked. 'It is too far for you to walk. I'll take you home, have breakfast and then I'll come and see if a couple of chaps I know will help get your car out of the dyke.'

'It isn't my car; it belongs to a friend,' Annie said. 'He is one of the doctors at Addenbrooke's and warned me to drive carefully. I hope I haven't done too much damage.'

'Not your fault – that road is a sheet of ice,' Artie told her.

'Except that it was a bit daft to be driving on roads like these in the first place.'

'Yes, I know. As I told you, in Cambridge, the roads looked fine and they were, but it is a different story when you leave the main road.' She eyed the tractor doubtfully but managed to climb into the cab with him.

'I'm afraid you'll have to stand behind me,' Artie said. 'There's only one seat and I don't think you'd better drive. Just hold on to the struts, or me if you prefer. Sorry it's such rough transport, but if I left you standing until we got the car out, you'd be frozen.'

'I'll be fine,' Annie assured him. 'I'm used to rough travel where I've been, but it was quite a bit warmer out there.' She gave a little shiver.

Artie nodded. 'Jeanie says you've been nursing at a field hospital somewhere?'

'Yes...' She smiled at him. 'We don't talk about it a lot, but it was hot and dry and hard work, though it had its rewards. I had a nasty fever over Christmas. That's why they sent me home for a rest.'

'Perhaps you shouldn't have tried driving yet,' Artie said, but she didn't answer.

After that, he didn't attempt to make conversation, just told her to hang on tight as he started the engine. Jeanie was used to travelling this way, sometimes hanging on in the cab with him and at other times riding in a trailer at the back, but he wasn't sure her sister was ready for the bumpy ride and the cold bite of the wind as it blew through the cab. He was lucky to have a cab at all, Tom's old Ferguson didn't have one, but then they were used to all weathers on the farm and this girl wasn't used to the cold yet.

He risked a glance over his shoulder as he approached the

crossroads to turn off down the Witcham Road that led to Mepal village. It was the long way round, but there was no quick way now they'd closed the road that had once led through farmland and had been taken for an aerodrome. Even as he cursed the inconvenience, he heard a plane take off and fly straight over their heads; it was followed by several more. Artie wondered briefly where they were going and then forgot them. His mother and Lizzie sometimes went to lie in the ditches at night and count them in and out, worrying when they didn't all get back, but Artie didn't bother. For a while, he'd felt out of things, stuck on the farm, half envious of the adventures his brothers were experiencing, but then, both Tom and John had been wounded and he'd decided he was better off where he was, though sometimes he felt guilty for being the one to stay home while his brothers went off to fight. His father said they were fighting the war in their own way, because without the farmers the nation would starve. He was right of course.

It had never seemed a longer journey home, because Artie was conscious that he had Jeanie's sister behind him and he felt every bump in the road for her, though she didn't cry out or make a sound. She must be freezing cold back there and it wasn't an ideal way to travel after her slide into the ditch, even though it hadn't hurt her or the car much. He just hoped she wouldn't catch her death of cold.

At last, he drew into the farmyard and stopped the engine. He turned to look at her. She was shaking and pale, so he reached out and lifted her down, looking into her face. She was quite pretty, but not as bright and lively as Jeanie, he decided.

'You're frozen,' he said as he felt her hands. She didn't even have gloves on. 'I'll get you inside. Mum will look after you.' He took her arm to assist her, but she shook her head.

'I'm all right. I can walk...' Annie said, but her teeth were chattering.

'Come on, I don't want you slipping over on the ice,' he said and grabbed her arm firmly. 'Jeanie would have my guts for garters if I let you come to harm.'

Annie didn't say any more as he guided her over ground that was uneven and, in some places, very icy where the mud holes were filled with frozen water.

Pushing open the kitchen door, Artie released her into the warmth and comfort of the big old kitchen with its smells of wood burning, spices, herbs and cooking. His mother was at the stove. She turned to him with a smile and a greeting and then glanced at the young woman.

'So who is this then?' she asked.

'It's Annie – Jeanie's sister. She got lost in the fog and went into a ditch at the top of Painter's Lane. I brought her home on the tractor and she is frozen.'

'Oh my lord! Are you all right, love? Not hurt?' Pam cried in shock and horror. 'Fancy letting her ride on that thing in this weather!'

'Well, I couldn't get the car out alone and I couldn't let her stand there and freeze to death.' Artie frowned. 'What else was I to do?'

'I am all right, Mrs Talbot, no cuts or broken bones,' Annie said. 'I'm sorry to arrive like this, but I only have a few days' leave and then I'll be working in Addenbrooke's until they send me abroad again.'

'Come and sit down and have some toast and a cup of tea,' Pam said, her worn but still attractive face wreathed in smiles of welcome. 'Get warm by the fire for a few moments first. You look so cold, Annie. I am sorry you haven't had a better welcome to our home.'

'Your son has been very kind,' Annie said, glancing at him as Pam handed him a plate heaped with fried bubble and squeak and an egg.

'No bacon for any of us today,' she apologised. 'The hens aren't laying well either in this weather. I'm afraid the best I have to offer you, Annie, is a piece of toast with a little farm butter and homemade jam. I have to feed the men and Jeanie first as they do the hard work.'

'That is more than enough,' Annie said quickly. 'I don't expect you to feed me, Mrs Talbot.'

'Oh, I shall have enough pie to go round for lunch,' Pam assured her. 'I can make the meat stretch, but I rely on my hens for eggs. They don't like this bitter weather. I might have to bring some of them inside to warm them up.'

At that moment, the door opened and Jeanie entered, her face red from the cold, though she was well wrapped in scarves, a woollen hat, gloves and wellington boots over her slacks. 'It is you!' she cried, delight in her voice and her eyes. 'I saw Artie draw up and help a woman down from the tractor. I thought it looked like you but couldn't believe it!'

'I was ill over Christmas so they sent me home for a rest,' Annie said and rushed to meet her. They embraced and hugged and kissed, laughing excitedly. 'I'm working at Addenbrooke's for a few months and then they will send me abroad again – at least I think so...'

'Does Mum know you're home?' Jeanie demanded. 'She didn't tell me...'

'No. I haven't told her yet,' Annie replied. 'I know she'll want me home if she learns I've been ill. I've got a few days' leave before I start at the hospital, so I thought I'd visit you first and then Mum – I thought we might go up to London together? If you can be spared?'

'I'm not sure. I'll ask Mr Talbot when he gets in,' Jeanie said. 'Oh, I forgot, Pam. He has gone down the road to help unfreeze Mrs Jacobs' water. She only has an outside tap in that old cottage and it froze last night.'

'I wondered where he was,' Pam said. She looked at Artie who had finished his breakfast and was drinking his mug of tea. 'What are you doing today apart from rescuing Annie's car?'

'Did you have an accident?' Jeanie demanded.

'Just a gentle slide,' Annie assured her. 'I'm fine, love, don't worry.'

'Good.' Jeanie accepted a plate of fried bubble and squeak with an egg from Pam and sat down. 'Do you want some of this, Annie?'

'This is fine,' Annie assured her as Pam slid a plate of hot toast, spread with a little butter and margarine, and thick blackberry jam. 'I'm going to enjoy this, thanks, Mrs Talbot.'

Jeanie tucked into her food, clearly hungry.

Artie bent over her and whispered something in her ear, which made her glance up and laugh, and then looked at his mother. 'As soon as the car is out, I'll be back if you've got any jobs for me?'

'I want some bits fetching down from the attic,' Pam said. 'If you feel like it, you can mend my mincer. It has clogged up somewhere again and needs taking apart. Oh, and there's the door handle on Tom's old room; it has come loose again.'

Artie grinned. He'd known there would be a string of little jobs when his mother got started. She would think of half a dozen more by the time he got home, but it was better than being outside on a cold day. He didn't relish the ride back to Sutton in the draughty tractor or the task ahead, but knew it was down to him to get Annie's borrowed car from the ditch. Someone in the village would lend a hand, despite the weather... He would see if it could be driven back here if the roads improved later, otherwise he'd have to tow it to the garage in the village.

'See you all later then,' he said, shrugged on his waxed jacket, then picked up his waterproof leggings, pulled the woollen hat down over his ears and went out. His trousers had more or less dried by the fire, but there was no point in changing them because he would get soaked again rescuing the car.

He smiled to himself as he climbed into the tractor seat. Jeanie had looked thrilled to see her sister. It would be nice for her to have the company. She was a lovely girl, his Jeanie. Artie thought of her as his, though as yet he hadn't got round to asking her to marry him. For the moment, he was content to take her out and kiss her goodnight, but maybe he should think about putting a ring on her finger...

2

'So, Jeanie went off to London with her sister, then?' Arthur said that evening as they settled in front of the fire. The scuttle was filled with logs Artie had chopped to save on coal and coke while the Betteshanger miners' strike continued in the Kent coalfield. Some folk who relied on coal were going short, but on the farm, they had plenty of wood, because Artie had stacked a big pile when a tree had come down in the winter storms. 'Just as well we're not in the middle of harvest, I suppose.'

'Don't grumble, love.' Pam Talbot looked at her husband affectionately. He looked a stern old thing, but underneath he was a softie. 'She works hard when there is work to be done. Yes, I know she had time off at Christmas to see her mum, but she asked and I said yes, so that's it.' She didn't often lay down the law, but when Pam said something Arthur listened.

Arthur nodded. 'What did Artie have to say about it? He'll be doing her job until she comes back, as well as his own – not that there is much land work he can do in this weather. He can't even clear ditches; they are frozen hard.'

'I know. The yard was like a skating rink when I went across to the hens. They're not liking it, Arthur. Just four eggs between the lot of them this morning.'

'Put them in the scullery,' he suggested. 'It's warmer there. I'll bring a bit of straw in for them and a cardboard box. They can nest down there; it is what my granny used to do and she always had eggs.'

'Yes, I know. I was thinking of the baby. I sometimes leave him in his cot by the range and go upstairs for a moment. I don't want hens flying up and sitting on his face.' John's child was mostly referred to as the baby; he hadn't been christened yet, because it should be his father's choice to name him.

Arthur contemplated his pipe for a moment. 'Mebbe I could fix a little gate across the door to the scullery so if the door gets left open, they can't wander straight in.' His stern-looking face softened. 'How is the little lad then?'

'He's doing well,' Pam assured him and smiled in pleasure. It was a delight to have her son's baby to care for, though she would much rather his mother had been here, too. She would have enjoyed teaching Faith how to care for her baby, but she felt blessed to have him and was so relieved Faith's mother wasn't interested in taking him. From what she'd heard, the unfortunate woman spent most of her life in bed, though whether from grief or illness she wasn't sure. Faith's father visited his grandson now and then, but seldom mentioned his wife. 'We're lucky to have him, Arthur. When I think how he was born and his poor mother dying all alone...' She was silent for a moment. 'I wish they'd got to her Uncle Ralph before he died in that car accident. He should have paid for his crimes!'

'I've told you not to think of it,' Arthur said, shaking his head at her. 'It does no good, love. We can't bring the poor lass back and it wasn't your fault. I know it's there at your shoulder all the time; it's the same for all of us. I think even Artie was affected by it, though he can seem a cold one if you don't know him. He asked me if I thought Faith would've died if she'd given birth in the naturally rather than after being brutally attacked by her uncle. I told him no. She was a normal healthy girl and should have been fine.'

'He's been worrying over what John will think,' Pam agreed. 'I believe he half blames himself. He was in the cowshed milking while that was happening only a few yards away. I told him none of us could have guessed something like that would happen. Do you know what he said to me?' Arthur shook his head. 'He asked me whether John would believe that we were all here and yet could do nothing to save her?'

'He thinks John will blame us?' Arthur frowned. 'How could he? It was the act of an unstable man. From what I've been told in confidence, the London police suspect him of being involved in gangland murders.'

'No!' Pam stared at him in horror. 'You don't think of that sort of thing happening round here.' She hesitated for a moment, then, 'Do *you* think John will blame us for not taking better care of her? If I'd only told her to stay here until Lizzie got home...'

'Now then, none of that,' Arthur said and sighed before relighting his pipe. 'You couldn't know that madman was on the loose. Faith was happy with us and she wouldn't have done any different. She was entitled to think she was safe and so were all of us. I am sure John will understand that.'

Pam nodded. She did blame herself sometimes, but knew it was silly. None of them could have prevented it, however much they might wish they could have. 'In time, I know he will come to accept it, but it is going to be so hard for him on top of his injuries.' John had broken his left leg and arm and also had cuts and bruises all over his body, as well as knife wounds to his shoulder and arm, which no one yet understood. John hadn't been able to tell the doctors about what had happened to him thus far, because he was still in and out of a fever. 'I do wish they would let us visit him, Arthur.'

'And if you could – what then?' her husband asked. 'Supposing he asks you about Faith? What will you tell him?'

'I don't know,' Pam said honestly. 'I'm not sure whether it's best to tell him the truth or wait until he is well enough to come home before I explain.'

'Let him recover and I will tell him,' Arthur instructed. 'It would be too hard for you, Pam. You would cry and we mustn't give way to it. John needs time to accept and come to terms with his grief. Besides, they've told us, best not visit until he's well enough to welcome a visit.'

She sighed and accepted what he said. Arthur was usually an easy-going man and like his wife seldom put his foot down, but he had over this and, to tell the truth, she was dreading it. 'I know you're right but—' A little sob escaped her. 'I'm sorry, but I can't help it when I think of how John will feel.'

'It's a hard burden to bear and no mistake,' Arthur agreed. 'We all wish it hadn't happened – but now, let's put it away. We all have to think to the future. It will soon be Lizzie's turn to bear a child. Tom isn't likely to be back for the birth. I am going to suggest that she moves in with us until afterwards.'

'Yes,' Pam smiled her agreement. 'I suggested it to her this morning and she says she will, so I'll be able to keep an eye on her.'

'Good.' Arthur grunted and stood up. 'I don't fancy it, but I must just check on the beasts. Bitter cold night or not, I've always done it and I always shall...'

Pam didn't answer. He always went out for a last walk round, whatever the weather, and didn't need her permission. After he'd gone, she got up to fill a kettle and put it to heat on the stove.

They would go to bed soon now, but she would make a hot drink before they went up and a hot-water bottle would not come amiss. She picked up her knitting, but even as she looked for her place in the pattern, a wail from upstairs summoned her. John's son needed attention. He'd had his bottle before sleeping so she thought it was probably a nappy change.

Smiling, because it was a pleasure to have a young baby in the house again, she went up to his room and over to the cot. It was as she thought, a wet napkin.

'We'll soon have you warm and dry, love,' she told him as she gently lifted him and kissed his soft cheek. 'Your daddy will be home again one day soon, I hope. I wonder what he will make of you, my little darling.'

John would love the child, of course he would. Yet what would he feel when he learned that Faith had died alone and in pain?

Pam shook her head. It didn't bear thinking about, so she wouldn't.

* * *

Arthur stood looking up at the sky. Was that bright light a star he could see in the clear sky or a plane gently winging its way back to base? It seemed to be descending, so it must be one of the Allied planes on its way back from a mission. Every day, the brave lads, who came from as far afield as Australia, New Zealand, Canada and some from America, to join their British friends in the fight and help win this war, were risking their lives in the struggle against what seemed to be the overwhelming might of the Germans. No one had expected the Germans to be quite this strong, but for the moment it seemed that Hitler had the upper hand. Arthur shook his head over it. After the Great

War, they'd all hoped it could never happen again, but it had and once more men were dying in their hundreds and thousands. Such a waste of young lives.

London and all the major industrial cities had suffered too from the intensive bombing. Night after night, the sound of planes and of the ack-ack of guns on the ground could be heard in towns and cities all over the country. Whole streets had been destroyed, innocent women and children left dead or maimed. In the country, they'd got off lightly, though a plane had crashed into the roof of a house in Sutton and there had been a loud bang or two up on the aerodrome, though Arthur didn't think it was a full-on air raid. In some areas of the country, there would be an unused bomb carelessly dropped, causing damage to an outlying building or a home, though the destruction was mainly centred on the cities and the factories or the airfields, but there were too many airfields for them to attack all of them and it hadn't happened here yet. He shuddered as he prayed it never would.

'Keep my family safe,' he said aloud, and rubbed at his chest. Damned indigestion again! 'I've never asked for much, Lord, but I'm asking now. We've suffered enough. That's all. I'm not making any bargains. I've never offered harm to another and hope that counts for something – and I know I am an old fool, talking to the moon.' He shook his head, laughing to himself, but he'd always had a childlike faith in God. It was his habit to talk to the Almighty, but he had mostly thanked Him over the years for all the good things. 'And thank you. I know I am lucky to have my Pam and the children.'

Arthur smiled to himself as he completed his round of the farmyard. Good thing there was no one here to hear him. They would either think he was mad or blaspheming, but he truly wasn't, because his God knew him and they'd always been on easy terms. One day, when the time was right, Arthur would go quite happily to his Maker.

He heard the sound of an engine. Artie had been to visit a friend, to thank him for rescuing Jeanie's sister's borrowed car. It was parked in the yard behind the barn with a blanket over it and would stay there until the girls returned from visiting their mother in London. Hopefully, the weather would have eased off by then so she could drive it safely back to Cambridge and return it to its rightful owner. Unfortunately, the paintwork had become scratched. Artie said some of the damage had occurred as they hauled it out of the ditch, but it was still roadworthy and that was something, he supposed.

'That you, Dad?' Artie said as he got out of his car. 'You should get in in the warm. It's bitter again tonight.'

'Aye, it's cold enough,' his father agreed. 'You get on all right?'

'The roads were a bit slippery coming home.'

'Daft you going out in it,' Arthur muttered. 'I'd be messed up if anything happened to you.'

'I only went as far as Witcham – a couple of miles down the road – and they are gritting it now.' Artie smiled as he approached. 'I hope the girls got home all right. I suppose Jeanie hasn't rung?'

'Not unless it was after I came out,' Arthur replied and chuckled. 'Why don't you ask the girl to marry you, you, daft lump?'

Artie laughed. 'Yeah, I know I am and I will – soon.'

'She's just the sort of girl we need on the farm,' Arthur said. 'A proper farmer's wife she'll be, just right for you – and she likes you, Artie. If you asked her, she might say yes.'

'I will. I hadn't reckoned on getting wed for a few years yet, but I didn't expect to feel like this,' Artie said and lit a cigarette, he offered the pack to his father, but Arthur refused. 'Did you ask Mum as soon as you knew she was the one?'

'She was courting strong when I first saw her – but then he was killed and she was alone with our Tom on the way. She took me then, but I'm not sure she loved me right off...' He looked at Artie. 'I was older than you are though – what is it, twenty-four this year?

Artie nodded. 'Mum thinks the world of you!"

'She does now, I know it.' Arthur smiled contentedly. 'It took her a while, but she got there – Jeanie cares about you. Make sure you don't lose her, lad. She's the one for you.'

'Yes, I agree.' Artie laughed again and gave his father a little shove on his shoulder. 'No need to keep telling me. I'm not daft.'

'You will be if you let her slip through your fingers.' Arthur thought it was what Artie needed to settle him down.

Arthur led the way inside the house. He could smell baby powder and smiled. Pam had been changing the baby and she must be upstairs getting the boy off to sleep again. He didn't have a name yet, because that would be for John to decide. Another John in the family might be confusing, but perhaps Jack...? He smiled to himself. It wouldn't be long before he'd have another little chap trotting at his heels and begging to be allowed up on the tractor or to help carry the pails. Mebbe more than one if Lizzie had a boy too...

3

Lizzie picked her way carefully up the lane and through the farmyard. It had snowed again in the night and there might be black ice beneath it. She didn't want a fall at this late stage of her pregnancy, it could bring the birth on suddenly and risk her child. She was feeling a bit wearied by it now and her back ached. Pam had wanted her to move into the farmhouse for the birth and Lizzie was glad of the invitation. She didn't fancy risking giving birth on her own after what had happened to Faith, though she knew it was the head injuries that had caused her death rather than the actual birth. Had she been able, she would surely have tried to reach help at the farm.

A little shudder went through Lizzie as she shook off the memory of that terrible day. It was so hard to believe that Faith had gone. She'd just been getting to know her and love her and then...

No, she wouldn't let herself dwell on it, hard though it was to accept. Lizzie had her own child to look forward to and knew she was luckier than a lot of women right now. Because of an injury sustained on active duty that had left him with a permanent limp, her husband Tom was now training men, but it was all hush-hush and he couldn't tell her much, other than that he was unlikely to be sent to the front again.

'They need fit men for this job,' he'd told her. 'I might have been put on the scrap heap if they hadn't thought I'd be good at inducting new recruits to the kind of tough training they need. It means I'll get home a bit more than if I was serving abroad, Lizzie, and we have to be grateful for that, love.'

Lizzie was grateful. She had never allowed anyone to see how anxious she'd been for Tom when he'd been actively engaged in dangerous secret missions, but it was a relief to know he wouldn't be posted overseas again for a while at least.

'There are all kinds of specialist groups being formed and most are experimental,' Tom had told her as they lay side by side in bed, the last time he was home. 'This war won't be fought in the trenches like the last one. That was a stupid slaughter with thousands of men being killed over a few miles of territory. We can't just sit and wait to be shot at; we have to take the war to them – and that's just what a group of very brave men are doing right now. You probably won't ever hear about them, but the papers will record a victory for us in some far-flung place.'

Lizzie hadn't asked questions. Tom told her as much as he could, which wasn't a lot, but she knew he was busy and happy in his work so that was enough.

'We're not winning the war yet,' he'd told her before he returned to his base. 'But we shall. Just keep your chin up and look after yourself for me. I love you, Lizzie, and think of you all the time I am away.'

Lizzie did her best to think good things and not worry, for the sake of her baby. She had spent her evenings knitting and sewing little blankets for the cot she'd managed to buy. It had come from a second-hand shop, as had the pram she had standing in her front room. Both had been in good condition and she'd cleaned them thoroughly and painted the cot white with some gloss left over by the builders when they'd decorated the house. It was easier than trying to buy new. There wasn't much in the shops to choose from and if you could find anything it was expensive. Perhaps in London, but she'd asked her friend Vera Salmons to look and she hadn't seen what Lizzie had wanted.

'It's all pretty basic,' she'd told Lizzie when she'd rung her. 'Those lovely prams with the big wheels you used to see in the park just aren't about at the moment.'

'I've seen a Silver Cross second-hand,' Lizzie had said. 'I'll probably just get that and clean it up.'

'That's what I had with my first,' Vera had told her. 'Give it a good scrub – and make lovely new blankets and that's all you need.'

'This one still has its waterproof cover,' Lizzie had replied. 'It is almost like new, so it makes sense.'

Tom had wanted to buy her all new things for the baby, but he didn't earn that much in the army and neither of them had asked his parents for more. Arthur and Pam had already been more than generous. It was no use expecting anything from Lizzie's mother. Maud grumbled she didn't have enough to live on as it was whenever Lizzie visited. She lived with her friend in the railway town of March, some distance away, and they shared expenses, but it was never enough for Maud Johnson.

Lizzie sighed. It was a chore rather than a pleasure to visit her mother sometimes. Why couldn't she have been warm and loving like Tom's mother? Lizzie loved Pam Talbot and Arthur too. They'd made her welcome right from the start, and even when she and Tom had broken up for a while, they hadn't been judgemental.

Lizzie hadn't been to visit her mother for a couple of weeks and she didn't think she would until after the birth. It was too far for her to drive to the town of March and would take too long on the bus. She wasn't due for another couple of weeks, but sometimes babies came early and she didn't fancy being stuck on a bus giving birth on a lonely fen road. Her mother would complain when she saw her again, but that couldn't be helped.

Lizzie's wandering thoughts fled as she opened the door to the big warm kitchen and saw Pam busy kneading dough at the long pine table. Her mother-in-law's face lit up with pleasure as she saw her.

'You never lugged that heavy suitcase all this way,' Pam scolded, fussing over her as she came to draw her in and take the case, depositing it near the door to the stairs. 'Artie could've fetched it. You just leave it there and he'll take it up for you, Lizzie.'

'It was heavier than I thought,' Lizzie agreed, thankful to put it down. 'I'm all right, Pam. Doctor Price said it is best to carry on as usual. Resting just slows everything down.'

'Well, I'm not certain he is right,' Pam said, 'but I dare say you feel restless. I scrubbed the kitchen and the stairs two hours before Susan was born.' Susan was Pam's eldest daughter and Angela her youngest child. Three sons and two daughters; it was a large family, but just what she and Arthur had wanted.

Lizzie laughed and went to fetch the kettle. She filled it at the deep stone sink and then placed it on the hob to boil. Pam had her dough proving by the fire now and a plate of fresh-cooked plain buns on the table.

'They might taste faintly of almond,' she told Lizzie, indicating the cakes she'd baked earlier. 'I used the last of my almond essence, but there was hardly enough. I don't know when I'll get any more.'

Lizzie nodded her understanding. Pam had a lot of people to feed and it wasn't easy to get hold of the ingredients she needed. The basics were still in the shops but in short supply at times and just now it seemed impossible to buy dried fruit or flavourings of any kind.

'I'll ask Vera to see what she can find,' Lizzie promised. 'Sometimes they have more of that kind of thing up there, though we do better for eggs and butter and fresh veg here than she does.'

'Yes. Tell her I'll exchange a few eggs for anything like that... or I will once the hens start laying again.'

'Have you brought them in as Arthur suggested?'

'Yes.' Pam laughed. 'He made a sort of pen in the scullery. I keep—'

Whatever she was about to say next was lost as the peace of the morning was shattered by a loud bang, followed by several more and a whooshing sound. The two women looked at each other in alarm.

'Was that up on the drome?' Lizzie asked, feeling shaken.

'I think so...' Pam said just as the door opened and Arthur rushed in.

'I think there has been a crash or something on the drome. Stay here, both of you. Artie and I are going to see if there's anything we can do...'

He was gone again in an instant. Lizzie and Pam looked at each other in consternation. 'I don't think it was a bomb, do you? If it was an air raid, there would be more explosions.'

'I think Arthur is probably right. One of the planes must have crashed on landing or take-off...'

'That is awful,' Lizzie said. 'I hope the crew are all right.'

'Oh God, I hope so.' Pam nodded. Lizzie could see she was anxious, as she was herself. 'Those poor men...'

'We don't know what happened yet. Arthur will tell us when he gets back.' Lizzie got up and went to the window, but all she could see was some smoke issuing from behind a hedge. 'I wish we knew what was happening...'

'Now don't you go upsetting yourself,' Pam said and then, to change the subject, 'Arthur went up to the base again the other day and issued an invitation to any of the men who wanted to come for a meal. We expected someone to turn up but they haven't yet.'

'I know some of them go regularly to houses in Sutton. It is probably closer for them,' Lizzie suggested, though it wasn't much different really. She hesitated, then, 'Should we go out and look?' She felt restless and anxious about what was happening.

'Arthur said to stay here – but I suppose we could look from the yard...'

By mutual agreement, they put on their coats, hats and scarves, and went outside to look. All they could see was a cloud of black smoke curling into the air, but it seemed to be coming from their top field rather than the drome itself. It looked as if the plane hadn't quite been able to make the landing strip and had crashed into the fields. In the distance, they could hear a siren and, overhead, another plane was circling as if its pilot was uncertain of where to land.

'Come on,' Pam said, seeing Lizzie was shivering. 'Let's go back inside. We can't do anything yet, but we'll put the kettles on just in case we get some visitors. I don't want you catching a chill, love.'

Lizzie nodded. If it hadn't been so close to her time, she might have set off across the fields to see if she could help, but

Artie and Arthur had already gone and there was nothing more they could do.

'Do you think the pilot got out?' Lizzie asked as they hurried back inside the warm kitchen, but she knew Pam couldn't answer. Sometimes the planes were damaged by the ack-ack on their mission and could hardly manage to get back. Some of them didn't. Lizzie always worried when there was a plane missing, though she hadn't been to count them in recently, because she was too far gone to lie in a ditch and it was bitterly cold.

'I pray so,' Pam said, white-faced, and Lizzie knew she was thinking of John. None of them had yet been allowed to visit him in hospital and she knew that was eating at Pam, even though she didn't say much about it.

* * *

A loud knocking at the door startled them both. No one ever knocked, they just walked straight in. 'Is it all right to come in?' a voice asked as the door opened and a girl's anxious face peeped round. 'It's awfully cold out today and I had to walk from Witcham Toll as the Military Police have a roadblock up and the bus dropped us there...'

They stared at the young dark-haired girl standing in the doorway, suitcase in hand, and then Pam's face cleared. 'I am Pam Talbot. You will be Frances Grant – the new land girl. Come in, lass. It's a terrible day to arrive. Why didn't you let us know? We expected you next week.' She offered her hand to the girl, who was pretty but rather thin and pale, probably in her early twenties. Pam thought she looked different from most of the land girls, who necessarily needed to be strong and fit.

'I know I am early, but my landlady wanted my room, so I thought I might as well come. I was supposed to be on leave, but

I really had nowhere else to go...' Frances seemed nervous and uncertain as she hovered just inside the door.

'We don't mind you being early,' Pam said. 'One of the men would have met you if we'd known. Come and get warm by the fire. You must have seen the smoke on the hill – you probably heard the explosion, too?'

'Yes... I saw the plane circling, trying to get down, but it was a bit foggy and I think the pilot must have missed the runway or just run out of fuel or something. A friend of mine says they often only have just enough to get back and if they get caught up in the flak, they can't always make it all the way home – if it leaks or something.'

'Your friend is in the air force then?' Pam said, looking at her with interest. 'My youngest son is, too – he is in hospital now. We are lucky he is still alive.'

'I am sorry to hear your son was injured...' Frances nodded, a faint smile on her face as she moved towards the range, holding her hands out to the fire. 'My friend David hasn't been shot down yet, but he's had some near escapes. We used to live next door to each other when we were kids. Neither of us had fathers; mine was a fireman and killed two years after the end of the last war. I moved away after my mother died and hadn't seen David for years, until I met him and his wife recently.'

'I'm sorry to hear that you've lost both parents, Frances,' Pam said. 'In a few minutes, I'll show you to the room you will be sharing with Jeanie – she's away now. This is my daughter-in-law, Lizzie. She is my eldest boy's wife. Besides, John, who I told you is in the air force, I've got Tom, in the army; Artie works on the land with Arthur, my husband, and then I've got two daughters. They are both at school. Susan is seventeen now and will be going to college in the summer and Angela is our baby, ten soon

– though we've got John's baby, too. His mother died giving birth...'

'Gosh, there are a lot of you,' Frances said and looked over-whelmed for a moment. 'I'll soon get used to you all. I was working in the munitions factory, but I wanted a change. Thought I'd prefer something safer in the country. Besides, the factory is out of action at the moment; there was a nasty explo-sion and some of the night workers were hurt.'

'Oh dear, and then you arrived here just as a plane crashed up on the drome,' Lizzie said. 'We've been lucky enough not to be bombed yet, but with the aerodrome so close it could happen, I'm afraid.'

'Oh, I was told it was here,' Frances said and grinned, suddenly looking very pretty. 'I'm not that worried, but the factory was a scary place to work. We had lots of little accidents and some of the girls got killed when mistakes were made.'

'That must have been frightening,' Pam agreed. 'We've got a pot of tea on the go – are you hungry? I can make you some toast and marmalade if you like?'

'Oh, yes please,' Frances said. At that moment they heard a wail from upstairs. 'Is that the baby? Can I go and bring him down?' Her face had lit with anticipation and after a moment's hesitation, Pam agreed.

'He is in the bedroom to the right of the stairs at the top,' she said. 'I've got his cot down here. I expect he needs changing...' She smiled as Frances looked about her. 'The stairs are behind that door there.'

'I'll fetch him for you,' Frances bent to pick up her case.

'Leave that for now, Frances. Artie will take it up later.'

'Oh, I can manage to get it up the stairs,' Frances said. 'I am very strong, even though I don't look it.'

She picked up the case and opened the stair door, disappearing up the stairs as Lizzie and Pam gazed at each other. Lizzie wanted to laugh, but Pam shook her head at her, so she held it in. Frances might still be within earshot and they didn't want to offend her, but she did make you smile. She so obviously wanted to please.

'She will do,' Pam said after a moment. 'I can see her fitting right in—'

Just then, the outside door opened and Artie entered. His face was flushed with the cold and excitement. 'It wasn't one of our boys that crashed, it was a German bomber plane and that's why there was such a loud bang and so much smoke. There is a huge hole in the top field, and an unexploded bomb, so we've been warned to stay away until they deal with it later – but a couple of men got out alive. The poor devils were dazed and hardly able to stand, no danger to anyone. The Military Police were all over them and they've taken them off in an army ambulance, the live ones and the others.'

'I'm glad it wasn't one of ours,' Pam said. 'I'm sorry that some of the crew was killed though...'

'I'm not,' Artie said. 'They were returning from a bombing raid but got caught by the flak; they must have been losing height for a while. If they hadn't crashed in our field, they would have dropped their last bomb on the drome or us.'

'German or not, they are some mothers' sons,' Pam said sternly. 'I know they are the enemy and I know what they've done, but a life is a life. I just wish it was all over and we could stop killing each other and I know in Germany somewhere a woman will grieve for her son or husband.'

Artie shook his head at her. It was obvious he didn't agree but wouldn't argue with his mother further over it. 'Do you want me to take your case up, Lizzie?'

'Yes please, Artie.' She was inclined to agree with Artie. The enemy was the enemy at a time like this, though Pam was right too, of course, and it was a shame that anyone had to die, but war was war.

Artie bent to pick the case up just as the door to the stairs opened and Frances came through it, carrying the baby. They stopped and stared at each other for a moment.

'You'll be the new girl, Frances,' Artie said after a moment's silence. 'Where is your case? I'll take it up for you.'

'At the top of the stairs, just to the left,' Frances said and blushed a delicate pink.

He nodded and went past her.

Frances walked towards Pam with the baby cradled in the crook of her arm. 'Can I change him?' she asked. 'I know how. A friend of mine lets me change her baby sometimes.'

'Yes, if you want to and if you're careful,' Pam said. 'You like babies then, Frances?'

'I love them,' Frances confirmed with a smile. 'I always have.'

She sat down in the chair by the fire and removed the dirty nappy and then wiped the baby's bottom with a cloth and some warm water Pam had provided, dried it carefully and powdered his skin before applying a pad of cotton wool, a clean muslin napkin and then a terry one and pinning it carefully with the big safety pin, slipping her hand under the folds so that there was no chance of it sticking into the baby, but she did it so well that that could never have happened.

'Well done,' Pam nodded her approval. 'He looks quite content. Give him to me and I'll lay him down for a while so you can have your tea and toast. He is awake and watching us so he'll bide here for a few minutes before we put him back in his big cot upstairs.' Baby waved his chubby hands at her as if to agree.

'I think I'll go up and unpack,' Lizzie said. 'I'll be down in half an hour or so if you need me to do anything, Pam.'

'You have a rest, Lizzie,' Pam told her with a smile. 'Frances is here if I need a hand. Come down when you're ready – but you are here to be looked after, my love.'

Lizzie nodded and smiled as she walked up to the room that had once been Tom's. She liked the new girl. Frances looked as if she would fit into their family very well.

4

After delivering Lizzie's case to Tom's old room, Artie carried the new girl's bag up the next flight of stairs to the attic she was to share with Jeanie. He inhaled the scent of Jeanie's perfume – Yardley lavender, he thought. He knew she liked that and the room smelled of her. He was reluctant to think of the new girl sharing it, though that was plain daft. They needed more help on the farm, or they would do once this pesky snow cleared and they could get on with the busy routine of ploughing, harrowing and then setting the seed for the new harvest. The winter wheat was already in the ground, of course, safe under the blanket of snow; it was still beneath the earth and would be fine. It was the spring barley and the potatoes and other root crops they would be pushed for time on if this inclement weather lasted much longer.

Artie sighed. He missed working with Tom, the easy companionship between them as they discussed the work with their father, had made the hours fly by, and he cursed the war that had taken his brothers far from home – and yet the war had brought Jeanie into his life.

He smiled as he thought of her. She would be back the next day. He would like to take her somewhere nice, but unless the snow cleared, they couldn't risk going to a dance and driving home late. His father would be in a pickle if he put them in the dyke. He wasn't old, but Artie had noticed him slowing down a bit of late, moving a bit stiffly – but arthritis was common enough amongst those who worked on the land in all weathers. This freezing weather was guaranteed to put anyone out of sorts. Sometimes the snow lingered for weeks. Artie hoped it wouldn't this time.

If he was going to ask Jeanie to wed him, it had to be a proper proposal; he wasn't going to just pop the question in the cowshed! That meant careful planning – an outing somewhere. He wished now that he'd spoken to her at Christmas.

Artie shook his head. There was surely no urgency. If Jeanie liked him enough – and he was fairly sure she did – she would be there when the time was right. He would have to think about a ring as well. Perhaps she would like to choose her own. Artie wasn't sure there would be as much choice in the shops as usual, but he'd have a look next time he went to March or perhaps Ely. Fishers was an old-fashioned jeweller and might just have some good rings still in stock.

His thoughts turned to the little flurry of excitement in the fields that morning. Although, he hadn't told his mother, Artie had been the first on the scene. He'd rushed to the crashed plane and dragged a couple of men clear, one of them already dead, a shard of jagged metal straight through his throat, which had given Artie a right shock. The other had been alive and thanked him in broken English. Artie hadn't gone back to the plane, but the last survivor had stumbled out as the flames began to shoot up – and then the MPs from the airfield had arrived and taken over. They'd begun to hose the burning wreck, and prevented it from reaching the unexploded bomb, for which he'd been grateful as his father had arrived by then.

There was already a huge hole in the field, right in the corner, which was a nuisance. He doubted if he'd be allowed near it for weeks even if the thaw came. That would put the ploughing back again, which was something he could have done without. Artie didn't much like working this heavy clay land; he usually left it to Tom if he could. Maybe he would get home leave soon, he thought hopefully. They could discuss things then...

As he walked back downstairs, towards the kitchen, Artie heard the sound of voices and laughter. That sounded like the new girl, he thought. She was pretty enough when she smiled and before he'd got interested in Jeanie, he might have tried his luck with her. He shook his head. Jeanie would have his guts for garters if she caught him flirting and his chances of getting her to say yes to marrying him would be nil... No, he would stay well clear of this one, because he had a feeling, she might be trouble.

* * *

It was as he was returning from feeding the pigs the next morning that Artie saw Jeanie enter the farmyard and walk towards the kitchen. She halted as he drove the tractor into the yard and waited for him to switch it off and come to her.

'Where is your sister?' he asked. 'I thought she was coming back with you?'

'Mum wanted her to stay a bit longer,' Jeanie said. 'She rang her friend who lent her the car and he said there was no hurry to return it as he hasn't got any more petrol rations for the moment. So she'll stay another week and then collect it on her way to Cambridge. It isn't in the way, is it?'

'No. I'll move it if I need to,' he said and smiled at her. Her red hair gleamed with health in the wintry sunshine and the tip of her nose was pink from the cold, but she was lovely. 'Did you enjoy your time with your family?'

'It was nice seeing Annie again after such a long time,' Jeanie said, 'but... this seems more like home to me now.' She blushed faintly and avoided looking at him. 'Have you missed me then?' Suddenly, the gleam of mischief was in her eyes. 'Did Dora kick you?' Dora was their most stubborn cow but responded to Jeanie much better than to Artie.

'Yes, she did,' he confirmed ruefully. 'You're the only one who can milk her – and I don't think the new girl will be much use with the milking. She cleaned the sheds out this morning, but I noticed she was nervous of the cows.'

'She's arrived then, that's good. I was a bit nervous at first,' Jeanie reminded him. 'I soon got over it. Most of them are as gentle and patient as you need – it is only the odd one that kicks.'

'And when they do it hurts,' he said but laughed. 'Yes, I did miss you, Jeanie, and not just because of the milking...' They had reached the kitchen door now and stopped by mutual consent. He bent his head and kissed her. 'I care a lot about you, you know?'

'Yeah, until the next pretty girl comes along,' she teased, but her eyes lit up.

'She already did,' Artie replied, 'but I still prefer you.'

Jeanie arched her brows as he pushed open the door to let her precede him. The sound of a girl's laughter made Jeanie stop and stare. She turned to look at Artie and then back to the newcomer.

'Hi, I'm Jeanie Salmons,' she said and offered her hand. 'You must be the new girl. We shall be sharing a room...'

The other girl hesitated and then moved forward to take Jeanie's hand, or rather just touch it with her fingertips. 'I'm

Frances Grant. Pleased to meet you.' She said the words, but
there was no warmth behind them and Jeanie shot Artie a
puzzled look.

He gave a little shake of his head, but he too had caught the
instant when Frances' greenish eyes had registered dislike. She'd
masked it quickly, but it had been there. Why? He wondered.
Who could possibly dislike Jeanie?

'Oh, Artie,' his mother said, interrupting his train of thought.
'Can you fetch in the steps for me and help us clear the top
shelves in the pantry please? I want to wash them down and if
there is any whitewash, we could do the walls while we're up
there. I'd like a nice clean pantry, to start us off before the spring.
Not that I'll be able to make many preserves this year, unless I
can cadge some sugar from someone...'

'I know someone who might be able to help,' Frances said,
making them all look at her in surprise. 'Bill – he used to work at
the munitions factory with me – can sometimes get extra stuff
like that; it is a bit dearer, of course.'

'You're talking about black market stuff,' Pam said. 'Thank
you for the kind thought, Frances, but I don't approve of that – it
has to be stolen or misappropriated in some way. It means
someone has to go without elsewhere and I won't take someone
else's rations, but some folk don't always use them and I
exchange some eggs and a chicken for sugar when I can.'

Frances looked at her oddly and then blushed. 'I didn't mean
any harm by it, Pam. I don't know where Bill gets his stuff, but he
says it is all legitimate...'

'I'm sure he does and you were only being helpful, but I won't
have black market stuff in my house. We might have stored a bit
extra before the war and Arthur might kill the odd pig that
wasn't reported to the Food Ministry, but we don't sell it or profit
by it other than a nice meal or two.'

Frances nodded.

Artie shot a warning look at his mother, but she wasn't looking at him. He thought her unwise to speak of his father's little bit of deception in front of the new girl. They didn't know her well, and although she seemed a friendly open girl, he had a feeling there was more to her than met the eye.

Pam had turned her attention to Jeanie and was telling her more of what she had planned for the morning.

'You don't need to do the cleaning, Pam,' Jeanie told her. 'Frances and I can do that while you get on with your other jobs. I'll go up the steps and hand the stuff down to Frances – if that suits you?' She looked at Frances, her brows raised.

'Yes, I don't mind,' Frances said. 'I'm here to help. I've never used whitewash but I'll have a go.' She turned her wide gaze on Artie. 'If you show me where they are, I can fetch the steps in.'

'I'll fetch them and I'll give you both a hand,' he said and went off.

Maybe he was wrong about her, but he would keep an eye on things for a while. He was probably misjudging a fleeting glance, but instinctively he didn't trust Frances, despite her eagerness to fit in and help.

5

'He's nice, isn't he – Artie?' Frances remarked to Jeanie when they went up to wash and change after their busy day. 'The dark silent type. I like men that way – don't you?'

'Artie is all right,' Jeanie answered casually. She wasn't going to let Frances see how she felt about him just yet. The new girl seemed decent enough and she'd certainly done her share of the work, but she hadn't missed a chance to catch Artie's attention. 'We get on.'

'I think he likes you a lot,' Frances replied. 'Why don't you give him the go-ahead?'

'I don't know what you mean,' Jeanie said, though she thought she did.

'Flirt with him, get his interest,' Frances persisted. 'I would if he looked at me the way he does at you.'

'Artie has been out with a lot of girls but doesn't get serious with them,' Jeanie told her. 'I'm a marriage or nothing girl and I'm not sure he's ready for that...' She cursed herself as Frances' eyes gleamed. 'If I was interested...'

'You should watch out some other girl doesn't snatch him

from under your nose,' Frances replied. 'I'm not bothered about marriage. My mum never married.'

'You told Pam your father was a fireman and killed a couple of years after the end of the last war?' Jeanie looked at her in sudden suspicion.

'Oh, he was, a hero was my dad – but he never married Mum. He had a wife somewhere, but they didn't get on, so he left her when Mum was expectin' and lived with my mother. They had two kids but never married... my brother died of typhoid when he was ten.'

'I'm sorry,' Jeanie said. 'Did you find the fact that your parents weren't married difficult at school? I know some children can be cruel about that kind of thing.'

'Nah, a lot of the kids in my school were in the same boat. The snooty ones left us alone, because we bashed 'em if they didn't.'

Jeanie nodded. It sounded to her as if Frances had had a hard life as a child. She wasn't yet sure how she felt about her. She could be good company, but sometimes she seemed to go into herself – and Jeanie was pretty sure she'd flirted with Artie a few times despite knowing that they liked each other. There was some mystery about her – and she wasn't sure Frances liked her either.

'Are you ready? Shall we go down? I'm starving.'

'You go down first,' Jeanie replied to her questions. 'I'll be down in a few minutes.'

Jeanie looked at herself in the mirror after Frances had gone. She'd always thought herself attractive, but Frances was equally so, especially when she smiled. Supposing Artie tried flirting with her, the way he had with Nancy, the land girl before her? Nancy hadn't been interested, but Frances might be. Perhaps

Jeanie ought to have told her he was off limits, but she wasn't sure he was hers.

It was obvious her life hadn't been easy from the few hints Frances had dropped, and Jeanie knew she'd been lucky with her loving and hard-working parents, but she couldn't quite *like* the girl. If she allowed her feelings to show, it would make life difficult on the farm so she would have to hide them and put on a show of being friendly with Frances or it would sour the happy atmosphere that made life so pleasant here at Blackberry Farm.

* * *

Frances knew Jeanie had fallen asleep as she heard the gentle snore later that evening. Despite the hard work she'd done, Frances was unable to let go, to let herself sleep. Was she safe here? The family were friendly and Pam was kind. She liked Artie a lot but wasn't sure he liked her – but she had learned the hard way that men could be deceiving.

Memories from her past, when she'd been just seventeen and suddenly alone after her mother died, flashed into her mind. She'd been so young and innocent and so alone... A little sob broke from her and was hastily buried in the soft pillows. She mustn't let anyone see beneath the friendly, chatty face she showed to the world. Most of the time now, she was able to forget; she had other, happier memories to replace the bad ones – but sometimes they came back to haunt her.

A shiver went through her as she buried her head in the pillows. If ever *he* found her... But he wouldn't. *He* couldn't. She must be safe here. She'd changed her name and the colour of her hair, shading it darker; it made her look very pale, but she'd needed to change her appearance and her name. *He* must never find her! Derek had helped her with that...

Now tears were on her cheeks. She'd felt safe with Derek; he had healed the pain inside her, taken away the humiliation and the shame, but then he was gone – away to the war, never to return.

The tears soaked her pillow now as she muffled the sobs. She needed to feel safe again, to know she was protected. A thought entered her mind then – Artie Talbot was strong. He would protect the woman he loved. If Frances could just make him look at her the way he looked at Jeanie Salmons...

It wasn't fair, she thought as her tears dried. Why should Jeanie have everything and Frances nothing? To live here in this warm farmhouse, far from London and the danger that lurked there, would be a kind of paradise. A feeling of jealousy made her thump her pillow. If she had a husband to care for her, she wouldn't need to fear *him*... the memory of what *he'd* done to her forever lurking in the dark shadows of her mind.

6

Annie arrived in a taxi the following morning. She'd been told there was a large intake of wounded men in the hospitals and was going back to work, even though she was officially still on holiday. Pam invited her to stay for a breakfast of bubble and squeak and a fried egg, which she gratefully accepted before going out to her car.

'I'll come and see you in Cambridge next time,' Jeanie offered. 'You can ring me here when you are free and I'll come over on the train from Sutton.'

'Good. We can go shopping together. You need some new clothes and a haircut,' Annie said in her big-sister mode and hugged her. 'Take care of yourself, love – and I like your Artie.'

'If he is mine...' Jeanie replied pensively. She'd started to wonder since Frances had arrived.

'Of course he is,' Annie told her. 'Don't ever doubt it, love. Artie is yours when you want him. I know by the way he looks at you – and Mum told me he cares about you.'

'How can she possibly know that?' Jeanie asked with a frown.

'Mothers know these things,' Annie said wickedly. 'At least

that is what she says – and she knows I've been breaking my heart over someone who never looked at me, though that is finished. He got married.'

'Annie! No!' Jeanie gave her another hug. 'I'm so sorry. I didn't know. You never told me.'

'I only discovered it yesterday. My friend told me the news. He married a girl in the Wrens...' Annie pulled a face. 'Perhaps it is just as well. I'll have to get over him now, won't I?'

'I am so sorry, love,' Jeanie said, concerned as a look of sadness passed across her sister's face. I wish I could do something.'

'No one can. Mum told me to put it behind me and move on – it is part of the reason I am returning to work sooner. I won't have time to think about him when I get back to the hospital.'

'I don't suppose you will,' Jeanie said. 'Choose someone nicer next time, love.'

'Oh, he was nice and kind – that was a part of the problem. If he'd been bad-tempered like some of the other doctors, I wouldn't have felt the same, but he made you feel you were special – only I wasn't; just another nurse he was kind to.' Annie's voice wavered a little. 'Take no notice, Jeanie. I shall be fine when I start work.'

She stood back, gave Jeanie a lopsided smile and got into the borrowed car, driving off with a wave of her hand.

Jeanie stood staring after her for a few minutes and then the sound of a boot crunching made her turn just as Artie came up to her.

'Daydreaming or missing your sister?' he asked as she met his enquiring gaze.

'A bit of both, I suppose,' Jeanie said and sighed. 'Annie just heard a doctor she was keen on got married.'

'I'm sorry she was hurt,' Artie's voice dropped, then, 'You know I would never hurt you, Jeanie, don't you?'

Jeanie was startled by the sincerity of his tone. Artie didn't often say things like that; he usually teased her or took her for granted. 'Do I?' she asked, tilting her head up at him. 'Do I know that? Can I, Artie?'

'Jeanie, this isn't the time or place for what I want to say, but surely—'

'Hey, you two,' Frances' voice cut across whatever he was about to say. 'Mr Talbot wants you to take him to Chatteris, Artie. He needs something from the ironmongers and he says this thaw isn't going to last long; he says it will freeze again tonight and he needs a part for the big trailer so he wants to go now.'

'Dad can drive,' Artie snapped, a note of irritation in his voice, but headed towards the kitchen with a look at Jeanie that spoke volumes.

Jeanie kept her sigh of disappointment inside as she turned to the other girl. 'Why does Mr Talbot need Artie to drive him?' she asked.

'I think the axel is heavy and he doesn't think he can lift it – or Pam said he shouldn't,' Frances replied. 'You two looked very close when I arrived? Artie trying it on, was he? He asked me out last night, but I said I'd think about it.'

For Jeanie, the words were like a knife thrust to the heart, but she kept the hurt inside. Artie had seemed so sincere. Was he playing with her? 'Why didn't you say yes if you like him?'

'I will next time. I don't want him to think I'm too easy,' Frances replied. 'He said there is a good film on in Ely at the Rex and that he would take me.'

Jeanie nodded and headed for the cowsheds. She had some mucking out to do and a bit of back-breaking shovelling would do her good – stop her hitting Frances to make her shut up! She needed to be alone with her thoughts, to think about Artie and her feelings towards him.

* * *

Artie found her there three hours later. She'd changed the straw, filled the hay racks with fresh fodder for the cows and scrubbed the pails and churns. He looked about him, brows raised.

'Good job,' he told her. 'I would have helped you if you'd waited, love.'

'I am not your love,' Jeanie said and bit her lip, jerking her head away. 'Don't think you can play fast and loose with me!'

'What do you mean?' Artie stared at her. 'Who has upset you, Jeanie?'

'No one...' She refused to look at him, but he spun her round and made her face him. Temper made her blurt it out, 'Why did you ask Frances out if you care about me?'

'I love you,' he muttered fiercely, his fingers digging into her upper arms as he gave her a little shake. 'And I didn't ask her out.'

'She said you were taking her to the cinema—'

'She is lying. Mum told her that there was a good film if she wanted to see it on Saturday night and she asked how she could get there. You know Mum. She looked at me and I said I would take her into Ely if the roads were OK. I thought *we* could drop her off and go somewhere nice...'

'I thought...' Jeanie stumbled over the words. 'Frances is very pretty... so pale and interesting...'

'I am not such an idiot as to get mixed up with her, Jeanie. There is something not quite right about her. I sensed it the minute I saw her,' Artie said and pulled Jeanie close. 'I wanted to take you out so that I could propose – I didn't want to do it here in the cowshed, but it looks like I am. Will you marry me, Jeanie?

I do truly love you – and I've never said that to a girl before. I thought you might like to go into Ely and choose your own ring one day?'

'Oh, Artie...' Jeanie felt the tears on her cheeks, but she couldn't help her emotion. She'd been torn with uncertainty and now it seemed that all her hopes had come true. 'I must look such a mess – and I stink...' She gave a watery laugh, her uncertainty turning to pleasure as she felt a surge of love toward him . 'Of course I'll marry you. I've been waiting for you to say something for ages. I wasn't sure it was what you wanted.'

'Sweet idiot,' he said gruffly. 'You should know I'm not much with words, Jeanie, but the way I look at you should have told you. I can hardly keep my hands off you.'

'Artie...' Jeanie giggled. 'I love you so much, but I was afraid to show it in case I was just another girl to you.'

'You're *my* girl,' Artie told her. 'You have been for a while, but I was too set in my ways and too slow. I'm sorry I chose such an unromantic place to ask you.'

'What is unromantic about a cowshed?' Jeanie asked and threw her arms about his neck, kissing him with all the passion she'd kept pent up inside her. Artie returned the kiss and squeezed her so tight she could hardly breathe.

'Let's go and tell Mum and make if official,' he suggested, offering his hand. 'Then you can get cleaned up and we'll take a drive into Ely and buy you a ring. I looked in the jeweller's in March but didn't see anything nice, but they will have some good ones in Fishers in Ely. That is where Dad bought Mum's, so hopefully we will find something you like.'

'I'll be happy with anything you give to me,' Jeanie said.

She felt as if she were glowing as they walked hand-in-hand up to the kitchen. She'd known in her heart Artie was the one for her ever since he first took her out but had been uncertain of his feelings and now, well, she was bubbling over with happiness.

Pam looked up from her baking as they entered, her eyes going to their faces; she nodded contentedly. 'So you've made up your minds then,' she said. 'I'm glad, Artie and Jeanie. She'll make you a lovely wife, Artie – and he'll be a good husband to you, love, or he'll answer to me.'

Jeanie rushed to her and hugged her. 'You always knew how I felt, didn't you? I do love him, Pam, and I love you, too,'

Pam hugged her tight. 'Arthur will be delighted and so will Lizzie and the others. Welcome to our family, love. When will the big day be? I can't promise you a proper cake with icing, but we'll find something nice...'

'We are going into Ely to buy the ring this afternoon,' Artie said. 'We haven't discussed dates yet – but, as far as I am concerned, the sooner, the better.'

'You'll have to pop up to London and talk to Jeanie's mum and dad,' Pam said. 'They will need to give permission as Jeanie isn't twenty-one yet, but I doubt you will have any trouble there. Vera has been asking me if I thought it would happen since Christmas!'

'That was what Annie said – and I haven't told them anything yet.' Jeanie gave a little gurgle of pleasure. 'I'll ring them this evening when Dad gets home from work. I'd better go up and wash and change. I can't go into Ely like this.'

* * *

'Congratulations, you, sly cat,' Frances said when she and Jeanie were alone in their room before supper that evening. 'Making out you weren't particularly interested and then grabbing him as soon as you got the chance.'

Jeanie's fists curled at her side, but she bit back the angry retort. 'We don't all talk about our feelings,' she said coldly. 'We've been courting after a fashion for a while, but now we've made up our minds.'

'Fair enough,' Frances shrugged as if unconcerned, 'but I still think you might have told me you meant to have him.'

What business was it of hers? Jeanie nearly snapped the question at her, but nothing had changed about the necessity to get on with Frances. For the moment, they still had to share a room and even when she was married, they would need to live and work together in harmony, so there was no point in provoking her. Frances might be trying to needle her, but Jeanie wouldn't give her the satisfaction of seeing her lose her temper.

'It's a nice ring,' Frances remarked. 'A solitaire and a decent size – that is what comes of marrying the boss' son, I suppose.'

'Artie wanted something good.' Jeanie shrugged, not wanting to share her pleasure with the other girl. The ring was gorgeous but any ring would have been fine for Jeanie; it was knowing that Artie loved her that mattered. 'I'm hungry. I'm going down for supper.'

She left the room. Frances' jealousy when she learned that Jeanie was engaged to Artie had been swiftly hidden, but Jeanie knew it was there and her spiteful remarks in the privacy of her room hadn't surprised her. She would have to suffer the other girl's occasional spite without complaint if they were to work together. Frances would get over it and find someone else to fixate on in time Jeanie was sure, but for now she was undoubtedly miffed. If they hadn't needed her help on the farm, Jeanie would have had it out with her, but they did – or they would once the land was fit to work again. It was still bitterly cold and the snow was lingering, waiting for more to fall so the farmers said. Their forecast was for a cold, few weeks to come.

* * *

Left temporarily alone, Frances closed her eyes as a tear escaped. She could've bitten off her own tongue. She hadn't meant to be so nasty, but her envy had overcome her. Now Jeanie would hate her and she might have to leave the safety of Blackberry Farm. If that happened, she had no idea where she would go...

Swallowing her disappointment, she painted on a smile. It wasn't as if she had a thing for Artie Talbot, but she had thought it would be all right to be his wife. Yet, in her heart, she suspected that he didn't like her or trust her – and perhaps he was right, because, after all, she was living a lie. Frances Grant wasn't her real name. She'd managed to get new ration cards in that name by telling the authorities that she'd lost all her papers in a bombing raid. It happened all the time now and no one questioned too closely. Derek had found the gravestone; a girl her age had died some years earlier and he'd managed to get a copy of her birth certificate.

'It will keep you safe until I get back and then we'll marry and no one will hurt you then,' Derek had told her. 'I love you and I don't care about what happened before we met...' He'd kissed her on the lips, but then he'd gone off to war... and he wouldn't be coming home. She'd only ever had one letter from him, though she'd written several times.

Tears stung Frances' eyes at the memory. If only they'd met when she was just seventeen and alone with no money and no friends. If she had never met *him*...

Rubbing the tears from her cheeks, Frances lifted her head. She had no choice but to go on with the life she'd chosen, but she would have to watch what she said, because otherwise they might send her away.

7

Jeanie woke in the night when she heard the scream. It had come from just down the hall and her immediate thought was of Lizzie. Jumping out of bed in her warm pyjamas, she pulled on her dressing gown, slipped her sensible flat shoes on, and went quickly down the stairs to the next level just as she heard the next scream. When she reached Lizzie's bedroom, it was to find that Pam was already there and it was clear the baby was on its way.

'Ah, I'm glad you're here, Jeanie,' Pam said. 'Artie has gone for the midwife and I need someone to start boiling water. We'll need hot water later – and Lizzie could do with a cup of tea, so could I. We shall be a few hours yet, I think...'

Jeanie smiled at Lizzie reassuringly. 'We'll look after you, love,' she said, suspecting that Faith's awful death might be on her friend's mind. 'I'll get us all a lovely cup of tea.'

She went down to the kitchen, where Arthur Talbot was poking at the range fire. 'I think it is hot enough, Jeanie love,' he told her. 'I have filled a couple of kettles ready.'

'Thanks, Mr Talbot,' she said. 'I'll make a pot of tea as soon as the water boils and then put some more on ready for when the midwife needs it.'

'Artie went to fetch her, because she was a bit dubious about driving on these roads. It couldn't have been a worse night; it was snowing a blizzard again earlier. This damned weather just seems to go on and on.'

'At least Lizzie is here with us,' Jeanie said. 'I think together we are capable of delivering her baby safely even if the midwife doesn't get here.'

Arthur looked at her in surprise. 'Do you know anything about the process?'

'Yes, a bit,' Jeanie said. 'Mum is a midwife, as you know, and she used to tell us about her mothers, sometimes – and when I went home with Annie, I asked her what we needed to do if Lizzie gave birth in the middle of the night before the midwife could get here. She talked me through a straightforward birth, step by step. Of course, if there are complications, I wouldn't be sure what to do, but there won't be.' She crossed her fingers behind her back.

'You're a confident young miss,' Arthur said with a gleam in his eye. 'We see birth on the farm all the time, with the animals. Tom and Artie have sorted more than one breach birth before now, so as you say, we should manage between us.'

* * *

Their skills were not put to the test as Lizzie's labour went on for some hours and the midwife was with them when her son was finally born. She had coped with the pain brilliantly and was crying and laughing when the child came into the world with a swoosh and started making himself known immediately.

'He is a noisy one,' Pam said, smiling down at the mass of

dark hair clinging wetly to the babe's head. 'Tom had a lot of hair, too, when he was born and a good pair of lungs. If he is anything like his father, you'll have your hands full with this one, Lizzie.' She took the child and wrapped him in a towel while the midwife finished her work. 'He is beautiful, love, and perfect. What did you decide to call him?'

'Tom thought he might like to call a boy Archie. I think it is nice and we can't call him Arthur; we have two of those already in the Talbot family.'

'Archie Thomas Gilbert,' Pam said and nodded. 'You'll add Tom to the middle, won't you? Or did you want your father's name?'

'Not this time,' Lizzie said and smiled at her and then at Jeanie, who had brought them yet another cup of tea. 'Thank you both – and you, Mrs Jones, for helping me.'

'I wish all my mothers were like you,' the midwife answered with a nod of approval. 'Give him a little feed when you feel up to it, but he's a big lusty lad, so he's fine for the moment and all he needs is a cuddle.'

Pam put the baby into Lizzie's arms.

Jeanie watched her, saw her look of tenderness and her heart caught. Lizzie looked so beautiful in that moment, her hair lank with sweat and her face devoid of powder, but dazzling with her love and maternal pride.

'He's really lovely, Lizzie,' she said. 'You are so lucky to have him. A boy first time.'

'I hope I will have a girl somewhere along the line,' Lizzie said, stroking her baby's head with one finger. 'But I'd like at least three – two boys for Tom and a girl for me.'

'The boys are less trouble until they grow up,' Pam said with a snort of laughter. 'Wait until this one starts crying all night before you make up your mind, Lizzie.'

'You wouldn't be without any of yours, Pam,' Lizzie said, arching her brows.

'No, I wouldn't,' Pam agreed, 'but they can be hard work. Still, there are plenty of us to help when you're ready to go back to work – but you won't for a while, will you?'

'Not until he is weaned anyway. I'll do part-time then, just pop in for a morning or afternoon. It's lucky I learned to drive last summer. I can take him with me and make sure everything is all right at the shop, but I have good staff now so it should be fine.'

'Well, you're not going anywhere for a week or two,' Pam told her. 'Now give Archie to me and get some rest. I'll take him and show him to his grandfather and uncle. His aunts, too, if they are up. I think Susan might be, though nothing wakes Angela.'

'I doubt anyone got much sleep,' Lizzie said ruefully. 'Sorry I made so much noise and thank Artie for fetching Mrs Jones for me.'

The midwife looked at her and nodded. 'He is a good lad, your boy, Mrs Talbot. I'll go now and he can run me home. I've got two more mothers to visit and another very close to her time. I'll call in one morning to see how you're getting on, Mrs Gilbert.'

'Oh, please, call me Lizzie.'

She nodded and smiled. 'I'll say goodbye then.' She left them and followed Pam downstairs.

'I'd better leave you to rest,' Jeanie said. 'I must help Artie with the milking, but if you need anything first just say...'

'No, I'm just going to sleep,' Lizzie replied and yawned. She lay back and closed her eyes, dropping into a quiet slumber as Jeanie softly left the room.

* * *

Downstairs in the kitchen, Jeanie could hear Artie and Arthur laughing and Susan was talking excitedly. When she entered, Pam was sitting in her chair by the stove with the new baby in her lap. Artie looked at Jeanie, his eyes warm with love.

'He looks just like his father. Tom will be proud when he sees him. We shall have to write and let him know he has a boy.' He got to his feet. 'Well, I'd best get on. I'll run Mrs Jones home and then come back to clean out the sheds.'

'I will start the milking as soon as I'm dressed,' Jeanie said.

'You've been up half the night. Go back to bed and rest. Frances can help muck them out when I've done the milking on my return.'

'You've been up ages and you've got to take Mrs Jones home first. I'll get ready and make a start while you're gone.'

Artie hesitated, then inclined his head. 'Fine. You can rest afterwards. There isn't much to do elsewhere in this weather – but make sure Frances does her share.'

'Is she up yet?' Jeanie said, glancing round, but there was no sign of the other land girl. 'She was still asleep when I got up to go to Lizzie.'

'Then it's time she was up,' Pam said. 'I can hear Jonny crying, Susan. Can you fetch him down for me, please? I dare say he needs changing.' She'd decided they couldn't go on calling John's child 'baby' so would give him his father's name, until John came home anyway. 'We shall have a busy few days with two babies in the house. If one isn't wanting something, the other one will be...'

* * *

Jeanie returned to her room to find Frances just getting up. She gave her a strange look as she saw her. 'Did Lizzie have her baby?' she asked. 'I heard a commotion but decided not to investigate. I thought I might be in the way. I know nothing about all that stuff...'

'I thought you liked babies?' Jeanie questioned as she went behind the screen and pulled on her working clothes. Frances was still sitting on the bed yawning when she was ready. 'Artie is driving Mrs Jones home, so I need you to help with the mucking out, please. I'm going to start milking now...'

'Before breakfast?' Frances stretched and looked reluctant. 'It is so cold. I need some tea and toast before I get going.'

'I made us all tea and toast in the night,' Jeanie replied. 'I'll last until I get finished and then Pam will have something cooked. I think she has some bacon today.'

She went out and left Frances to it. The other land girl normally worked hard once she started but was often reluctant to get going first thing.

It had stopped snowing when Jeanie let herself out of the kitchen. Pam and Susan had disappeared somewhere, upstairs probably. Jeanie breathed in the cold crisp air. The snow was still pristine on the fields. It was lingering this year, she thought. Pam said they shouldn't grumble. She said they might need the moisture the thaw brought later in the year if they didn't get enough rain.

'A hard winter often means a hot summer,' she'd told Jeanie. Jeanie had just smiled. Farming folk were always predicting the weather.

Making her way to the cowsheds, she felt the heat of their bodies as she entered. It was always nice and warm in here when the cows were in residence. They lowed in greeting as she went in and fetched her stool and pail. There were ten cows to milk, but the fat stock had gone off to market before Christmas. There would be more calves to rear soon and then the whole cycle would start again. The heifers would be kept for breeding and the bullocks went out in the fields to graze on the rich pasture by the river all summer long. There was a kind of rhythm and permanence about the sequence, like the rotation of the crops that Jeanie liked.

She smiled as she bent her head to the task, coaxing the warm milk from full udders with gentle fingers that stroked rather than demanded, hearing the gentle murmur of satisfaction from the cow as she was relieved of her heavy load.

When her pail was full and the cow had given all its milk, she tipped it into a churn and went on to the next one. She was on number seven when Artie entered the sheds and looked about him.

'I'll finish up now,' he told her and frowned. 'You go and get your breakfast, love.'

'What about you?'

'I'll be along in a few minutes. Why isn't Frances here helping you?'

'She said she wanted her breakfast first,' Jeanie said and yawned as she stood.

Artie took the full pail and tipped the contents into the churn.

'The cows like you,' he said as he saw how much milk they'd given. 'They don't always give me as much. Go and have your breakfast. I'll be there soon.'

Jeanie did as he suggested and left him to finish the milking. She saw Frances coming towards her as she reached the farmhouse. She was wearing make-up, including a bright red lipstick, and had obviously taken her time getting ready for work. She nodded to her, but neither of them spoke. Jeanie frowned as she entered the kitchen to the smell of bacon frying. She wasn't sure

Frances was truly cut out for work on the farm, but it wasn't up to her to say anything.

'Ah, there you are, Jeanie,' Pam said cheerfully. 'I'll bet you are ready for this?'

'Yes, I am. It smells good, Pam.' She smiled as Pam pushed a plate of bubble and squeak that was browned on top, an egg and a slice of streaky bacon in front of her.

'You've all got one slice of bacon this morning and I'm glad to say the hens are laying again. I'll have plenty of eggs now for baking as well.'

'Is Lizzie still asleep?' Jeanie asked, tucking into her plateful of delicious hot food.

'Yes, I imagine so,' Pam replied, looking happy. 'That all went beautifully, didn't it? I wondered if we might have problems, but it was straightforward in the end.'

'Lizzie did really well,' Jeanie said. 'I am so glad after...' She met Pam's gaze and knew it had been in her mind, too. 'How is little Jonny? Is he well?'

'Yes, it was just a wet nappy. I thought he might start Archie off, but he didn't, thank goodness. Lizzie needs to rest for a while.'

She looked up as Artie entered the kitchen and went to wash his hands. 'The milking is done. I left Frances to get on with the feeding and the mucking out. She can earn her keep for once.'

'That's not fair,' his mother gave him a sharp look. 'She hasn't been here long, Artie, and she worked well enough for me cleaning the pantry.'

'She doesn't much care for the yard work,' Artie said. 'I know milking isn't for everyone, but if you work on a farm you have to do your share – and at the moment there isn't much else.'

'Which means you could have stayed and given her a hand,'

Pam said, putting his plate in front of him. 'You don't have much to do either.'

'I have to feed the pigs,' Artie said. 'And I've arranged to meet a friend of mine. He has some bits and pieces that we need for machinery repairs, which he will sell for a price.' He ate hungrily. 'Besides which, she wasn't up all night fetching the midwife.'

'Give her a fair chance,' Pam warned. 'I know she isn't like Jeanie, and she can be moody, but not all the girls settle at first. I am sure she will do her fair share when you can get on the land – and until then, she can help me in the house. I do need a bit of help with the work a couple of babies make.'

Artie glanced at her and then inclined his head. 'As long as she does her share,' he said. 'Though what she thinks she is about, prancing in late in full make-up I don't know.'

'Some girls don't feel dressed without it,' Pam said. 'Jeanie always looks lovely even if she doesn't get time to put on some lipstick, but other girls need it. Frances hasn't had a particularly happy life.'

'You don't want to believe all the things she says,' Artie said dourly. 'She tells lies.'

'Artie!' Pam looked at him crossly.

'She does make things up,' Jeanie said and then stopped as they both looked at her. 'No, I won't say what – but I think she isn't very keen on land work, at least not with the cows. She will probably be fine on a tractor.'

'Well, I feel sorry for her,' Pam said. 'All I ask is that you both give her a chance before you condemn her.'

8

Frances finished forking the last of the soiled straw into the wheelbarrow and took it outside to the muck heap to empty. It smelled foul and her stomach roiled, bringing the taste of bile to the back of her throat. Sometimes, she felt she must have been mad to come here! And Artie seemed to give her all the worst jobs. She could have found another job in a factory if she'd tried – but then *he* would have found her. Frances had come here to hide.

Tears stung her eyes and she lifted a hand to wipe her cheeks, leaving a trail of smelly dirt and smudged make-up on her face. How she wished she'd never met Roy Bent – his name suited him so well. He was a small-time gangster, but she hadn't known that then. Her thoughts were bitter as she remembered how handsome he was and how flattered she'd been that he was interested in her – a little girl from a slum in London's East End. When he'd stopped in his flashy green car with a model of a leaping Jaguar on the bonnet, her heart had jumped with excitement. She'd smiled at him shyly. She'd been shy then, an honest working girl who lived in one room and never had more than a couple of shillings to spend on herself.

Roy had promised her the world. He'd told her he loved her and would look after her. She'd surrendered her innocence to him one night after he'd taken her dancing and plied her with gin and orange until she hardly knew what she was doing. Then he'd taken her back to his apartment – a place of wonder to a girl from the slums. He had clean fresh sheets on the bed that smelled nice and soft furniture that you sank into. Cabinets gleaming with precious items that he'd showed off to her, and thick carpets on the floor. Frances had been in heaven. The next morning, he'd given her all kinds of luxuries, food she'd never tasted, new clothes and silk stockings, real leather shoes.

She was his now, he'd told her. He would never let her go. She just had to do a few things for him now and then. Nothing she wouldn't like – but she had hated those small favours. Although she had willingly given herself to him, she was a good girl deep down and his suggestion that she should have sex with some men he owed money to had horrified her.

Frances had run from him then, but he'd fetched her back. He'd locked her in the bedroom and that night he'd given her something that drugged her senses. She hadn't really understood what was going on, but the man who came to her had used her like an animal, and she'd been bleeding when she woke up and realised what had happened to her.

She had been forced to 'be nice' to Roy's friends after that a couple of times most weeks. In between, Roy had made a fuss of her, taking her out and giving her things, but she'd been trapped, his slave to do whatever he told her. It had gone on for several months, long enough for her to have given up all hope of ever escaping, of being happy.

Then a different man had come along. His name was Geoff

and when they were left alone together, he'd asked her if she enjoyed the life. At first, Frances had been afraid to answer, but he'd gained her confidence by talking quietly to her and making no demands, and once she told him she was a prisoner, he'd promised he would help her.

Geoff had kept his promise. He'd come to the apartment one day when Roy was out and told her to leave with him. Frances had no idea how he'd got the keys, but he'd told her not to waste time or worry about it. She'd gone with him, hoping that he would be kind to her and look after her, but he'd taken her to the police station and they wanted her to tell on Roy – tell them how she had been forced to go with other men.

After some coaxing and reassurance that she would be taken somewhere safe, she had given them the details they'd wanted. Roy had been arrested and Frances had been able to get a job and live her own life – for three years. It was all the judge had given him. With time off for good behaviour, he was out of prison in two years – free to come after her. She'd had some narrow escapes, moving from one lodging house and one job to another. Twice she'd seen him watching her and that was when she'd decided to leave London.

She had gone to Birmingham for nearly a year, always looking over her shoulder, wondering if he would find her – and then the war had happened and she'd met someone. A young soldier named Derek. He'd been lovely to her, kind and gentle, not judging her but making her feel that she was loved, and she'd slept with him before he was sent overseas. Frances had felt safe and managed to put the sordidness of her life with Roy behind her, to begin to live again. Derek said he would write to her as often as he could, but, after the first one, no letters came from him and it was a letter from his best friend that told her he was dead.

Frances had gone out and got drunk that night. It wasn't fair that the one man she'd loved had been killed. In her grief, she'd risked returning to London, where she'd been born and felt more at home, and found herself a job in a munitions factory. She hadn't much liked the work, but the girls were protected and lived in a hostel, and it was years since seen she'd last seen Roy. Perhaps he'd forgotten her.

If she'd put her hopes in his forgetting her, Frances had a rude awakening on leaving the factory one night. She was in the company of other women and the male supervisor, so she'd been untouchable, but she'd seen him watching her from a distance and she'd known she had to get away. Roy had found her and the look on his face had told her he wanted revenge.

Frances knew now that his money came from his activities as a gangster. Roy wasn't a Mr Big in the underworld – no, he was the one who did their dirty work. He beat people up to make them pay protection money and he'd used a knife more than once; the police had told her. They'd hoped her evidence would bring others forward with proof of his worst crimes, but no one had dared. They feared him – and with good reason.

So, Frances knew that she had to disappear. She'd managed to avoid being alone when she left work and had persuaded her manager to let her apply for land work. Now she was here in this lonely, godforsaken place, hiding from the man who terrified her. She was sure Roy wouldn't think of looking here in the country-side. Why would he? He knew she liked the town and nice things, having fun. He knew her so well. Right from the start, she'd been an open book to him and he'd known just how to take advantage of her desires – her longing to be loved and for the better things in life she'd never had.

Derek had been the opposite of Roy, a kind and generous lover. She'd told him of her past and he'd sworn it didn't matter.

One day he would give the man who had used her the biggest beating of his life.

'He'll never harm you or another girl ever again,' Derek had vowed as he'd held her in his arms and let her cry. 'I'll look after you, my love. I promise.'

Frances had believed him. Derek was big and strong and afraid of nothing. She would have been safe with him – but the war had taken him. She would never see him again.

She'd liked Artie Talbot and thought he would be strong and protective, like her Derek – but he was taken. Frances felt bitter. It wasn't fair that Jeanie Salmons had everything Frances wanted. Love and security – and a smashing diamond ring. Derek had promised her a ring on his return, but he hadn't been able to keep his promise.

A little shiver went through Frances as she brought her mind back to the present. She didn't much like this job, but she was stuck with it, at least for a while – until she could work out a new plan. Going back to London wasn't an option, though it was what she wanted. She'd been safe in Birmingham but hadn't been truly happy there – finding it difficult to understand what a lot of people said when they talked quickly. Derek had been from London but posted to a base nearby and they'd met while he was on leave before he was sent overseas.

If only he hadn't died, Frances thought.

She wheeled the barrow back to the sheds. One more load and she was finished. Then there were just the pails to wash.

A sigh escaped her. Sometimes she felt so alone. She couldn't even tell the Talbot family her real name...

'Frances...' She turned as Jeanie spoke to her. 'Have you nearly finished?'

'Just the pails to scour,' she replied.

'I'll do those,' Jeanie offered. 'Go in and get warm. It won't take long and then I'll join you. Pam wants us to help her this morning. I've offered to do the ironing and there is a pile of nappies to wash. You can either do them or scrub the scullery?'

'I don't mind either or both,' Frances said. 'It will be warmer in there.'

'Yes, it is bitter today. It does get better when the weather turns, believe me. Some of the land work is pleasant – like haymaking and harvest. Everyone gives a hand and it is fun.'

Frances nodded and then met Jeanie's gaze. She felt a little stab of guilt for her behaviour. Jeanie had been willing to be friendly from the start but Frances had been too wary, too bitter and hurt to accept that friendship. Now, she realised that it was stupid to blame Jeanie for her own unhappiness. 'Thanks. I know I haven't exactly made myself popular with you. I suppose I envied you. Will you be friends if I say I'm sorry?'

'Yes, of course I will,' Jeanie responded warmly. 'I dare say you felt a bit out of things when you arrived.'

'Perhaps – anyway, I am sorry and I'll try not to be spiteful again.'

Jeanie nodded and went off to clean the pails and get ready for the second milking session that evening. Frances soon had the shed cleaning finished and then Artie arrived with fresh straw. She went off, leaving him to finish replacing the old bedding, and up to the kitchen. It smelled lovely, of baking and babies, and she smiled, relaxing for the first time in a long while.

'Have you finished, love?' Pam asked her.

'Yes, thanks. Jeanie and Artie came and did the last bits – so I'm free to do whatever you like.'

'Have a cup of tea and a jam tart before you start – and then you can rinse out those nappies for me in the scullery.' Pam nodded to her as she washed her hands at the sink. 'Let yourself relax and you will soon settle in. These are hard times and we must help each other.' She mixed her dough with a firm hand. 'If the weather allows it, you and Jeanie can go into Ely and do some shopping for me this afternoon. Have a walk round and perhaps a cup of tea in the café. Make it a little outing...'

'Thank you, Pam. You've been kind to me...' Frances hesitated. She wanted to tell her employer's wife the truth about her reasons for being here, but she was afraid that Pam wouldn't like her if she knew what she'd done. She was a bad girl. If she'd been a decent girl, she wouldn't have got in with Roy Bent in the first place, though she'd only been an innocent seventeen-year-old...

9

It was a bit warmer at last. After lunch, the sun had come out and the lingering snow had melted away. Jeanie and Frances caught the bus into the small market town, though despite its size, Ely was actually a city, because of its magnificent cathedral.

Frances hadn't seen much of it on her arrival, because she'd jumped straight on the bus at the station that had taken her to Mepal. Now they had the chance to look round and visit the shops as they searched for the items Pam wanted. A board outside the newsagent's had something on it about American troops who had arrived in Belfast in January. It was February now and another headline spoke of a strike by Chinese seamen in Liverpool. Jeanie decided to buy a paper and a women's magazine.

'There might be some good knitting patterns,' she told Frances when she came out of the newsagent's with, her paper, magazine and a bag of toffees, which she opened and offered to Frances.

'I can't knit,' Frances said. 'Mum couldn't either.'

'I could show you,' Jeanie offered and Frances thanked her

but wasn't enthusiastic.

After their wander around the shops, they went next door to the Lamb Hotel and had a bun and a pot of tea, then walked down the high street and past Woolworths on Forehill to stroll by the river. It was still cold, but, in the sun that afternoon, you could have been forgiven for thinking that it was nearly spring.

As they walked by the river, Jeanie talked about her home in London. Frances was hesitant at first and then told her about the school she'd gone to as a little girl. 'David – I told you he is in the air force now. He used to walk home from school with me. It was a rough area and—'

What she had been about to say was lost as they both saw a boy slip from the quayside, where three of them had been playing, into the icy but free-flowing water.

'Oh my God, it is deep there,' she heard Jeanie cry, looking about her for help. 'I can't swim well...'

'I'll get him,' Frances muttered and ran towards the river, hardly thinking about what she was about to do, her concern for the drowning boy all that mattered.

* * *

Jeanie watched, feeling stunned as Frances kicked off her court-heeled shoes and dived straight in.

'Frances—!' Jeanie was shocked and dazed as she saw Frances seize the boy by his jacket as he was going under for a third time. She pulled him to her and, supporting his head, towed him back along the river to where the ducks waddled in the shallow sloping area. Jeanie ran to meet her, but she was no longer alone. Suddenly, other people were there.

'What a brave thing to do and on a winter's day like this, too!' A woman's voice made Jeanie look at the newcomer. She'd brought blankets and, as Frances emerged, dripping with water, and weeds, she threw them around both her and the boy. 'Well done, miss! That was wonderful.'

'I think he's all right,' Frances stuttered, her teeth chattering with cold as she hugged a blanket to her.

'Oh, Frances, I thought you would die in that water,' Jeanie said, going to her and rubbing her hard to get her dry. Several men and women had now gathered on the quayside and she caught the flash of a camera but was too concerned about Frances to see who had taken a photo. 'It was such a brave thing to do...'

'Someone taught me how to...' Frances said, shuddering with cold. 'I have to get out of these wet things.'

'Come into my house, my dears,' the woman with the blankets was drying the little boy now as his friends wandered off towards their homes. 'I'll get you all hot drinks and lend you some clothes while yours dry. You need some reward, miss.'

'C— Frances,' Frances said, teeth chattering now. 'Thank you, Mrs...?'

'Bates. I live just here by the quayside and I saw what you did from my window. You didn't even hesitate.'

'I knew he might die because his friends were yelling that he couldn't swim.'

'—Then his mother shouldn't let him play by the river.' Mrs Bates tutted over her shoulder as she led the way inside her home. 'I've seen more than one youngster in trouble here. They will play on the railings and then they slip into the river. My husband has fished a couple of them out before now – but he wasn't here today, so it was a good thing you were, Frances.'

Someone called to Jeanie as she followed them in. 'What's her name, miss?'

'Frances Grant. She is a land girl...' Jeanie said. 'Why?'

'I'm from the local paper,' he replied. 'Folk will want to know!'

Jeanie nodded and closed the door behind her. Mrs Bates had taken the boy and Frances straight through to her big warm kitchen, where the radio was playing music. 'I like my radio for company,' she told them. 'Did you hear that new show on the BBC Forces Programme? It's called *Desert Island Discs* – and Roy Plomley was the first presenter... ever so interesting it was.'

'No, I haven't,' Jeanie replied.

Frances was drying herself with a fresh dry towel and the boy had been stripped and wrapped in a thick blanket. Frances went into the scullery and took her things off, coming back in yet another blanket to sit by the fire and sip the hot cocoa Mrs Bates had now made for them, chattering all the while.

Jeanie looked at the child. He couldn't be more than six or seven. If Frances hadn't acted so promptly, he would almost certainly have died.

'What is your name?' she asked him as he warmed his hands on the cup of creamy cocoa. 'Do you live near here?'

'Billy,' he replied. 'I live just down the road wiv me gran. Mum's dead and Dad's gorn off ter beat the Germans. So I live wiv Gran. She won't care, but she'll be cross if she knows what I done...'

'She will have to know,' Mrs Bates said. 'Hasn't she told you not to play near the water?'

'I've only been 'ere a week,' he replied. 'They sent me down 'ere from London 'cos me home was bombed and me mum killed.' He sniffed and rubbed his nose on the blanket.

'It was very nearly the end of you, too,' Mrs Bates said. 'You are a very lucky boy, Billy. If it hadn't been for Miss Grant, you would have almost certainly died.'

Billy looked at her and then turned his big sad eyes on

Frances. 'Fanks, miss. Me dad will be pleased. Me gran says I'm too much trouble for an old woman, but me dad will come back fer me, 'cos he promised.'

'You're welcome,' Frances said. 'Be careful next time. I shan't be here to jump in and get you.'

'Can I come and live wiv you?' Billy asked and Jeanie's heart caught as he looked from Frances to her. 'I'll be good...'

A knock came at the door then and Mrs Bates went to answer it. She returned shortly with a grey-haired woman who was bent over and leaning on a stick to support her. Her eyes flashed angrily as she looked at Billy.

'You bad boy,' she said harshly. 'Causing all this trouble. You'll be the death of me...'

'It were an accident...' Billy sent her a scared look. 'I'm sorry, Gran.'

'Here, put these on,' she said and shoved a bundle of clothes at him. 'You are in trouble, lad. Any more of this behaviour and I'll send you to an orphanage...'

'He is frightened and scared,' Frances said. 'Please, don't scold him.'

'You'll be the one that jumped in after him, I suppose,' the old woman said. 'I ought to thank you, but it would have saved a lot of trouble if he'd drowned. His mother's dead – not that she ever bothered about him – and his father's gone to war. I shan't live long and then what will become of him?'

No one answered and she grabbed the boy's arm and dragged him off.

'I'll come back for his wet things later,' she muttered and then took herself off towing Billy behind her without another glance at Mrs Bates or Jeanie and Frances.

'Well...' Mrs Bates was lost for words as the door slammed behind her. 'What a rude woman. I am so sorry, my dear. After you risked your own life to save Billy. She might have thanked you properly.'

'I'm not that bothered about my life,' Frances said, and then as both Jeanie and Mrs Bates looked at her. 'I mean, I never thought. I just wanted to save him. Poor little chap. It isn't very nice to know you're not wanted...'

'Your life is important too,' Jeanie said. 'I think what you did was wonderful, Frances, and I know Pam and the others will be proud of you. I feel sorry for Billy, but perhaps his gran was just cross because she was worried.'

'Somehow I doubt that,' Frances replied. 'I think she genuinely doesn't want him. He looked so sad – and so scared.' His sad little face had touched something inside her, breaking through the barriers of self-protection. She too had known what it felt like to be alone and scared.

'Yes, he did,' Mrs Bates agreed. 'Well, don't you worry, my dear. I shall keep an eye out for him. I get a bit lonely on my own, with my husband away a lot due to the war. Billy can come here for his tea sometimes. I'll speak to his gran about it another day...'

'Yes, that would be nice,' Jeanie said. 'You are very kind and helpful. Thank you for bringing us in and getting Frances warm again.'

'You can borrow my things and bring them back another day when you have time. Leave yours here and I'll wash and iron them for you – you might both come to tea one day if you'd like.'

'That is kind of you,' Frances said and for a moment Jeanie saw tears in her eyes. 'We'd better go, Jeanie, or we shan't get our bus... Oh, what about my shopping bag? I dropped it as I ran...'

'I picked it up,' Jeanie said. 'Pam is going to be so pleased we managed to get almond essence and ground almonds, as well as the rice. She can make Artie's favourite cake now.'

'Yes, we were lucky,' Frances agreed and smiled. Jeanie knew it for a genuine smile and felt pleased. Their afternoon shopping and then Frances' heroic deed had brought them together and she felt they were now friends, instead of just work colleagues. 'We'd better go – but I will visit if I may, Mrs Bates?'

'Of course. Whenever you can manage it, dear.'

She saw them to the door and they ran all the way up the hill and along Market Street to the bus stop. It was just about to leave, but the conductor saw them and held it until they clambered on. Sitting down with a plop of relief, they looked at each other and then laughed.

'Well, I never expected that,' Jeanie said. 'Just wait until I tell Artie what he missed...'

'Don't make a big thing of it,' Frances flushed. 'I told you, I just did it without thinking.'

'It was the bravest thing I've ever seen,' Jeanie said. 'I can't not tell them, because they are bound to hear what happened. Besides, Pam will wonder why you're dressed like that...'

Frances looked down at herself and laughed, because the skirt was down to her ankles and the jacket was cinched in at the waist in the fashion that was popular thirty years before. 'Yes, they aren't exactly the clothes I like to wear, but she was so kind I couldn't refuse them.'

'No, of course not,' Jeanie agreed.

* * *

Pam stared at Frances in amazement when Jeanie told her what she'd done.

'I was paralysed with fear, because I could never have done it,' Jeanie said. 'Frances didn't even stop to think. She just dived in and grabbed the boy by his jacket and hauled him to the shallow bank where the ducks and swans gather.'

'That was a dangerous thing to do,' Pam said. 'You don't know what is in that river. You could have hurt yourself and, in this weather, it is a wonder you didn't freeze to death.'

'We were taken in by a lady who lives close by,' Jeanie said. 'She was so kind and looked after us – even loaned Frances some of her clothes...'

'Yes, so I see,' Pam said and chuckled. 'Not much of a reward for such bravery, Frances. Come and have a sit by the fire while I get tea ready.'

'I'm not cold,' Frances said. 'This suit is old-fashioned but it is good tweed and kept me warm. I know it was a bit daft, but the alternative was to stand by and let the child die.'

'His gran fetched him,' Jeanie explained. 'She is old and I think he's too much for her. She said it would have been just as well if Frances had let him drown.'

'Wicked woman,' Pam riposted, her blue eyes flashing with anger. 'How could anyone say such a thing?'

'His mum died and his father is in the army or one of the forces,' Frances said, accepting the hot cup of tea with a smile. 'I felt sorry for him. Jeanie did too. Poor little kid. No one to care about him...'

'That isn't good,' Pam said and sighed. 'I dare say there are many more sad cases because of the war. We didn't have any evacuees when they sent the London children to the country...'

'You had a houseful,' Jeanie said. 'You still do, Pam.' A wail from upstairs confirmed that she was right. 'That sounds like Jonny. Shall I go and fetch him?'

'Yes, please, love. He's been crying on and off this afternoon. I don't know if he heard Lizzie's little one, or whether he's sickening for something.'

'I'll get him.' Jeanie left the kitchen. Jonny's wails had increased as she reached his bedroom. Picking him up, she was relieved that his cries ceased and decided it was probably just a wet nappy upsetting him.

'Is that you, Pam?' Lizzie's voice called from her bedroom.

Jeanie went along the hall carrying Jonny in her arms.

'It's me,' she said from the doorway. 'Do you need something, Lizzie?'

'Just some company,' Lizzie said. 'I was going to ask Pam if she wanted to have Jonny's cot moved in with me. I think he knows there is another baby in the house and he wants to be with us.'

'I was just going to change him,' Jeanie said. 'I can do it here if that's okay?'

'Would you? Thanks so much.' Lizzie smiled at her.

Jeanie placed a towel on the bed and then gently deposited the warm baby. The soiled nappy was whipped off, bottom patted dry and clean wrappings applied.

'I'll take this down in a minute or two,' Jeanie said and sat on the bed beside Lizzie. 'How are you feeling now?'

'Still a bit sore and tired, but I'll soon be better,' Lizzie replied. 'Just fed up with lying here. The midwife said I could get up now and then, but she thinks I should have bed rest for two weeks. I don't think I can manage that. If I feel okay in the morning, I'll come down to the kitchen.'

Jeanie had placed Jonny in the cot with Lizzie's baby, Archie. He was sleeping contentedly. 'I think you were right; he seems to have settled fine now.'

'Just wanted company – and a dry nappy,' Lizzie said, smiling fondly at the two little boys lying side by side in Pam's big cot. It was a large, dark wood cot that was suspended so that a gentle hand could rock it and the motion helped to ease fractious babies into peaceful sleep. 'Pam said you'd gone into Ely with Frances. She hoped it would help you two to get on better – did it?'

'Yes. I think I may have misjudged her,' Jeanie said. 'I still think she might have lied to us, and she is definitely hiding something – but she did a very brave thing and I admire her for that...'

Jeanie described what had happened and Lizzie nodded. 'Yes, that was brave, but why do you think she lied to us?'

'She contradicted her story once and then – well, when she was telling Mrs Bates her name, she started to say something different – a name beginning with C. Then she changed it to Frances...'

'Strange, but perhaps she was going to say something else?'

'Yes, perhaps.' Jeanie frowned. 'I think she didn't like me at the start, but we're all right now.'

'Good. Pam was a bit worried about it, but I told her you would cope.'

Jeanie smiled as Archie gave a little burp and then snuggled closer to Jonny. 'They will be like brothers growing up.'

'Yes, it is good for them both,' Lizzie smiled and then her smile faded. 'Pam told me that Arthur has been told he can visit John in the hospital. It seems he has begun to remember things at last and he asked for his father and Faith...'

'How will they tell him?' Jeanie asked, feeling a great sadness wash over her. 'It is such an awful thing for him – to know the truth will be devastating.'

'Pam says Arthur insists on being the one to see him first and he isn't going to tell him exactly how she died, just that it was after her child was born.'

'Does John even know that Faith was having a child?'

'I'm not sure he does, because he went missing before she

really knew, so I don't see how he could...' Lizzie frowned. 'We all thought John was dead... Faith believed it to the last. We didn't hear he'd been taken to hospital until it was too late for her.'

Jeanie nodded. 'It is going to be hard for him, discovering that he is a father but that Faith is gone.'

'Pam – and all of us really – will look after the baby, but we can't restore what John has lost.'

'It is too sad,' Jeanie said and wiped away the tears that were trickling down her cheeks. 'It puts everything else into perspective, doesn't it? I mean, who cares if Frances isn't who she says she is? She works well and she is brave – and compared with the grief this family is carrying, it is nothing.'

'As long as you can work with her that's all that matters. Pam was afraid they might have to let her go if you couldn't.'

'Oh no, that would be mean,' Jeanie said. 'I'm sure we'll get on fine now. I'd better go down and see if Pam needs anything. I'll come up later and we can chat – if you'd like that?'

'Yes, I would,' Lizzie said.

Jeanie left her to rest and went back down to the kitchen. Arthur and Artie had come in while she was upstairs. Jean could hear them talking; Arthur was speaking.

'I'll go in the morning then,' he said to Pam. 'I'll talk to the doctors about getting John moved nearer home – and then you can visit.'

'I still wonder if we're doing right, not telling him the whole truth,' Pam murmured as she brought a deliciously aromatic, herby pie to the table. 'If he discovers it from someone else, it will be worse...'

'He's not up to dealing with it just yet,' Arthur said. 'If I'm wrong, he can blame me. Please let me be the judge of what's right for him just now, love.'

'Yes, I know you're right,' Pam gave in, but Jeanie could see by her face that she was anxious.

'Jonny is in Archie's cot,' she told Pam. 'He was wet, but I changed him, and Lizzie said to put them together. She wants to get up tomorrow.'

'She is getting fed up with staying in bed,' Pam replied, smiling now. 'Well, why not? I was up and about within days of having my Tom. You can tell her there's a letter for her when you go up. Arthur took it from the postman and had it in his pocket all afternoon.'

'Is there anything you want me to do for you this evening, Pam?' Jeanie asked.

'No, I don't think so, love. Frances has volunteered for the ironing, so you can do whatever you like.'

'I thought I'd spend a bit of time with Lizzie.'

Artie sent her a quizzical glance. 'Does that mean I can go down the pub then? There's a darts match I'd like to watch this evening.'

'Not playing then?' Arthur said and Artie shook his head.

'No, I'm not as good as Tom. I'll watch and buy a few pints – and then come home.'

'Don't be late, because it is turning bitter again,' his father said. 'Walk. Don't take your motorbike. I don't want you coming off it and being laid up for weeks on end...'

Artie raised his eyebrows at Jeanie. She giggled, but Pam was calling them all to table and Frances entered the kitchen wearing her own clothes again. Artie looked at her, respect in his eyes.

'Mum told me what you did. It was brave, Frances. I just hope you don't get pneumonia for it.'

'I shan't,' she said. 'It was nothing.'

Artie looked at Jeanie. She shook her head, so he said no more.

10

Arthur was met by a senior nurse at the military hospital, when he gave his name and told them he'd come to see his son, John Talbot. She was dressed in the uniform of a nursing sister and her expression was serious, even though she smiled as she saw him.

'You are John's father?' she nodded as he offered his hand. 'It was a log journey for you to Portsmouth, I think. Come with me, please. I'd like to talk to you in my office for a moment before I take you to him.'

'Sister...'

'Morrison,' she confirmed and led the way to a small office, indicating that he should sit in a rather hard elbow chair. 'I don't know how much you've been told about John's injuries?'

'I understand he had several broken bones and was feverish for a while – but no serious internal damage.' Arthur looked at her anxiously, fearing worse news.

'Yes, that is the extent of his physical injuries, apart from a knife wound, which had turned septic through neglect but has at last healed. However, it was a long time before he came back to us mentally, Mr Talbot. The doctors think there was some trauma – perhaps unconnected to his main injuries. He seems to be troubled about something that happened, but he won't speak about it to us. He ought to be able to come home in a week or two, but he may not be *stable* – mentally...'

'I see.' Arthur frowned. 'You have no idea what is troubling him, I suppose?'

'No. After his plane crashed, he was wandering in a semi-dazed state for a while. The knife wound appears to have happened sometime after the crash injuries, and it caused a lot of grief because it went untreated for too long. We know he was taken in by nuns and nursed through the worst of his wounds, before being smuggled to Switzerland and from there put on a hospital ship for England. John has very few memories of that time – indeed, he had few memories at all until recently, when he suddenly spoke of his family and someone called Faith.'

'Yes, he was engaged to her,' Arthur said. 'They were to have married...'

'That will be something for him to look forward to—' Sister Morrison began and then stopped as she saw his face. 'Something happened to her?'

'Faith died having his baby,' he said simply. 'His mother wanted to come today, but I decided it had better be me. I was thinking to tell him at least some of it, but perhaps I shouldn't?'

'He is going to ask,' Sister Morrison replied. 'I think you must tell your son the truth, Mr Talbot, but be prepared. He may react badly, and if he does, please ring the bell and I shall come personally.'

'Thank you.' Arthur stood and followed her back into a long corridor. They walked halfway down it and then Sister Morrison stopped and tapped a door, before taking him into the small room, where John was the only patient. He was lying on top of the bed, his eyes closed, and Arthur's heart stopped, as he saw how thin and pale he looked. He had some scars on his cheek and forehead, which had started to heal but were still red and a little puckered, and his right hand was bandaged, his arm in a sling. Other than that he seemed to be intact.

'John, your father has come to visit,' Sister Morrison announced and he opened his eyes.

'Dad...?' John inched his way up the pillows, looking bewildered for a moment. 'Is Mum here?'

'We advised only one visitor for a start,' Sister Morrison told him. 'I will leave you alone together – but I'm not far away, if you need me.'

'Your mum wanted to come, but I thought it should be me this first time,' Arthur said. He sat on the hard wooden chair provided beside the bed. 'How are you feeling, lad?'

'Like I've been run over by a traction engine,' John said and gave a short laugh, then winced. 'It hurts when I laugh. Sorry to bring you all the way down here. I asked when I can come home, but they said not yet.'

'I'm going to ask if they will send you to Addenbrooke's in Cambridge,' Arthur replied. 'Everyone wants to see you and it will be easier there.'

'What about Faith?' John said, his face lighting with sudden eagerness. 'Does she know where I am? I thought she would write – but I haven't heard from her.'

Arthur paused. He wished he could draw on his pipe but knew he couldn't light it here. 'Did you know that Faith was expecting your child?' he asked and saw the way John's face went white and then pink. 'No, we thought you might not know. You have a son – a beautiful boy. Your mum is looking after him.'

'Mum...?' John stared at him in bewilderment, clearly struggling to take this knowledge in. 'I don't understand...' He shook his head to clear it. 'I know we... I know it is possible but... What happened? Faith's parents will be so angry. She must have had to give up her nursing and it's all my fault. Does she hate me now?'

'I am sure Faith loved you,' Arthur said. 'She was a lovely girl, John, and we all became fond of her. She lived with Lizzie until...'

John stared at him. 'You're talking as if...' He leaned forward and gripped his father's wrist. 'Tell me, where is Faith? What happened?'

'I don't want to hurt you, John – but she died soon after her child was born. Jeanie was with her at the end and Artie called the doctor – but it was too late.'

'No!' John's eyes darkened with horror and pain. 'No! She couldn't die like that, she couldn't! You're lying to me! She was young and strong and full of life...' He clawed up wildly, gave a moan and fell back again, his eyes closing. Putting a hand to his head as if it hurt, he said, 'How could she die?'

'I think she fell and hit her head,' Arthur said. 'I am so sorry, John. Perhaps I shouldn't have told you yet...'

'I knew something was wrong,' he remarked, his eyes still closed. His fingers massaged the side of his head, clearly in some pain. 'I got someone to write to her as soon as I knew who I was, but no reply came – the letter was returned. I thought she was angry with me.'

'No, she was never angry with you. She wanted your baby, John.'

'It's my fault... my fault...' John said with a cry of despair. 'I killed her. I'm to blame...'

'No, you're not,' Arthur said firmly. 'Put that idea out of your head, John. Faith had a little accident and it was that that killed her – not your child. In no way were you to blame.'

John closed his eyes. 'Thank you for coming, but please leave me now.'

'John...' Arthur stared at him indecisively. 'I'll go if you want – but know this, we all love you and your son needs you. Come home to us soon. Your mother is breaking her heart over you, lad.'

Arthur gave his son one last lingering look and walked out of the room, closing the door softly behind him. Outside, he leaned against the wall and breathed deeply, cursing himself as he rubbed at his chest. Blooming indigestion! He'd had it a few times recently, but this was worse. Must have been that cheese and pickle sandwich he'd eaten on the train. Now, look what he'd done. He'd made a mess of it somehow. Pam would have done it better. For a moment, Arthur considered returning and telling his son how Faith had really died, but then a voice interrupted his thoughts.

'How did he take it, Mr Talbot?'

'Hard – he blames himself,' Arthur said. 'It wasn't his fault, Sister Morrison. In no way was John to blame for what happened.'

'It is natural that he should feel that way for a start. I know that men often do if a woman dies in childbed. In time, John will understand that he was not to blame for her death.'

'Yes, I suppose...' Arthur hesitated, wondering if he should tell her the whole truth, but then decided against it. It was family business and too unpleasant to discuss with a stranger. 'He is very upset. He asked me to leave.'

'Yes, I feared he might. I think we must give him time, Mr Talbot. If the doctors agree to his being moved to Cambridge, you will be able to visit him again sooner. Leave him to grieve. It is for the best...'

Arthur nodded. He bid her goodbye and knew that she was going to then go and check on his son. Mayhap a senior nurse was the right person to deal with John now. He was just a simple farmer and he didn't understand the workings of a distressed mind. If John hadn't been so ill, he would have told him the truth straight out and told him to buck up and face it like a man – as he would if he'd been in his shoes. John's son needed him. Yet he knew that his son must be in agony now. He felt another stab of pain in his chest and grimaced. That would teach him to eat on trains!

There was nothing he could do to help John through his grief. Surely, it was better for him to believe Faith had a little accident than be told the brutal truth. Even Arthur had found that hard to take and he considered himself tough. No, he'd done the right thing. Perhaps one day they would have to tell John everything, but he longed for it all to just disappear under the carpet. It didn't have to be right now anyway. Give the lad time to get himself right. He'd been ill for months and he still wasn't right – it looked to Arthur as if he was getting pain in his temples.

Arthur lit his pipe once he was out in the bitterly cold air. There was going to be more snow before long if he was any judge. He would be glad to be home, but he wasn't looking forward to telling his wife of John's reaction to the news of Faith's untimely death.

* * *

'I knew he would take it hard,' Pam said, looking at him anxiously as he recounted John's disbelief and then his self-blame. 'I still think it might have been better to tell him all of it. When he finds out, he will be angry with us for keeping it from him.'

'I'll tell him it was me who made the decision,' Arthur said. 'I wonder now if I should have told him anything about her or the boy. He is still in a fragile state mentally. They reckon something happened after he was in the care of the nuns. Something that he can't or won't talk about...'

'Why – what do you mean?' Pam asked. 'I thought he'd got his memory back?'

'Yes, he has. He knew me – and he'd tried to contact Faith. But they told me there was something haunting him... I think he might be having nightmares or funny turns... I know it happens to some of the lads when they've been through a bad time.'

'My poor boy,' Pam said. Her eyes were wet and she blinked away her tears. 'I should go to him...'

'They will probably move him to Addenbrooke's soon and you can all visit him then,' Arthur said. He sighed heavily. 'I should probably have let you go this time. You'd have made a better job of telling him than me.'

Pam stared at him, then her expression softened. 'Don't be silly, love,' she murmured. 'No one could have made that any easier for him – and perhaps I'm wrong to think it would be best out in the open. Don't go blaming yourself, Arthur. It isn't your fault that Faith's uncle was such a wicked man. He was the one to blame, no one else. If he wasn't dead, I could kill him myself.'

Arthur looked at her and then smiled reluctantly. 'You'd have to stand in line. Artie feels the same and I think I'd break his damned neck for all the pain he's caused.'

Pam put her arms around him. 'John is going to need a lot of love and understanding by the sound of it. The sooner he is home with us, the better.'

Arthur nodded and hugged her. He wasn't sure that the kind of injury that John was suffering from was that easy to cure, even with all the love his mother would pour over him. His physical hurts were healing and he would have been home before now had it not been for whatever was haunting his mind. Arthur had seen horror in his son's eyes before he closed them and knew that John was going to have to fight a lot of battles in his head before he could be the carefree lad they'd known and loved again.

* * *

John lay with his eyes open, staring at the ceiling. Faith dead – because of an accident that had made her give birth prematurely. He wished now that he'd asked for more details... but it hardly mattered how it had happened. Faith – his Faith – was dead and he knew he was being punished for what he'd done.

He was an evil man and he'd caused a woman to die and for that he was being punished. Bitter tears trickled down his cheeks.

'Faith... forgive me... forgive me,' he whispered. 'I never meant to hurt you. I love you... I love you so much.' He closed his eyes, but the pictures in his mind were too awful to remember and he shook his head. 'Go away. Please go away... I never meant it to happen...'

John stared at the ceiling again. He focused on a slight crack. Perhaps if he looked at that crack long enough, he could crawl into it and never come back. Never have to face his pain and the guilt... but he knew that he had caused the death of an innocent woman, a nun. She had been young and beautiful; though her head was covered in a wimple, her face had had the sweetness of an angel, but because she'd helped him, she was dead, and she'd died in a terrible way.

Pictures of her broken and ravaged body haunted him when he tried to sleep. The doctors asked him what was torturing him, but he couldn't tell them – didn't want to remember exactly. He only knew that he'd asked her for a hot drink and she'd gone to fetch it.

John had heard the terrible screams from his room hidden behind a false wall in the kitchen. He'd struggled from his bed, his head pounding; he'd had to fumble for the lever that opened the secret door, before going to investigate – and he'd seen her lying there on the floor, bloody and yet still alive. The man in uniform had stared at him before lunging at him, knife in hand. He'd smelled the fumes of strong drink on his breath. John had fought him with a strength he hadn't known he possessed, and somehow, he'd used the man's own knife to kill him. He'd finished him off by slitting his throat and turned to the young nun who had been so savagely attacked.

'Maria…' he'd said, bending over her, blood from wounds to his hand, arm and shoulder mingling with hers as she lay there, eyes staring up at him in pain and fear. 'I'll get help.'

'No, please…' she'd whispered. 'Just stay with me, please…' John had seen the puddle of blood that had run from her stomach where she'd been stabbed several times. 'He was looking for you. He knew we had you hidden. I wouldn't tell him. You must bury him before more soldiers come—'

'I need to help you…'

'No one can,' she whispered and closed her eyes for the last time.

The nuns had come then, frightened and shocked. Two of them had carried Maria away, and a third – an older, stronger one – had helped John to take the body of her murderer and bury it under a stack of manure from the cows the nuns kept for their milk.

'I was too late to save her. She died because she wouldn't tell him where I was hidden...'

'She did her duty,' the strong nun replied. 'Now you must prepare to do yours. Someone will come and take you away. We cannot risk keeping you here any longer.'

'Yes, I know. I am sorry. I would have given my life for hers...'

'That is foolish. Maria did God's will as she saw it – but we must send you away.'

When they returned to the kitchen, the floor had been scrubbed clean. John was banished to his hidden room, to wait there until a man came to fetch him. Their journey to Switzerland had been hard, travelling at night and hiding in daylight, and John's wound had festered over the days spent travelling. He'd hardly noticed it at first, wrapping it in a piece torn from his shirt. Had he told the nuns earlier, they would have tended it, but he had felt too guilty and hardly an hour had passed before he was taken away. His guilt had grown along with the pain in his arm.

The doctors in Switzerland had told him he was lucky to be alive. They asked how it had happened, but he told them he couldn't remember. It was true that he'd forgotten his own name for a long time, but the incident in the convent kitchen had brought it back to him. He was just too tortured by his guilt and shame to tell anyone his name until after they had shipped him home to England. Yes, it was war and these things happened, but John believed his hesitation – his cowardly hesitation – had been the difference between life and death and he could not forgive himself.

And now he knew he'd been punished for what he'd done. If he'd left the safety of his room the instant he heard the first scream, Maria might still live. He'd hesitated, fearing to be captured and imprisoned, and his cowardice had cost the life of an innocent woman.

John was too ashamed to tell anyone – he hadn't even wanted to go home at first. Now, Faith was dead, having his child. He'd killed her, just as he'd killed that nun. He was a coward and he deserved to suffer for what he'd done...

11

Artie was the first one to see the article in the local paper. He'd gone into Ely market, to pick up some new parts for the plough and saw an intriguing headline on a billboard outside the newsagent.

LAND GIRL IN HEROIC RESCUE

Artie went in and bought a paper, grinning it as he opened it to see a picture of Frances being led away with a blanket wrapped around her. The little boy was also in the picture and Jeanie was following them.

'Well, well,' he murmured as he read that Frances worked as a land girl for the Talbot family. All the details of the rescue were there, but whereas, Jeanie and Frances had played down the risks, the paper had gone into lots of details about the dangers of diving into icy cold water without knowing what was there – and, according to the paper, there was all kinds of rubbish dumped in the River Ouse where it passed through the Cathedral city, especially near the quayside.

As well as the large front-page article, there was more inside from the bystanders, all of whom had an opinion to give. He hadn't expected to see pictures of Blackberry Farm, but there were some inside the paper. Clearly the editor had wanted to make the most of the story. Artie hadn't noticed anyone taking pictures of the farm and wondered what the Air Ministry would think to the mention of the airfield. Surely that sort of thing should remain confidential. It was only one line, but still, in the wrong hands, the information could cause trouble. However, it was just a local paper with a limited circulation and most of the population in the area would already know of its location. Probably the enemy did, too, Artie decided and dismissed it from his thoughts.

He was grinning to himself as he drove home. He showed the paper to his father first.

Arthur frowned over it. 'Don't see why they needed to take photographs of the farm,' he grumbled. 'You can just see the edge of the airfield too. Bit stupid that, if you ask me.'

'If I'd seen them, I'd have warned them off, but I didn't – did you?'

'Nope. Never entered my head anyone would think of it,' Arthur grunted. 'Frances deserves to be congratulated, but nothing to do with us.'

When Artie took the paper into the kitchen, his mother and Lizzie were changing babies. They both looked at the front page, nodded and smiled.

'She was very brave,' Lizzie said. 'I don't think I would have done it. I might have got a rope to throw out to him or an oar from one of the punts that are moored there, but I don't think I would have been brave enough to jump in, even though I can swim.'

'Tom would have,' Pam said, 'but none of the menfolk were there. I think she deserves praise.'

'What do you think of that then?' Artie showed them the pictures of the farm.

Pam frowned. 'Not a good thing to put that about the airfield in. I'm surprised the editor didn't censor that. I mean, all the locals know it is there, but you shouldn't hand out information like that – there are saboteurs in the country, so the papers say, and they are always warning us that careless talk costs lives.'

'I doubt if anyone outside Cambridgeshire will read it,' Lizzie said. 'But it was irresponsible.'

'What's that then?' Jeanie and Frances entered the kitchen together. They had been mucking out the cowshed again and took off their filthy boots at the door, placing them outside before padding across Pam's clean floor to warm themselves at the fire.

'Artie saw this in Ely,' Pam handed her the paper. 'You're famous, Frances – well locally. They took pictures of the farm too and mentioned the airfield – that's what we thought wrong.'

Frances stared at the photograph of herself and all the colour drained away. 'No! How dare they do this? I didn't want my picture in the paper...' She looked at Jeanie. 'When did they take this? I didn't see anyone—'

'I saw someone take a picture, but I didn't think this would happen,' Jeanie said. 'I know you didn't want a fuss made, Frances, but they are only applauding you for your bravery.'

Frances shook her head and turned away. 'Excuse me. I have to be alone...'

They all stared at each other as she hurriedly left the room and they heard her pounding up the stairs.

'What is that about?' Artie asked. 'She went as white as a sheet when she saw that picture of herself.'

'She looked frightened,' Pam said. She handed Jonny to Jeanie. 'Here, he's changed but doesn't want to sleep for a bit. Jiggle him on your knee while I go to Frances.'

She followed Frances from the room, the steady tread of her feet up the stairs being heard until Artie broke the silence.

'That girl is hiding something. I sensed it when she first came – something isn't right about her, but I don't know what.'

'I thought the same,' Jeanie replied, 'but I've come to like her. She saved that child from drowning and she always does her share of the work. I do agree that she is hiding a secret, though.'

'Pam is right, she did look scared,' Lizzie said. 'She seems a nice, friendly girl most of the time, but then she goes silent – as if she has some deep sorrow she can't bear. I'd be inclined to give her the benefit of the doubt if I were you. Don't judge her for having a past she doesn't want to divulge. Not everyone comes from a good home or a happy life.'

'Lizzie is right,' Arthur remarked from the doorway. He'd followed the girls in after fitting some machine parts that Artie had brought home. 'The girl seems decent enough to me. She works well and now that she and Jeanie have sorted themselves, I think she will fit in. We must accept that perhaps she has her reasons for not telling us everything.'

* * *

Pam found Frances sitting on the edge of her bed. She had her head in her hands and was shaking, clearly shocked and distressed by the photograph in the paper.

Pam sat down beside her. 'Don't upset yourself, love. It's unlikely that whoever you are afraid of will see the paper. The circulation doesn't go that far.'

Frances' head came up and a little gasp escaped Pam as she

saw her despair. 'You don't know for sure he won't see it...' she said, her voice thick with fear and a hint of tears. 'If he does, he will come after me – and he will hurt me.'

Pam nodded. She'd guessed it was fear of a man when she'd seen the terror in Frances' eyes before she'd abruptly left the kitchen for the seclusion of her room. 'Can you tell me about him – what he did to you?'

Frances looked at her for a moment, then tears began to trickle down her cheeks. 'You won't want me here if I tell you what he made me do...'

Pam reached for her hand and held it. 'I liked you the minute you came,' she said. 'I've seen there was something you were hiding, but whatever this man made you do doesn't matter to me, Frances. I'm not shocked or angry, except for your sake. I may live quietly in the country, but I know what some cruel men are capable of, my dear.'

Frances gave a little sob. 'I've been so alone since my mother died. He was there; I was just seventeen and I needed a friend. I thought he was my friend – but he wasn't. He forced me to do things – bad things. I can't bear to tell you...'

'I understand, love,' Pam said. She put her arm about Frances' shoulders and felt the girl crumble against her, holding her as she wept into her chest and kissing the top of her head. 'That's it, let it all out. Whatever he made you do, he's the one to blame not you.'

'You're not disgusted? You won't send me away?'

'No to both questions,' Pam smiled as she soothed. 'You are one of us now, Frances. We shall do our best to look after you.'

Frances sat back and wiped her face. 'Supposing he sees that paper? Supposing he comes here after me?'

'I doubt that will happen,' Pam reassured. 'But we will deal with him if he comes – I promise. Both Artie and Arthur would see him off and so would I. He won't be allowed near you. Will you tell me his name, love?'

'Roy Bent,' Frances said in a low voice. 'I hate him. He is a vile crook and a bully and I wish I'd never met him.'

Pam nodded. 'Believe me, Frances, it is a chance in a million that he will see that paper – but if he does, we'll sort him. You try to put it all behind you, love.'

'You won't tell the others?' Frances threw her a desperate look.

'I will tell them to be careful if a stranger comes looking for you, Frances. I will tell them there is man who has harmed you in the past, but that's all. No one needs to know details, my dear. Just accept that we are your friends and be as happy as you can.'

'You don't think I should go – find somewhere else to hide?'

'Are you going to run from him all your life?' Pam asked. 'It won't help, Frances. If the worst should happen, face up to him. Tell him you want nothing to do with him.'

'I have, but he still tried to force me to go back to him...'

'You were alone then. Now you have us,' Pam said. 'You must be as brave as you were when you jumped into that river after young Billy...'

Frances lifted her head. 'I didn't think about that, I just did it.'

'I'd make sure a pitchfork is somewhere not too far away,' Pam said with a chuckle. 'He'd retreat fast enough if you stuck him with that – and I've got my broom and a marble rolling pin. We'll make mincemeat of him.'

Frances laughed and stood up. 'You make me feel so much better – all of you do. I've never had a big family. It was just my mum and me for years, until she died. I never knew my dad.'

Pam nodded. 'So your dad wasn't a fireman then?'

'I made that up and other things too. My real name is Cathy

Bristow, but I lost my papers in a fire and took the chance of changing it to Frances. Everyone was very kind and gave me new ration books and all I needed, because it was happening all the time with the gas leaks and the air raids, so they didn't question much.'

'What do you want us to call you?' Pam asked her.

'Frances. I want to leave Cathy behind with all the bad stuff. I'm Frances now. Frances was a real person, but she died in an air raid. A friend of mind saw her gravestone. I took her name. She didn't have a family; they all died together. I don't think she would mind, would she?'

'I don't expect it matters now,' Pam replied. 'We'll go on calling you Frances then, and now, my dear, you should come down and have some docky. You'll be milking before long, because Artie and Arthur are doing maintenance work on the machinery.'

* * *

It was late in the evening and Frances was in bed when her worries came back to haunt her. Pam had kept her busy all day and she knew that was done on purpose. Her employer's wife was so kind. She'd made Frances feel better about herself, even though she couldn't forget.

She knuckled her eyes to stop the tears of self-pity. Frances wasn't going to feel sorry for herself. All that stuff was over, in the past. She had a new life now and had begun to feel that she fitted in, and was liked for herself. Her silly little lies had done no harm and Pam hadn't condemned her. She would tell her family just enough for them to understand why Frances had been upset by the photograph. Frances trusted her and was glad that she need not feel guilt any more because she was living a lie. Pam knew the truth and she was still welcome here. It was a nice feeling.

Frances wanted to stay here in the peace of the countryside for as long as possible. She'd begun to enjoy the work – even the cows no longer frightened her and she'd got used to the smell of their waste. She believed that, as time passed, she would come to love the time spent outdoors, certainly when the better weather came.

Perhaps she might find someone she could love. If she married a farmer, she would never have to go back to London – but she knew she might never really care for anyone again.

Frances smiled as she glanced across at Jeanie. The other girl was her friend now and she'd seen that Jeanie knew just how to manage Artie; they were suited and Frances was happy for them.

Was there still a chance for Frances to be happy? Pam would have her believe it. If she could face up to what had happened and put her fear behind her, perhaps in the future she could find her own contentment.

12

John was lying with his eyes closed when the nurse spoke to him. Her voice sounded familiar and her words made him open his eyes and look at her as he struggled to place her face.

'I am sorry to see you back here, Lieutenant Talbot,' the nurse said. 'I understand you have been very ill – but hopefully on the mend now.'

'You were here when I was in Addenbrooke's before,' John spoke uncertainly. He'd been moved the previous day and slept most of the time since. Despite being transported in an ambulance, he'd found the journey exhausting. 'I am sorry. I can't recall your name.'

'It's Lucy,' she said with a shy smile. 'I told you about my brother, Josh, then... but it was a while ago...'

John's frown cleared. 'Yes, I do remember now. It was when I injured my ankle in that difficult landing – seems a lifetime ago. Your brother is RAF ground crew, isn't he?'

'Yes, he is,' Lucy agreed and her smile deepened. 'I have some lovely news for you, Lieutenant Talbot. Your mother is coming to see you this afternoon.'

'Is she?' John closed his eyes. 'I'm not sure I'm up to that yet...'

'Yes, you are,' Lucy replied firmly. 'You were tired when you got here, but your injuries are mostly healed now – it was just the infected ones to your arm and shoulder that kept you in hospital so long. The doctors think you are ready to go home – so the sooner you face up to it, the better.'

John opened his eyes and focused on her. She was a nice-looking girl, but her manner was strict, very different from his gentle Faith. Clearly, a capable nurse, she wasn't going to let him malinger here in the hospital. 'Must I?' he asked and sat up. 'I don't like being fussed over and my mother will smother me with love.'

'Don't you care about her feelings?' Lucy scolded. 'Imagine what she has been going through all this time – not knowing if you were alive, and then being told you were badly injured and had lost your memory. Don't you care that she must be worried to death?'

'Yes, I do care,' John said. 'I love her – but I don't deserve it...'

'Rubbish!' Lucy declared in a no-nonsense way. 'You fly boys are all heroes. I don't know what you think you've done wrong, but it's only what you had to do. It was your duty to kill the enemy and you can't feel guilty over it.'

'You don't know what I've done,' John replied. 'You wouldn't like me if you did.'

Lucy laughed and shook her head at him. 'Who says I do like you? You are my patient, Lieutenant Talbot, and it is my job to make sure you are well enough to go home.'

John inclined his head, but smiled. 'Won't you call me John?'

'I'm not allowed to call you John while I'm your nurse,' Lucy said, but her eyes twinkled. 'Stop feeling guilty and sorry for yourself, Lieutenant Talbot. You are alive and in one piece. You've had a bad time but you're nearly mended now. A lot of men aren't that lucky.'

'I told you. I don't deserve it.'

'What did you do that was so bad then?' she demanded.

'You'll hate me if I tell you...'

'Try me,' she invited.

For a moment, John almost did. He wanted absolution. It would be good to tell someone and have them say he wasn't to blame for that girl's death – but it wouldn't be true. His hesitation had cost Maria her life and she'd been instrumental in saving his.

'I can't tell you or anyone,' he said. He closed his eyes. 'My head aches.'

'I'll leave you to rest,' Lucy conceded, 'but I don't think you're a bad person, John. Whatever is upsetting you wouldn't bother you if you were.'

John didn't answer her. He couldn't. He felt guilty. Maria was dead because he didn't save her and Faith had died because he'd selfishly made love to her and then left her to cope with the consequences. Lucy wouldn't like him if he told her the truth. John didn't like himself.

* * *

Pam's heart caught as she saw her youngest boy lying with his eyes closed. He looked pale, the scar across his forehead still red and puckered, even though it must have been healed for a while. Injuries like that took a long time to fade and would never go completely. John's angelic looks had gone forever. He was still handsome, but older and bearing the scars life had dealt him, both mental as well as physical.

She approached cautiously. The pretty nurse had told her

John was still tired after the move. His eyes flicked open as she reached the bed. For a moment, he looked at her and she wondered who this man was, but then he smiled and it was John.

'I knew it was you,' he said and smiled. 'I could smell your lavender water. How are you, Mum?'

'Better now I can see you,' Pam replied, longing to hug him but afraid of hurting him. 'I've been so anxious for you, my love. We were all afraid we'd lost you when you were missing, presumed dead. I know you've had a terrible time.'

'Not as bad as some.' John sounded weary. 'I was lucky the nuns took me in and hid me when I was badly injured. They nursed me until I was able to make the trek to Switzerland. I would be a prisoner if it wasn't for them – or dead...'

'Then I shall pray for them,' Pam said, her eyes reflecting her concern. 'One day I may be able to thank them, but until then I will pray for their safety. They must be very brave ladies to hide you when you were in enemy territory.'

'You have no idea how brave,' John said, and then, because it was her and because he was overcome by emotion, he continued: 'Mum, one of them died, because she wouldn't give me up. I should have been the one to die, not her.'

'That was her choice,' Pam replied. 'You couldn't have done anything, John. You were ill...'

John closed his eyes. It was true and yet not true. He had been ill, but had he acted instantly at the first scream Maria might still live... But he couldn't tell his mother that shameful truth. She wouldn't condemn him, but he would see doubt in her eyes.

'How is everyone at the farm?' he asked, changing the subject, because her gaze was too knowing, too understanding, too full of love and kindness. 'Are Lizzie and Tom all right? And

Dad...? I was a bit off with him when he came. Tell him I am sorry.'

'Tom has a son too now, and Lizzie is well. Artie and Jeanie are getting married.' She smiled and pressed his hand. 'Your father doesn't need you to say sorry. He understands how you felt hearing about Faith...' Pam hesitated. 'I know it must hurt you, love, but you do have a beautiful little boy who needs his daddy. What you've lost is hard to accept. I know what it's like, my son. You feel as if there is nothing to live for – but in time you will come to know and love little Jonny...'

'You called him after me?' John frowned, as if uncertain of his feelings and Pam sensed he was struggling, torn between an instinctive love for his child and the pain of losing his baby's mother.

'For now,' Pam replied. 'It will be up to you to decide his name, John. Arthur registered his birth, but you don't have to name him John. We will have him christened when you're home. We don't know what Faith would have liked, because she never said.'

'Did she suffer a lot, Mum?' John asked, his hands white, gripping the bedcovers at his sides. 'I keep thinking about it...'

'I shan't lie to you,' Pam said. 'I wasn't with her unfortunately, but I think she must have done – for a while. I am sorry, but there is no point in pretending. It was a terrible thing and you will grieve for her. One day it will hurt less, but until then you must live with it, my love.'

'I wish I'd been there for her,' John said and his face twisted with grief. 'Mum, I feel guilty. I killed her—'

'No, you didn't,' Pam said and reached for his hand, holding it tightly. 'You were not to blame. Faith was a healthy young woman and she should have had her child and lived. It was the... accident that killed her, not you, John. Please believe me.'

'I'd like to but...' John wrenched his hand from hers. 'I loved her mum. I wish she was still alive. It is too much to bear...'

'I know, my dearest,' Pam said. 'I wish we'd had better news for you. I am so sorry. She was with me until just before it happened – and I blame myself for letting her walk home alone. If I had been with her, she might still be here.'

John shook his head. 'I know what you are trying to do, Mum, but I know who is to blame. Don't worry. I shall learn to live with it. I know I must – but not quite yet. It's too raw.'

'I do know, John. I lost Tom's father when I was carrying Tom. I thought my world had ended then, but it didn't. You will go on, because you have no choice... and in time, you will be happy again, I promise.'

He nodded and smiled at her, something approaching his old shy smile. 'I love you, Mum. Thanks for coming. I know you are always there for me whatever I do.' John hesitated, then, 'Take care of my son – but I know you will.'

'Of course. I'll always be here for you and Jonny – and so will your father.'

* * *

Pam worried about her son on the train journey home. He was blaming himself for Faith's death, which was completely wrong – but there was something more lurking behind those eyes. She knew her John and he was brooding over something, carrying some other burden. Did he blame himself for the nun's death? Surely, he must know that it had been her choice not to give him up?

Pam sighed as the train stopped in Sutton. Either Artie or Arthur would be here to meet her. They would have taken her to the hospital and back had they been able to get enough petrol, but it was short these days, on ration like so many other things, including soap now, and they needed fuel for their work as well as trips into the nearest towns for supplies.

Artie was standing on the platform as she got off. He came to greet her and took her basket. She'd shopped in Cambridge before catching her train. Artie's eyes went over her, dwelling on her face. 'He's not up to much then?'

'He seems to be recovered physically,' Pam told him. 'He looks weary and sort of defeated, as if he has the world on his shoulders.'

Artie nodded. 'I expect he has been through a lot of stuff we don't know about, Mum. He might never tell us, but he will get over it. He'll be fine once he's home and eating your food again.'

'I hope so, Artie,' Pam said and smiled at him. 'I know I can rely on you to look after him when he comes home next week... His nurse told me they expect to send him home by then.'

'You bet,' Artie told her. 'I'll sort him out for you, Mum. I think Dad should have told him the truth, so I suppose John still doesn't know what really happened to Faith?'

'No. I wanted to tell him, because he feels guilty, thinking Faith died because she gave birth. I told him it was her accident. I couldn't bring myself to go against your father and tell him she was murdered.'

'I didn't expect you would,' Artie replied. His chin jutted. 'If he wants to know, I shall tell him. If he's going to be mad at anyone, it might as well be me...'

13

'Not going to school today?' Pam asked her eldest daughter, Susan, as she came downstairs dressed in her own clothes rather than the uniform she normally wore for the high school in Ely.

'No, I've been told to take a few days off to revise at home,' Susan told her. 'I'll have exams when I go back and then I'll be taking the exams for college later this year.'

'Yes, I remember.' Pam looked at her as she settled on the mat in front of the range with a pile of books. 'Are you still happy about the idea of going to college to study to become a teacher?'

'Yes, Mum,' Susan replied and smiled at her. 'It is what I want to do with my life. I thought about working with Lizzie as a hairdresser, but, after she let me help on Saturdays before Christmas, I decided it wasn't for me. I like children, playing with them and showing them how to do things – I miss having Tina here, don't you?'

'Yes, I do miss her. She was a delightful little girl, but she belongs with her family in London. Vera is her grandmother and she loves her. She only let her come to us because her mother died, her father was in hospital and Vera didn't have time to look after her. Now Terry is living with his parents and they have a girl to care for Tina when he is at work. Vera says he just does a few hours in the office each day so he gets plenty of time with his daughter.'

Susan looked at her and for a moment Pam saw a look of regret or sadness in her eyes. 'Yes, I know it is better for her and them to have her there – but I miss them...'

'Do you miss Terry as well as Tina?' Pam asked. She looked at her daughter curiously. Terry was eight years or so older than Susan – was she carrying some sort of torch for him? His war wounds and tragic story might make him a romantic figure in a young girl's eyes perhaps?

Susan hesitated and then nodded. 'I really like him, Mum. I sort of hoped he might settle here. He thought he might be able to drive a tractor once his new leg fitted him properly. I think he is getting on with it better now and will be able to try driving soon.'

'Who told you that?' Pam enquired, her tone neutral but her gaze intent on her daughter's face.

'Terry writes to me now and then,' Susan said and glanced up from her book. 'He is just a friend, Mum. I'm going to college so I have a secure future as a teacher. It is what I want to do – besides, I'm too young to think about getting married.'

'Are you saying that one day you might consider marrying Terry Salmons?'

'I might,' Susan admitted. 'I don't know yet. He hasn't said anything to me or me to him. I just like him better than any of the local boys I know.'

'Is that why you haven't been out much recently?'

Susan looked thoughtful. 'I'm studying hard, Mum. Once I pass my exams and get to college, I can think about having some fun in my spare time. I suppose I might meet someone there I like a lot – but most of the older boys from my school have joined up, so I wouldn't be able to see them anyway. Besides, I can't think of marrying for a few years – I wouldn't be allowed to teach.'

'And that's a stupid rule; they should change it.' Pam nodded. Her daughter sounded older and wiser than her seventeen and a half years. It seemed she knew her own mind and would make her own decisions when the time came. 'Thank you for telling me your thoughts,' she said. 'I am pleased that you feel able to trust me.'

'Of course I do, Mum.' Susan smiled at her. 'Now, I really have to study.'

'Yes, I know. I'd better see where Angela is. If she doesn't get up soon, she will be late for school.'

'I think she wants to stay in bed. She said she had a bit of a cold – but she just doesn't want to go to school.'

Pam nodded and went upstairs to the room Susan and Angela now shared. Angela was sitting up in bed reading an Enid Blyton book but tried to hide it when her mother entered.

'Why aren't you up?' Pam asked her youngest child. 'You know you have school today.'

'It's too cold,' Angela complained. 'Susan doesn't have to go in, so why should I?'

'Because she is studying for college and if you don't go to school, you will never be able to take those exams and go yourself.'

'I don't want to,' Angela said and coughed. 'I'd rather get married and look after a family. Please don't make me go. I don't feel well.'

Pam placed a hand on her forehead. It was perfectly cool. 'Don't make things up, Angela,' she said calmly. 'You aren't a bit ill. Now get up and go to school like a good girl. Perhaps you will get married young and you may not want to go to college – but you won't find a decent husband if you can't talk to him intelligently.'

'I know about cooking, farming and animals,' Angela said, pouting.

'Then perhaps you'd like to be a vet and look after them,' Pam said without raising her voice. 'You are my daughter and I want you to go to school and learn things that you can't learn sitting here in bed.'

'Do I have to?' Angela lingered.

'You have to,' Pam replied, smiling at her. 'Come on, be a good girl, Angela. I've got some streaky bacon and bubble and squeak waiting for you downstairs.'

'Oh, I love that,' Angela said and scrambled out of bed.

'If you don't come down in five minutes, I'll eat yours myself...'

Pam smiled to herself as she left Angela hastily dressing. Normally, Angela enjoyed her school, but of late she'd been reluctant. Pam didn't think it was just the cold weather Angela didn't fancy but wasn't sure. Angela hadn't said anything about being bullied at school, but she would keep a watchful eye and perhaps have a chat to her teacher. After the summer term, she would be changing school, catching the bus into the nearby town of Chatteris, unless she passed to go to the Ely High School and Pam didn't think that likely. Angela wasn't studious like her elder sister. She was more interested in cooking and farming and she probably would marry young – but she still had to get a decent education and they would think about the future when it happened. This war might go on for a long time yet, according to the papers, and who knew what would happen if – God forbid! – the Germans actually invaded England.

Invasion had been very close for a while, Arthur had been worried they would be taken over by the Germans, but it hadn't happened yet and hopefully it wouldn't.

Returning to the kitchen, she discovered that Lizzie was already there pouring a cup of tea for herself, Jeanie and Frances. Artie and Arthur had eaten earlier and gone out to the yard. It looked as if there might at last be signs of a let-up in the frosty weather and they wanted to get on with the ploughing in the Fens as soon as they were able.

Pam smiled at the girls as they chatted and drank their tea, then began to serve up the cooked breakfasts they so deserved after milking and cleaning the cowsheds.

'You two won't have much to do today,' she told them. 'Not until the second milking this afternoon. I don't have that much needs doing either. You could go out together somewhere if you wanted to?'

Jeanie looked at her. 'Are you sure, Pam? I would like to go on the train into Cambridge to do some shopping if it is all right? It is my mother's birthday soon and Annie's next month. I looked in Ely for a nice twinset for Mum but couldn't find what I wanted. I thought I might have more luck in Cambridge.'

'You go and enjoy yourself,' Pam told her. 'What about you, Frances?'

Frances looked at Jeanie uncertainly. 'I'd like a new dress – would you mind if I came to Cambridge with you?'

'I'd like it,' Jeanie replied, smiling. 'It means walking to the station in Sutton – it is a long way. We might catch a bus into Sutton if we hurry, otherwise we'll need to walk. No one has time to take us today...'

'I don't mind,' Frances said. 'I can be ready in ten minutes once I've eaten.'

The girls cleared their plates and raced upstairs to have a quick wash and change into clean clothes. The sound of their laughter could be heard in the kitchen and Pam smiled at Lizzie. 'What are you going to do, love?'

'Stay here in the warm, though I might go home for a short time and check everything is all right.'

'Artie will have made sure your range is going,' Pam said. 'He does it three times a day to keep the house aired for you – but if you'd like to look for yourself, then do so.'

'I could do with some different clothes,' Lizzie said. She looked down at the shapeless maternity dress. 'I am hoping I might get into the clothes I bought before I went into these things. I bought a size 38 and I'm normally a 36-inch hips. I plan to be that again if I can.'

'You'll go back to your old size if you're sensible,' Pam told her. 'I did until after Angela was born and then I put on two sizes and I've stuck at a 38-inch ever since. I was only a 34-inch when I married.'

'Gosh, I don't think I've ever been that,' Lizzie said. 'I don't mind being a bit bigger, but I don't want to pack on the pounds like some mothers do.'

'I think it is all a matter of eating sensibly and keeping busy,' Pam replied. 'I've never had time to sit about much. Tom was just running about when Artie was born and then, two years later, I had John. I didn't have time to sit around and just eat.'

'I'd never want to do that,' Lizzie said. 'I want to go back to working at the salon when Archie is old enough to leave.'

'I've told you I will have him whenever you want, Lizzie.'

'Yes, I know.' Lizzie smiled at her. 'Perhaps I shall leave him with you sometimes, but he can come with me in his carrycot for a start and then, when he starts to run around... perhaps there is a nursery school in Chatteris. I'll have to ask my customers if anyone knows of a reliable carer.'

'You already know one,' Pam told her. 'No arguments, Lizzie. I'm going to be here looking after Jonny for the foreseeable future, so I might as well have them both. I hardly ever go anywhere and if I do get treated to an evening out, you can repay me by babysitting Jonny.'

'Yes, I suppose that is true,' Lizzie agreed. 'If Mum still lived in Mepal, she might have had Archie now and then – but perhaps not...' She sighed and Pam knew it was because her mother didn't show her much concern or love.

'You will have to take Archie and show him to your mum when Tom comes home. Have you heard anything from him yet?'

'He wrote and told me how thrilled he is to have a son and hopes to get leave next month. He says they are in the middle of a concentrated training effort just now and he can't ask for time off, even though he is longing to see us.'

Pam nodded as she heard the sigh. 'You know Tom would be here like a shot if he could, don't you?'

'Yes, I do,' Lizzie said. The sound of clattering feet as the girls rushed into the kitchen and then out the back door with cheery waves and much laughter interrupted her. 'Tom wouldn't miss a chance for leave if he had the choice. He wanted to be with me for the birth, but that was a bit sooner than we anticipated...'

'Men aren't a lot of use when you're giving birth I find. They either look as if they're suffering worse than you or they clear off down the pub – as my father did when my younger brother was born!' Pam remarked.

'I didn't know you had a brother. I thought you just had a sister?'

'I have two sisters, Jane and Mary – and then there's Keith. He is in his late twenties now and I expect he has joined up. My sisters were older than me by several years – and they wouldn't speak to me after I had a child out of wedlock; my brother wasn't allowed to...'

'Oh, Pam, that was cruel,' Lizzie said. They heard the letters drop through the letterbox and she got up to fetch them. 'There are two for you, Pam – and one for me. The postie knows I'm staying here for the moment so he popped mine through your door.'

'Is yours from Tom?' Pam asked and Lizzie nodded, opening it quickly to read the first few lines. 'Tom is getting leave next—' She broke off as she saw Pam's white face. Pam had opened one of her letters and her hand was shaking.

'What is it?' Lizzie asked concerned. 'Not John...?'

'No, not John, thank God,' Pam answered, her voice hardly above a whisper. 'My youngest sister Mary has recently died – I wasn't told...' Pam sounded hurt.

'Oh, Pam, I am so sorry,' Lizzie said.

'Her husband was killed a few months back; I hadn't heard that either...' She shook her head in disbelief. 'Jane has written to ask if I will take Mary's son. He is just eight years old and she can't take him because she is ill... she says she doesn't expect to last the winter...'

'Oh, Pam, that is awful,' Lizzie said, coming to take the letter from her. She scanned the first few lines and shook her head in disbelief. 'How could she write a letter like this... saying it is your duty to take the boy? I mean, I know you would, but this letter is so unkind.'

'She blames me for my mother's death, told me it was a broken heart that had caused it,' Pam said, her eyes brimming with tears. 'Neither she nor Mary would speak to me – though Mary did start to send Christmas cards a few years back. Just after her son was born. She couldn't have a child for years and then she did, but it made her an invalid. I knew she was ailing, but I thought Jane was well...'

'She seems to be demanding you take the boy, as if it's your fault he's an orphan or something.' Pam already had a houseful to care for and it seemed unfair to Lizzie that Pam's sister should just expect her to take a child she'd never even met. 'Do you know your nephew's name?'

'Yes, George,' Pam said. She took out her handkerchief and blew her nose.

'It will make a lot of extra work for you if you take a young lad of that age on.'

'Yes, but what is the alternative?' Pam looked at Lizzie. 'I will have to speak to Arthur about it.'

'He will say it is up to you,' Lizzie assured her.

'I couldn't let him go to an orphanage and that is what Jane will do if I say no. He is my nephew...' Pam shook her head. 'I dare say we'll manage one more, Lizzie. It was just the shock of knowing Mary was dead suddenly. She didn't say a word about being worse in her card last Christmas.'

'You know I will do whatever I can to help – but it will make a lot of extra work for you.'

'You and the girls will help me when you can,' Pam said, but she knew Lizzie was right. Pam had a big enough family to cope with as it was, but what else could she do? It would be too cruel to condemn the boy to life in an orphanage without giving it a go.

14

'So you're kicking me out today then?' John said when the nurse he liked most came to give him some medicine. 'Abandoning me to my fate.'

Lucy looked at him and smiled. 'You're feeling a bit better,' she said. 'Are you looking forward to getting home?'

'Yes and no,' John said. 'I'm bored with lying in a bed half the day, but...' He shook his head. 'You don't want to hear me moaning...'

'I'll listen if you want to talk,' she said. 'I know you're uneasy over something, but if you won't tell anyone, we can't help you.'

'I told my mother some of it,' John replied. 'If I told her the rest, she would be disappointed in me and I couldn't face that.'

'I'm not your mother and I shan't be disappointed whatever you've done,' Lucy invited, but John had said all he was going to. 'Well, it is up to you – but if you need someone to listen, I'm not going anywhere.'

'Don't you want to be transferred to another hospital?' John asked, remembering that Faith had volunteered for a military hospital, even though it had meant they couldn't meet as often.

'You mean go out to the frontline?' Lucy frowned. 'I thought about it once, but then decided I was doing good work here, so I turned the chance down. Yes, I want to help those wounded men, but there are other people who need nursing as well. I want to help all of them wherever I can.' She flushed as he looked at her. 'Someone called me a coward for refusing, but I don't think I am. I hate thunderstorms and so I don't think I'd be the right sort to work under fire. If that makes me a coward, then so be it.'

'We all have our limitations,' John told her. 'I don't think you are a coward, Lucy. My little sister Angela is frightened of thunderstorms too. I heard her crying and screaming once and went into her. I lay on her bed with her and cuddled her until it was over. Angela isn't frightened of dogs or cows or horses, but she hates loud bangs.'

'How old is she?'

'She will be ten in the summer, I think. She is the baby of the family... or she was...' John met Lucy's eyes then. 'I've got a son, so my mother tells me. His mother died soon after he was born – does that make me guilty of her death?'

'Of course it doesn't!' Lucy cried. 'I've seen a few women die in childbirth, but that doesn't make their husbands murderers. It is just bad luck. It doesn't happen as much these days, but it used to be quite common in the old days.'

'Mum said she had an accident...' He frowned. 'I didn't ask for details; I couldn't, but I shall. It felt too much like a punishment for my sins...'

'Rubbish! Why should your wife die for your sins? That would punish her as much as you.'

'We weren't married. I wanted to marry her, but she needed to continue with her nursing.'

Lucy nodded. 'I think the hospital would have turned a blind eye if she'd kept it to herself. We are so short of trained staff because of all the war wounded that we can't afford silly rules that say women can't be nurses as well as wives. I know for a fact we have a nurse working on the wards here who was married before the war, but she is a good nurse and matron took her on – she doesn't wear her ring at work but we all know.'

'I asked her if she would risk it, but she said not for a while...' John closed his eyes. 'We wanted to be together that way... it wasn't just me.'

'Of course she did, so stop blaming yourself for what happened,' Lucy said.

'She would still be alive if I'd waited...'

'You don't know that,' Lucy told him. 'Stop feeling sorry for yourself and face the future, Lieutenant Talbot. Someone must be around for your son as he grows and you can't just leave him to your mother. I am sure she has more than enough to do.'

'You're quite bossy, aren't you?' John remarked, but his frown had lifted. 'So, am I free to go now?'

'Doctor will see you at eleven,' she said. 'Your family has been asked to collect you at twelve. You'll need some tablets to take home.'

'Can't I just get the train?'

'It has been arranged,' Lucy informed him. 'You are considered fit enough to go home, but once there you should not overdo things. You were ill for months and you need to ease yourself back into normal life.'

John nodded. 'Do you think the air force will have me back?'

'Oh, I imagine you'll be given a couple of months to recover and then they will give you a medical,' Lucy replied. 'That will be with military doctors, so I can't say if they will consider you fit to fly again.'

'The limp will go eventually,' John said more to himself than anyone. 'If I can get to the plane, that is enough surely.'

'Would it have been enough when you crashed?' Lucy questioned. 'I don't know what you went through then, but I imagine you needed to get away quick.'

He looked at her sombrely. 'I was dazed and injured, my leg broken, but I dragged myself clear before it exploded – and then I don't quite remember. I think I crawled for a while, but I kept passing out with the pain, and then... I was in a small dark room and I could hear voices. The nuns and their priest had found me and carried me to safety. They nursed me back to health...'

'You must have been strong and fit to manage that with your leg broken,' Lucy said. 'You had other small injuries – but the wound that was infected came later I know...'

'Yes...'

Lucy waited but he didn't continue.

'I must leave you to it,' she said. 'I shan't be here when you are discharged, Lieutenant Talbot. I have three days off now to spend with my family.'

'Oh... thank you,' he murmured. 'For everything...'

She nodded and left the room.

* * *

John lay back and closed his eyes. He'd wanted to tell Lucy how he'd come to be wounded again, but he couldn't. The plane crash and its aftermath were mostly a blur. They'd been hit by flak on their way home from a mission. The pilot had thought they were close to the coast and kept flying for as long as he could, but then they'd suddenly lost height and crashed into a hedge at the end of a field as he'd tried to land. After that, things got hazy. John thought he'd dragged himself clear and away from the crash, but he only had vague pictures of fire and flames and then an almighty explosion. He wasn't sure if any of the crew besides him had got out.

He couldn't remember much after that, though he thought he might have found a piece of wood to make himself a crude crutch at one point, limping for a while and then falling face down as the blackness washed over him. He might have woken more than once and tried to crawl further, fearing that he was being hunted for. John had known nothing when he was carried to the convent. It was some weeks before he was clear of the fever and could speak to the nuns, and for a while, he hadn't been able to remember anything – his name, his nationality or how he'd been hurt.

His memory had begun to come back slowly as his body recovered. He'd wanted to tell the nuns who had saved his life his name, but they begged him not to. It was best they knew nothing, they said. John had thought he might be safe, but he was still in enemy territory and the nuns were risking their lives to hide him from the patrols that were still searching for any survivors. Maria had told him she thought there might have been others, but she believed they had been picked up soon after the crash. She spoke English well, having lived there as a young girl. Most of the other nuns only had a few words of English and made themselves understood by signs. So Maria was the one who looked after him the most.

'You were lucky we found you,' she'd said. 'I think if you had been arrested and taken to a prisoner of war camp you would not have survived.'

'Yes, I was lucky,' John had replied. 'But I should go – I am endangering you all by being here.'

'We are trying to arrange it,' Maria had told him that evening. 'Soon, someone will come and help you get to Switzerland. There you will be safe and can get back to your home.'

'Thank you – you are all very kind,' John had said. 'I've been here too long.'

'You were too ill to move...' She'd seen him wince. 'You still have pain – where?'

'In my neck and head,' John had said. 'It comes and goes...'

'I will make you a hot drink.'

He'd thanked her and she'd left – and the next time he saw her she was bleeding on the convent kitchen floor. His memory had come flooding back later, after they'd hidden the dead soldier.

John shut the picture out of his mind. Even if his mother and Lucy were right and he wasn't responsible for Faith's death, he had let a young woman die in his stead and he was shamed.

* * *

John was ready to leave when Artie entered the room. He looked at his brother and for a moment felt as if Artie could read his mind, but then he grinned and it passed. 'You're ready then?' Artie said. 'I'll take your kitbag. How do you feel? Can you walk all right?'

'Yes, my leg has healed completely, I just limp a bit,' John replied. 'I think my arm was the worst, because it was infected – but I don't remember much about the rest of it.'

'You've had a rotten time,' Artie said and touched his shoulder in sympathy. 'Let's get you home and then you can start to get well again, properly well. You've lost weight. Mum will soon put that right.'

'I know she'll try.' John nodded, following his brother outside. He stopped a couple of times to speak to the nurses and thank them, though he already had spoken to most of them. He would come back when he could and bring them some chocolates.

Artie had their father's car parked out front and John eased himself into the passenger seat as Artie put his bag in the boot. He gave a sigh of relief, feeling glad to be on his way after a long morning of waiting around.

'I'm sorry about Faith,' Artie said in a casual tone. 'If you want to talk any time, come to me and I'll tell you.'

'Okay,' John muttered. If there was anyone he didn't want to talk to about Faith, it was Artie. He'd mocked him for being a virgin and John had resented the way he'd spoken about the girl he loved, as if she were just some casual, light-of-love he'd picked up, instead of the love of his life.

15

As well as buying herself a new dress to go dancing in, Jeanie had taken the chance to look for a wedding dress in Cambridge, though she hadn't found one she liked enough to buy. It was going to be an early summer wedding, May or June, they'd decided. Artie hadn't gone up to London to see her parents because of the dreadful weather, but he'd spoken to her father and her mother on the phone and they'd both promised to come down and stay before then.

'Your mum has met Artie a couple of times when she's visited and says he's all right,' Jeanie's father had told her when she spoke to him on the telephone. 'My only question is whether you are certain you are ready to marry someone whose life is in the country, Jeanie love.'

Jeanie had reassured him that it was indeed what she wanted and her father had given his consent.

They had an appointment to see the local vicar that following weekend to discover when they could book the church.

'Early in May if we can,' Artie suggested. 'We should be ahead with the work then so that we can get away for a honeymoon. In normal times, I would have suggested somewhere like Devon or Cornwall, but it's a long way and I doubt we could get enough petrol if we took Dad's car...'.

'I don't mind where we go,' Jeanie told him. She hesitated, then, 'Where are we going to live, Artie? Here for the time being or...?'

'Dad promised me a house in Sutton when I married, because I'll have the fen land one day,' he said. 'I'm not sure you'd like that, Jeanie. Would you rather I look for something in Mepal – so you are nearer to Mum and Lizzie?'

'If we could come across the airfield, it wouldn't be so bad,' she suggested. 'But as we must go the long way round via Witcham, I suppose I might feel a bit cut off up there. Everyone I know is here in Mepal.'

'That's what I thought,' he agreed. 'I happen to know there is a small house halfway along the road to Witcham, ten minutes' walk, at most. The lady who lived there went to live with her sister when they built the aerodrome. She didn't like the idea of living next to it, because of the noise of the planes taking off and landing. It might be in a bit of a state, but we can have it done up. It's being offered for rent or sale so we can do either.'

Jeanie had agreed it was a better option; she would be in easy walking distance of Blackberry Farm and her friends and they could rent for a while and see how they got on. Sutton was the biggest village of the little cluster, which was in a sort of lopsided triangle, none of them being far from each other. After the war was over, when it might be possible for her to have a car, she could drive down to see her friends, they might think of moving to Sutton to be closer to the fen land Artie preferred to the heavy soil around the farm. It wasn't that far on a cycle really, but there were times when you needed to be close to family.

Jeanie's family were based in London and she visited when

she could. It had hurt her to see her brother Terry looking so pale and withdrawn when he'd come to the farm to stay for a while after leaving hospital. It wasn't just his war wounds that had left him looking so drained, but the tragic loss of the wife he'd loved. At least he'd got a little of his strength back before he returned to London, but she thought it would be a long time before he was himself again; this war had a lot to answer for in terms of the suffering it had caused.

Jeanie had seen how drawn and thin John looked when Artie brought him home. He'd nodded to her and Frances, but his normal warm smile was missing. Jeanie had not been able to meet his bleak gaze easily. Seeing his suffering made her conscious that she had let Faith down. If she'd only heard her earlier screams; if she'd noticed that man hanging around or been there sooner... Despite knowing that it was the head injury that had killed Faith rather than childbirth, Jeanie felt guilt that she had not been able to help her more. She suspected that Pam did too.

John had gone straight up to his room that first afternoon. Jeanie had seen the look of grief in his eyes reflected in Pam's. Clearly, his mother felt his pain; she'd hugged him, but she had wisely allowed him to go to his room and come down when he was ready. Pam had gone up to his room to tell him when supper was on the table and he'd asked if he could have a sandwich in his room. Frances had offered to take it up to him with a cup of tea. She'd told them he was lying on his bed fully clothed, his eyes shut.

'I expect he's tired,' Pam had told them and no one argued.

John came down for breakfast the next morning. He'd told his mother he felt fine when she asked how he was and then said he was going to see his old boss. Jack Freeman was a small builder and John had been his main plasterer before he joined the RAF.

Jeanie had been out in the cowsheds most of that morning, but when she went in for docky John hadn't come home. He had got back at about three that afternoon and told his mother that he was going to help Jack with some plastering work for a few days.

Pam had been concerned and asked if he was well enough, but he'd assured her he felt much better. 'It will give me something to do while I'm waiting for my medical,' John had told her. 'You've got enough to do without me under your feet all the time, Mum. I'd help Dad out, but I don't think he needs much from me at the moment.'

No one had argued with him and for the past three days John had left the house early, returning in the afternoon. He ate his dinner with everyone else now but had little to say, unless his mother asked him a question. He smiled at her and answered, but Jeanie noticed that he hardly spoke to his father or Artie unless he was forced.

She asked Artie if he'd fallen out with his brother. He frowned, answering reluctantly. 'It's not on my side. John and me – we always argued more. He got on better with Tom. I used to tease him, but I never meant any harm...' Artie sighed. 'Unfortunately, I ragged him over Faith. It was just a bit of fun, but he took umbrage – and now...' His gaze darkened. 'I think he is angry over something and he's looking for a fight, probably with me.'

'You won't fight him?' Jeanie said. 'You can't – not after all he's been through.'

'I'm not an insensitive brute, even if my brother sees me that way,' Artie told her. 'Blokes say things to each other about girls sometimes. I didn't realise she was the one. I wouldn't have needled him about her if I had. I thought he would have loads of girls before he settled...' He drew a deep breath. 'I wouldn't like anyone to rag me about you, Jeanie. I dare say I was an idiot until I met you...'

Jeanie laughed and hugged him. 'Yes, you certainly were. It took a lot to tame you, but I did, didn't I?'

'Minx! I've a good mind to tan your hide,' Artie laughed and kissed her. 'I don't know about tamed, but you've made me a nicer person, Jeanie. I know John is hurting and I want to help him, but I don't know how. We've never hugged or been close. I tried to talk to him on the way home from hospital but he cut me off.'

'He's hurting inside,' Jeanie said. 'I think you just need to wait. Be patient until he's ready.'

'I know you're right,' Artie agreed. 'I was always a bit jealous of John. I thought he was Mum's favourite – and Tom is the apple of Dad's eye, even though I'm his eldest son – but when I thought John was dead, it was like being hit by a ton of bricks. I felt bad about Faith too. If I'd known – if I'd heard her scream or seen that devil hanging around, I would have thrashed him.'

'Your mum cares about all of you,' Jeanie said, giving him a squeeze. 'I am sure your dad does, too – but you aren't to blame for what happened to Faith. None of us are. We all feel it – your mum, dad, me and Lizzie. She was giving up work that day to be with Faith until the baby was born. Imagine how she feels – one day sooner...'

'It might not have made a difference,' Artie said. 'We'll never know for sure. It was lucky you heard that scream when you did. At least the baby survived...'

'Yes, and I am sure John will learn to be glad of that in time.'

'Mum says he hardly looks at Jonny when she tries to show

him the baby.' Artie shook his head. 'He needs sorting – maybe I should fight him just to wake him up a bit.'

'No!' Jeanie cried urgently. 'Promise me you won't, Artie. Please?'

'I might think he needs a good shaking, but I shan't be the one to do it, so don't look so anxious, my love.'

* * *

John stood looking down at the baby in the old-fashioned rocking cot. His eyes were a bright blue like his mother's and his hair was fair, as both John's was and Faith's had been. Looking at the child was to experience a deep stabbing to his heart, because he should have been in Faith's arms. John was torn with the longing to pick the child up and hold him close and the desire to walk away and never look into those eyes again.

'He is beautiful,' Pam said behind him and John stiffened. 'Don't you want to hold him, John? He is going to need you. You are his father...'

'I know...' John turned to her and his grief was writ on his face. 'She should be here with him, Mum.' A little sob broke from him. 'I want to love him but I can't... he's here and she isn't.'

'That isn't his fault, John. Don't blame him. He is so small and vulnerable and he needs your love.'

John nodded, dashing away a stray tear from his cheek. 'How did it happen, Mum? You said there was an accident?'

'Come and sit with me downstairs and I'll tell you,' Pam said. 'It won't be easy to hear, John, but I think you should know the whole truth...'

She turned and left the room, obliging John to follow.

No one was in the warm kitchen and Pam went to the kitchen door and turned the lock. 'I don't want anyone to come in and interrupt,' she told him as he frowned. 'Now sit down, John, and listen to the end.'

John did as she said. A tremor shook him as he realised that she was going to say something important and awful.

'Faith didn't die because she had a baby,' Pam told him, her voice firm and strong. 'She died because something hit her head and it caused internal bleeding. Somehow, her body gave birth while she was dying. The doctor said it was a miracle that the boy didn't die with her – but she held on to give him life. Remember that, John. Even though Faith was dying, she hung on long enough to give her son his life – and that must have been so important to her.'

'Yes...' He nodded, swallowing hard. 'How did she come to injure her head so badly, Mum? I know there's more.'

'We believe Faith was killed by her uncle, Ralph Harris,' Pam said and John's face blanched with grief and anger, but his eyes never left hers. 'He was waiting for her when she went back to Lizzie's house, where she was staying, and he attacked her. Artie and Jeanie were the first there, but it was too late, though your brother rang for the doctor at once and I went to her and did what little I could. Artie believes that Ralph banged her head against the wall but she also hit it as she fell or was thrust against the table.'

'Oh my God!' John swallowed hard, then, 'Why? What had Faith done that he should hurt her like that? She must have been close to having the baby...' His hands clenched, the knuckles tight with tension.

'Yes, Jonny was on his way – that was what saved your son's life. I don't know why that man did it – no one does, and he can't tell us, because he's dead.'

'Dead?' John closed his eyes briefly and then opened them again, tears of grief mingling with a burning anger. 'That's just as well, because I would have killed him. How did he die? I hope it was painfully...'

'He was driving like a maniac and ran head on into a tractor. I've been told glass pierced his eye and brain. I imagine it was quite quick.'

'Pity...' John had no sympathy for the man whatsoever. He looked at her hard. 'Whose idea was it to tell me it was an accident, Mum?'

'Your father thought it might be too much for you to bear, John. No one knew what to do for the best.'

John nodded. 'I wish I could kill the devil that hurt her, Mum, make him suffer for what he did to her, but I am glad you told me the truth.' He raised his head and looked at her. 'You said Jeanie and Artie were the first there?'

'Jeanie heard a scream as she left the cowshed after the milking was done. She ran straight there and Artie followed. I think you owe it to her that you have a son alive, John.'

He inclined his head. 'I am grateful for that, Mum. I know I haven't shown any love for him yet, but I shall in time.'

'I know.' She looked at him lovingly, reaching for his hand. John hesitated and then took it and held on tight. 'We all loved Faith. She came here to have her baby and stayed with Lizzie; they were good friends. Her mother didn't want to see her – but her father visits Jonny sometimes. She is buried here in Mepal, John. I take flowers, so does Lizzie and I think her father does when he visits.'

'Thank you. I did see her grave when I visited the church.' John bent his head, close to giving way, but he mastered his tears and raised his head. 'I wanted to visit her parents, but I thought they would blame me for her death.'

'Her mother might,' Pam admitted. 'I can only think that Ralph came here that day to quarrel with Faith because of her mother's distress. She took the news of Faith's pregnancy badly.'

'Yes, I expect she would. Faith said if anything happened her mother would disown her. If I hadn't been shot down, I would have married her before she told them…. Her father would have had to sign for her to marry as she wasn't twenty-one, but she said he might be all right.'

Pam nodded but made no reply.

'I should have waited,' John said and the bitter regret showed in his eyes. 'It wouldn't have happened if I'd been content to wait…'

'I know you didn't force her,' Pam said, smiling gently. 'I'm the last person to judge, John. I had Tom in similar circumstances to your own and Faith's. Remember that she loved you – and *she* wanted to be with you. Just treasure her memory like I do Tom's father.'

John inclined his head. 'I'll try, Mum – and thank you for telling me the truth. I needed to know – and now, I'll spend a little time with my son…' He smiled slightly. 'Tell Dad not to worry. I understand why he couldn't tell me. He isn't as brave as you…'

'Just forgive all of us for letting you down, John. We all wish it had been different.'

'You didn't let me down,' John said, pushing back his chair. 'I'll go up to my son now, Mum. I think I need to be with him for a while…'

16

There had been a subdued atmosphere in the farm since John's arrival. Frances had been introduced but just smiled and said hello. John scarcely noticed her anyway.

Artie and Jeanie were so close and obviously a pair, always smiling at each other and talking in whispers. Frances didn't feel jealous. Pam was kind to her and Mr Talbot never said much to anyone, but he'd been pleased with her when she'd helped him load the muck heap onto a trailer so he could take it to one of his fields in the Fens.

'It helps to keep the soil from blowing if you use this to bind it,' he'd told her. 'We can get on the land there much sooner than on the heavy clay soil. These fields near us will need a lot of drying out before we start or they'd go down hard, but as the fen soil dries it becomes vulnerable to a blow and the expensive seed you've sown can end up on someone else's land. We try to work enough manure into it before we sow and hope it holds it when the wind blows.'

Frances had volunteered to go with him and help spread the muck on the fields. She'd had to ride in the back of the cab and hold on; it was draughty and bitterly cold still, even with several layers of clothes on. The wind had been blowing hard across the flat open fields and she imagined what damage that would do if the land had dried out.

Frances had worked hard, climbing into the trailer to fork the manure onto the land as Mr Talbot drove it slowly up and down the field.

He'd thanked her when they got back to the yard with an empty trailer. 'That was a dirty job and too much for one person alone,' he'd said. 'You'll want a bath when you get in, Frances. Tell Pam I've said you can have the rest of the day off – just be back for milking.'

'Thanks, Mr Talbot.'

* * *

After spreading the muck on the fields, Frances went into the kitchen and then straight upstairs to take a quick bath. Because there were so many of them, the hot water didn't allow for everyone to bathe every day so they took it in turns, but Frances had been told she could have an extra one and as she looked at herself in the wall mirror in the bathroom she could see why. The wind had blown muck into her face and her hands smelled awful; it was a good job she had some of her favourite Yardley soap left. Now it was on ration, she might not be able to buy it for a while.

She ran the permitted allowance of water that they had to stick to. Everything was rationed these days, even the amount of hot water families could use. Although there was no way of regulating it, other than a line painted on the bath, which they did in hotels and boarding houses, most people played fair and stuck to the rules.

After she'd bathed, washed her hair, and changed into a clean pair of slacks and a jumper, Frances went down to the kitchen. She asked if Pam needed her, but she said no, just relax with a book or go to Ely if she liked.

Frances decided to go into Ely. It was time she returned the clothes Mrs Bates had loaned her and retrieved her own, She could have a wander round the shops, though she didn't have enough coupons to buy herself anything, having used them in Cambridge, and then she could go down to the river – and call on Mrs Bates.

* * *

Frances didn't see any children playing by the river, which was just as well as she didn't fancy jumping in again. Frances was smiling as Mrs Bates opened the door to her.

'Oh, my goodness,' she exclaimed. 'What a lovely surprise, Frances! I wondered if I should ever see you again, my dear. Please come in...'

Frances followed her into the hall and then straight into the large warm kitchen. It had a homely feeling, with its smooth dark oak dressers on which stood a hotchpotch of blue and white earthenware, the deep bucket sink festooned with flower pots, and bright blue and white curtains.

Mrs Bates invited her to sit down by the range, which gave out a comforting heat. 'I'm so pleased you've come. I was just sitting here on my own, reading the paper – Princess Elizabeth registered for war service, you know, and there is a lovely picture of her in uniform.' She showed it to Frances. 'It is so nice to have company. I've baked this morning. Billy usually comes to me for his tea now when he gets back from school. It saves his gran cooking for him and she seems to be glad to have a bit of peace. I take him home at seven and he goes to bed soon after.'

'Poor Billy,' Frances said. 'I expect he likes coming to you – his grandmother isn't exactly loving.'

'I think she is just too old and unwell to have the care of a young lad,' Mrs Bates agreed as she busied herself with cups and saucers and little plates. 'There's jam tarts and a pound cake, made with rice and a vanilla flavouring. Help yourself, Frances – and tell me how you've been getting on.'

Frances took a lemon curd tart and a small slice of cake, sipping her tea and nibbling the tart before answering. 'I'm enjoying my time at the farm,' she told her. 'I've made friends now – and I went to Cambridge with Jeanie... that's the girl who was with me when Billy fell into the river. It was nice and I don't mind the work, even though it is a bit dirty at times. I was muck spreading early this morning. I had a bath afterwards...'

'I can smell the soap on you,' Mrs Bates said comfortably. 'It is a nice scented one. You can't get things like that these days – at least I haven't seen any for ages.'

'It was given to me by a friend for a present before he went away...' Frances blinked hard. 'He was killed overseas...'

'Oh, you poor thing,' Mrs Bates said and frowned. 'That reminds me, dear. I had a visitor yesterday. He said he was a friend of yours but had lost contact due to the war. He'd seen something in the paper – one of the daily papers used that article from our local.' Mrs Bates went to the dresser and took out a paper, bringing it back. 'Look – it's in the *Daily Mirror*. Just a small piece inside and the photograph isn't as clear, but he thought he knew you.'

Frances felt the fear constrict her throat and for a moment she couldn't speak. Her hands trembled and she hid them in her lap. 'Did he give a name?' she managed at last.

'No.' Mrs Bates frowned. 'I did ask him, but he didn't answer – so when he asked if I knew where you lived, I didn't tell him. The paper didn't have as many details. It just said that you'd bravely rescued Billy and your name, not where you were living.'

Frances drew a deep breath, telling herself not to panic. 'I am glad you didn't tell him. If he was a friend, he would've given you his name. It was probably just another reporter looking for something new to write.' It couldn't be Roy! He wouldn't come all this way to look for her surely?

'Well, that is what I thought,' Mrs Bates agreed. 'So I didn't tell him anything. He looked annoyed, but then he went away.'

Frances forced a smile. 'I can't think of anyone I want to see who doesn't know where I am, so please don't tell anyone – if he should come again.'

'No, I won't dear.' Mrs Bates leaned forward and touched her hand. 'I shan't breathe a word to anyone, but I hope you will come back and see me again.'

'Thank you. Yes, I'll come when I can...' Frances glanced at the clock. 'Oh dear, I had better go. I need to get back in time for the milking.' She put her empty cup and plate on the table. 'Thank you for the tart and cake; they were lovely.'

'You are very welcome,' Miss Bates said. 'Don't forget your clothes; I have them made up into a parcel for you.' She handed Frances a brown paper parcel tied with string.

Frances thanked her again and left. She walked quickly towards the hill and up it, glancing over her shoulder now and then, but she wasn't being followed. She'd told Mrs Bates she would visit again, but as she gained the top of Forehill and then Market Street to queue for her bus back to Mepal, she decided she wouldn't risk it for a while. If someone had come looking for her it had to be him – Roy Bent, the man who had made her life hell until she'd escaped him.

How unlucky was it that he'd seen the newspaper article. Why had a big newspaper bothered to pick it up at all? As the bus arrived and she climbed on, Frances frowned. The papers looked for good news articles to counter against all the bad news from the war. Her little act of courage had filled a space for them, but it could hold dire consequences for her if Roy found her.

All the way back to Mepal and the farm, Frances worried at the problem. Should she leave Blackberry Farm and try to lose herself in a big city? A part of her wanted to run but the other half told her to stay put. She couldn't remember if the local paper had given details of where the farm was located or not – but there surely were no copies left. They would all have been used to wrap vegetable peelings or made into firelighters by now; these days there was never enough wood for fuel, because people couldn't get as much coal or coke as they needed, so they were buying logs.

Jeanie greeted her as she entered the farm kitchen. 'The vet was able to treat Daisy,' she said cheerfully. 'So we shan't lose her. Did you have a lovely day in Ely?'

'It was more fun when you were there,' Frances admitted. 'I visited Mrs Bates. She gave me cake, which was nice of her – she makes them for Billy, I think. He goes there for his tea every day.'

'Ah, that's nice,' Jeanie said and smiled at her. 'I was wondering if you would like to be one of my bridesmaids, Frances? We've set the day for the second Saturday in May and the vicar will read the banns for the first time this Sunday. I've asked Susan and Angela, but I'd like you, too – if you would?'

Frances hesitated and then nodded. Her panic had receded a little. She was enjoying her life on the farm now and she was part of a family. She didn't want to run away again. 'Yes, I'd like that,' she said. 'But shall we be able to get material for the dresses?'

'I've talked to Mum and Pam and they are both giving me their coupons. I think if we keep the dresses simple, we shall be fine. Dad and Mr Talbot are giving up theirs too. They both have suits in their wardrobes that will do, so they say.'

'I like shorter dresses,' Frances said, smiling. 'We have to wear them these days anyway if we want anything new – but we'll make the bridesmaid dresses, won't we?'

'Yes. Pam has a machine and both she and Lizzie are good at cutting out. I picked up some patterns in Cambridge and I saw some nice material on the market in Ely. I thought either a peach or a pale lilac. Which do you think would be nicer? Susan says peach, Angela says lilac.'

'I think probably the peach is easier to wear, but Angela could have lilac, I suppose.'

'Hmm, not sure they go together,' Jeanie said. 'I think I will settle on the peach if you agree. Pam said she wants to make Angela a new dress for Sundays so she might get something in lilac for her.'

Frances agreed that it was a good idea and they went upstairs still discussing the wedding. Jeanie had seen a dress in Cambridge that she wasn't sure about but thought she might go back when she got a day off and try it on.

'They might have some new stock next month,' Frances suggested. 'I think more weddings happen in the spring – or they normally do. At the moment, a lot of girls have to arrange it when their boyfriends are home on leave.'

'Yes, I know I am lucky that Artie is here,' Jeanie said, frowning. 'Artie isn't a coward, you know. He stayed on the farm because his father couldn't manage without him. Tom wanted to join the army and John was never interested in the farm.'

'I didn't mean it that way...' Frances hesitated. 'If all the men went to war, we'd have no coal and less food, because most of us land girls have no idea what to do when we first come.'

'I think Artie was very tempted to join up for a while last year,' Jeanie said thoughtfully. 'He was restless when John went missing all those weeks, but he felt it was his duty to help his father run the farm – and he seems to have settled now.'

'Both his brothers have been injured,' Frances said. 'Surely that's enough for Pam to cope with.' Yet she knew that some families had given all their menfolk to the conflict. The Talbot family had been lucky that both men had come home.

'Yes, she suffered a lot when John was missing,' Jeanie agreed. 'You weren't here when Faith was living with us... with Lizzie, really. She was beautiful. I've never seen a girl that pretty and John was mad about her. It's no wonder he looks as if he has the world on his shoulders.'

'He must have been through a lot,' Frances agreed. 'I think his left hand still doesn't work exactly as it should. I noticed it trembled a bit at dinner last night.'

'At least he is coming down for meals now,' Jeanie replied. 'I think he is taking more interest in his son, too. It must be so hard – he didn't even know Faith was having his child. She hadn't told him before he went on that last mission. I doubt she knew...'

'At least he has something real to remember her by,' Frances said a little wistfully. 'I sometimes wish...' She stopped and Jeanie looked at her.

'Are you thinking of a man you loved?' she asked.

'There was someone – he helped me through a bad time,' Frances said. 'I did love him, yes – but I didn't know him as long as I would've liked. He promised to come back and marry me – but I had a letter from his friend to say that he'd seen him killed...'

'I am so sorry,' Jeanie said, looking at her with sympathy. 'I can't imagine how awful that would be. I'd hate to lose Artie now.'

'You really love him,' Frances nodded. 'I didn't think you were that interested when I first came. I know I flirted with him – but I just wanted to belong and I thought that might be the way.'

'You do belong with us,' Jeanie replied impulsively. 'We're friends now, Frances, and I've forgotten what happened at the beginning. Don't think that you're not appreciated, because you are. Arthur was telling us how hard you worked spreading muck this morning.'

'He was kind, giving me a few hours off afterwards,' Frances said. She was tempted to tell Jeanie that someone had been looking for her but decided against it. If she got started, she might tell her everything – and Frances still felt ashamed of what Roy had forced her to do. It wasn't her choice, but she should never have fallen for his flattery.

'You deserved it,' Jeanie said. 'It is one of the worst jobs, especially if the wind is blowing across the Fens.'

'Yes, right in my face,' Frances said with a laugh. 'I needed that bath...'

'I'd love one tonight,' Jeanie said, 'but I am saving mine for Saturday, Artie has got tickets for a dinner dance in Haddenham – that's a biggish village on the way to Cambridge,' she explained. 'He managed to get four tickets. I don't know if Pam and Arthur will go...'

At dinner that evening, Artie revealed that he'd offered the extra tickets to his parents but they had refused them. 'That means John can come if he wants – and either Frances or Lizzie...'

'I am hoping Tom might get home by Saturday evening,' Lizzie said. 'Thanks for the offer, but I wouldn't go without him anyway.'

'He is welcome to my ticket,' John said instantly. 'Thanks, Artie, but I'm not in the mood for dancing.'

'I think we'd rather spend a little time together,' Lizzie said. 'Perhaps another time.'

Artie shrugged. 'My mate George is home for the weekend,' he said. 'I know he'd enjoy it – he is a good dancer. He doesn't have a girlfriend, Frances – so would you make up a fourth? George isn't bad-looking – is he Jeanie?'

'He is a nice person,' she replied. 'Why don't you come, Frances? It will be more fun if there are four of us.' She gave Artie a teasing look. 'George never treads on my toes...'

'I only did that once,' Artie protested, but he was laughing. 'He is better at dancing than me.'

Frances hesitated and then nodded. 'Thank you. I should enjoy it. I do have a nice dress. It isn't long, but it has a lovely full skirt.'

'I'm not wearing a long dress,' Jeanie said. 'Most of us don't – there will be jiving and hip-hop as well as ballroom dancing, so a long dress wouldn't work anyway.'

Artie glanced at John. 'You should've come, John, but George will be pleased to be asked.'

'Not interested in dancing.' John got up and walked from the table, disappearing upstairs without another word.

Pam frowned at Artie. 'You know he has a lot on his mind,' she reproved. 'You asked and he said no – now leave it.'

'It would do him good,' Artie said, sounding grumpy, but in fact cursing himself for upsetting his brother. 'I know he loved Faith, but he must try. He needs to be right with himself again before they call him back. If he goes into combat with an enemy plane in this mood, I don't give a lot for his chances.'

'Artie!' Pam sent him an angry look, but Arthur nodded his agreement.

'The boy needs to come out of it,' he said. 'I know it is a terrible thing he has to live with, Pam – but he has to make an effort to put it behind him.'

There was silence for a moment, then, 'He has tried. He helped me change little Jonny earlier. Don't expect him to want to go dancing – Faith loved to dance. How can John dance with someone else when he knows he will never dance with her again?'

They all looked at Pam. Artie frowned but said no more. Jeanie reached for his hand and squeezed it beneath the table. Frances looked down at the table. She didn't know John and she didn't particularly like the sullen man he was now – though Pam said he'd been vastly different before he'd been wounded so badly. She was clearly worried about him, but Artie was angry. It would result in a row between them one of these days...

Tom came home that Saturday evening. He arrived after the others had gone to the dance and found Lizzie and Pam sitting by the fire with the two children. Both women looked up with cries of welcome. He approached Lizzie instantly, looking down at the baby on her lap, and then squatted down so that he was on a level with his son.

'He's beautiful,' he said to Lizzie. 'I think he has your eyes, Lizzie.'

'His hair is like yours,' Lizzie replied and smiled at her husband. 'I am glad you approve.'

'Of course I do.' Tom leaned in to kiss her. 'Was it very bad, my darling? I'm so sorry I wasn't here for you.'

'You couldn't get leave, so it isn't your fault,' Lizzie excused him lovingly. 'I'm fine and so is he, so it doesn't matter now. I'm just glad you're home, darling. How long have you got with us?'

'They gave me ten days,' Tom told her. 'We've just finished training a batch of men for a rather difficult mission – and the new recruits won't arrive until two weeks from now. They've given all the instructors time off.'

Lizzie nodded. 'Do you want to hold Archie?'

'Yes,' he said.

Lizzie stood up and indicated that he should sit in her chair, before placing the baby in his arms. Tom took him gently but confidently and his son opened his eyes and then blew a bubble as he burped. Tom put him up to his shoulder and gently patted his back.

'Mum had four children after me...' he murmured with a grin at his mother. 'I know how to deal with a little wind.' His gaze came to rest on the baby Pam had just placed in his cot. 'And who is this little fellow?'

'That's little Jonny,' Lizzie said and Tom nodded.

'John's boy.'

'Welcome home, love. I put some dinner aside for you if you're hungry?'

'Thanks, Mum. I might have it warmed up later, but I ate something on the train coming here.' He looked around. 'Where is everyone?'

'Your father is out tending to one of the cows. She has an infected teat, but the vet gave Artie something for her. Artie, Jeanie and Frances have gone to a dance – and John is in his room. He went up straight after he'd eaten.' She frowned. 'He spends a lot of his evenings there alone.'

Tom looked at her. 'Is he still unwell? I thought he must be better when they let him come home.'

'John is grieving – and I think there's something else playing on his mind, but he doesn't talk about it much.'

'I'll go up and have a word later,' Tom said. He smiled as Lizzie brought him a cup of tea and he gave the baby back to her. She placed Archie carefully in his carrycot. 'Is he always this good?' Tom asked.

'No, he has been known to scream and cry for a couple of

hours at a time,' Lizzie replied with a smile. 'I thought we would have tonight here, Tom, and then move back home tomorrow.'

'Are you certain you feel up to it, love?' Pam asked her. 'You know I've always got room for you, Lizzie. George isn't due to arrive for another few days.'

'I know,' Lizzie replied. 'I'll be here often once Tom goes back, but I thought we'd have some time on our own, get me used to coping while Tom is around.'

Arthur came in at that moment, his smile broadening as he saw Tom sitting by the fire drinking tea. 'I thought I heard a car,' he said and came to the fire, rubbing his hands. 'No, don't get up, son. I can sit at the table. Did you have a decent journey?'

'Yes, pretty good,' Tom told him but vacated the chair that was Arthur's favourite place to sit. 'The trains were running a bit late due to a false alarm, and packed, but I got a seat most of the way. There are a lot of army chaps on the move now, so I expect there's another big push in the offing.'

Arthur nodded, sat down, and lit his pipe. 'Not been going too well for our chaps,' he said. 'It's time the Americans got going and helped us out.'

'We have been under the cosh,' Tom agreed. They'd been on the run on several fronts, but he thought the tide might be about to turn. 'I can't say why, but I think we will be giving the enemy something to think about soon, Dad. It is bound to help now the Americans have joined us. We've held them at bay, but we needed the Americans. They have a lot of money and firepower and we could do with some of that...'

'Roosevelt will do everything he can – good man,' Arthur said, nodding his approval. 'Damned war, but we've been lucky here in this part of the country. Haven't seen too much of it. The cities take the brunt of the air raids.'

Tom agreed.

* * *

Tom and Arthur talked for a while longer of various aspects of the war and then Tom excused himself and went upstairs. He visited the bathroom first and then walked down the hall to John's room, knocking on the door.

'May I come in, John?' he asked.

There was silence for a moment, then, 'Is that you, Tom? Yes, come in...'

Tom walked into the bedroom. His brother had been lying on the bed, but he swung his legs over the side, got up and came to meet Tom, offering his hand.

'Good to see you, Tom. It seems a long time...'

'Yes, a very long time.' Tom clasped his hand warmly. 'I've thought about you a lot, old chap. I'm sorry for all you've suffered – out there and when you got back. Rotten thing to come home to...'

'It knocked me for six,' John admitted. 'I couldn't take it in at first, didn't understand how, but Mum explained it to me. I understand now, but it doesn't stop it hurting.'

'Of course it doesn't,' Tom agreed instantly. 'I'd be devastated if I lost Lizzie. I still can't believe that bastard could do such a thing. I knew Ralph was a rotter and he hated me – but how any man can do that to a woman he is supposed to care about I don't know – his own niece!'

'Maybe he didn't mean to hit her that hard,' John said, his face torn with grief. 'I can't see why he would want to hurt her – it doesn't make sense. He used to be fond of her and buy her presents. She thought he was wonderful at one time, though I think she changed a bit towards him later...'

'Who knows what festers in the mind of a man like that? The police say he was suspected of a double murder in London, but they couldn't prove it. Maybe he let something slip in front of her and was afraid she might tell...' Tom shrugged. 'All I know is that if he hadn't been killed in that motor accident, I would have knocked his head off.'

'Artie said he'd have killed him,' John said. 'I'd have liked him to hang. He would have suffered more that way.'

'Thank God your son is thriving. I know you must be going through hell – but you must cling to the boy. He needs your love even more...'

'I know. It was so strange to be told I had a child. I didn't even know Faith was pregnant.' John shook his head. 'I do know I'm lucky to have him, Tom. It's just hard to accept she isn't here.'

'That's natural, but he is a part of her, John.' Tom hesitated, then, 'Do you feel like coming down, old chap? We could go for a stroll to the pub and have a half, if you like?'

'Take you away from Mum and Lizzie on your first evening back?' John gave a rueful laugh. 'They would have my guts for garters. Maybe another night – but I will come down for a while.' He hesitated, then, 'It's Artie that gets me. I know he doesn't mean to rile me, but he isn't the most sensitive of blokes.'

Tom laughed. 'He cares about you, John, but he is about as sensitive as a bull in a china shop when it comes to trampling all over your feelings. I could have punched him in the face more than once when Lizzie and I were at odds, but he's family and Mum would've given me hell, so I didn't.'

John grinned, looking more his normal self. 'It's good to have you home,' he said. They'd always got on well and, when he spoke to Tom, John experienced none of the animosity he sometimes felt towards Artie.

Tom turned and left the room and John followed him down, after pulling on some shoes and a sweater. Pam smiled at him as he entered but didn't say anything. His father looked up, nodded as if he'd expected it, and went back to his paper. Lizzie's baby was asleep in his cot and she was helping Pam stitch a new coat for little Jonny, who was sleeping soundly upstairs, by pressing the pieces with a warm iron. She just smiled and got on with what she was doing.

Tom went to the pantry and found a bottle of beer and two glasses. He poured the dark liquid into the glasses and pushed one towards John where they sat at the long pine table.

'There is more beer if you want one, Dad,' he said. 'Lizzie – Mum?'

They all refused, but John took a mouthful and nodded to Tom. 'It's a long time since I drank English beer. They gave me wine at the nunnery... it was rough and dark, but it helped when the nights were long. Their supplies didn't always include pain relief.'

'No. I suppose they relied on herbal remedies mostly,' Tom said. 'I was luckier in my hospital ship; they had strong pain relief.'

'Has your limp gone?' John asked. 'I doubt if mine ever will. The nuns did their best, but the scar on my leg is going to be with me for a long time – and I limp heavily if I try to walk fast.'

'Mine has improved a bit,' Tom said. He glanced at Lizzie and shook his head. 'Not sure it will ever go completely.'

John nodded. 'I'm hoping they will take me back in the RAF. I don't need to be fast on my feet to navigate a plane.'

'No, you don't,' Tom agreed. 'I suppose they might consider it would hamper you if you were brought down again.'

'Not likely to happen twice,' John said. 'It was a fluke – absolute miracle that I didn't die in the crash. I doubt any man would walk away for a second time.' His mother looked at him. 'Don't worry, Mum. It's more likely that I wouldn't be shot down again.'

'You wouldn't consider retraining as an instructor?' Tom

asked to cover the small silence. He knew his mother worried over her children, particularly those fighting for King and Country.

'I don't know,' John replied. 'I suppose... I've been helping Jack out with a bit of plastering, but I feel I'd be letting the side down. It is peaceful and good to be home but... I don't want to be a coward. I may not be the bravest, but I want to fight this war in the only way I know.'

'You've never been a coward,' Tom told him and held his eyes. 'We all have our limits, John. Some men struggle against fear each time they have to fight, chain smoking. Others pee themselves just waiting for the attack – but they do what they must do when the time comes, just as we all do – just as I know you do.'

John nodded but bit his lip.

Tom understood there was some issue here but knew his brother couldn't talk about it in front of others. He would get to the bottom of whatever it was before he went back to camp, but for now he would turn the subject.

'How is it with the airfield just up the hill then?' he asked the company in general. 'Does the noise disturb you at night when they take off or land?'

'Jeanie and Artie go and count them in some nights,' Pam replied as Arthur just grunted. 'The noise as they come back in the middle of the night can be disturbing – we had a crash in the top field earlier this year.'

'Yes, Lizzie told me in her letters,' Tom said. 'Not one of ours, though, was it?'

'No – German bomber. It still had an unexploded bomb on board, but they were able to defuse it,' Pam replied. 'Some of the crew died in the crash. Artie said he wished they all had because he hates Germans...'

'So why did he pull one of the blighters out then?' Arthur

said and nodded as they all looked at him. 'He kept quiet about that, didn't he? It was already burning. He could have been killed if it had exploded, but he dragged one clear and would have gone back for another if I hadn't yelled at him to get away before it went up.'

'So Artie is a bit of a hero then,' Tom said and chuckled. 'I bet he felt daft when he realised it wasn't one of ours. That's why he said they should all have gone, Mum. Annoyance that he'd saved an enemy.'

'Yes, perhaps,' she agreed. 'None of you really know Artie. He isn't as charming as you pair and he has difficulty with saying what he feels at times, but he's got a good heart. He might have felt a fool when he realised that he'd saved enemy airmen, but he'd do it again.'

Tom laughed. 'Yes, Mum. He's your son, so how could he be anything else but perfect?'

'Cheeky devil!' Pam said and threw a wet dishcloth at him. Tom ducked and it landed on the stove behind him. John laughed and so did Lizzie and even Arthur had a chuckle over it. The atmosphere had lightened and it was much like it had been before the war, when they boys were together, happy, and carefree. She smiled at him. 'It's so good to have you all home at the same time.'

18

'It is good to have you home,' Artie said the next morning when he and Tom had gone out into the farmyard together for a cigarette.

'Yes, I'm glad to be here. I'd like to come to the wedding, Artie, but don't rely on it. I might not manage it. I'm not sure where I'll be by May...' He smiled at his brother. 'I like Jeanie. She is a nice girl.'

'She's the only one for me,' Artie replied with a slight shrug. 'I would've asked you to stand up with me as best man, but I know you can't always get leave.'

'I'd have been here for Lizzie if I could – not that I was needed, but you know what I mean.'

'Yeah...' Artie grinned. 'You and John were both lucky to have a son...'

'Lizzie wants a girl next,' Tom replied, looking pleased with himself.

'Yeah...' Artie hesitated, then, 'I wanted to ask when you thought the bottom field would be ready for ploughing. It laid wet for weeks under the frost and snow.'

'I'll take a look at it,' Tom replied. 'I'll be helping Lizzie settle back at the house this morning, but I'll find time later.'

'Thanks,' Artie nodded. 'It's not the only reason I'm glad to see you home, Tom. I'm worried about John. He needs shaking out of himself. I know he is grieving for Faith, but he needs to get over it before they send him back. If he isn't right in his mind, God knows what he might do...'

'He didn't seem too bad last night, but I know what you mean,' Tom said and drew a last puff of his cigarette before grinding it out beneath his boot. 'Bad habit. I should cut it out.'

'I like a few cigarettes, helps the day through,' Artie replied. 'I worry that John might—' He shrugged as if not wishing to put his thoughts into words.

'Throw himself in harm's way?' Tom nodded. 'I've heard about chaps who do that in the army – just charge in and hope to get shot – but John is in a plane with others. I can't see him doing anything that might risk their lives. He is more likely to do something heroic and save them. Besides, he has a son to think of and he does care, even if he might not be able to smile about it just yet.'

'I hope you are right,' Artie said and glanced over his shoulder as Frances and Jeanie emerged from the kitchen and walked in the direction of the cowsheds. 'I'd better go and give them a hand. I'm on schedule with the fen land, but I haven't made a start on the heavy land yet.' He grinned ruefully at his brother. 'I know I made a mess of it the other year when I wouldn't listen to you. I've learned my lesson.'

Tom nodded. 'I'll take a look and give you a hand if it's right,' he said. 'Now, I'd better go and see if Lizzie is ready. I may take her to see her mum for a visit later.'

Artie watched his brother walk off and then made his way to the milking shed. He hoped Tom was correct about John, but he still had an uneasy feeling that his younger brother was hiding his desperation behind a mask of withdrawal.

* * *

John decided that he would go for a walk by the river. He wasn't needed on the farm; it had never been his job or his desire to work there. Jack Freeman had needed some help for a few days and would welcome his skill when he had more plastering to be done, but just now there wasn't a great deal of building going on. Jack had told him that it was mostly repairs and a few larger renovations to old property.

'We can't get the materials for building new, even if anyone wanted to put their money into it,' Jack had said when they were talking. 'All the men are needed for the army or one of the other armed forces. Oh, they man the mines and the docks and fire stations, but there's not enough labour to make bricks or other materials we need. Of course there's still some production going on, using older men and women too; the lasses are doing their bit, bless them, but nothing like as much production as before the war. Some of the raw materials come from overseas and we're still suffering too many losses in the Atlantic.'

'Yes, I know,' John had said. 'Anyway, I'll be going back to the RAF once they pass me as fit.'

'You wouldn't want it any other way,' Jack had said and looked at him straight. 'I know you've had a rough time, lad, but keep your chin up. It will come right. One of these days this nightmare will be over and you will be able to make a new life for yourself.'

John had just nodded. He wasn't sure he would ever get over this feeling of regret and loss as far as Faith was concerned.

His shame at what had happened that night at the convent

was tucked at the back of his mind, too. He wished he'd done something to save Maria's life, because she hadn't deserved to be murdered by that devil who had been searching for him. John didn't know how the man had discovered the nuns were hiding him. The loud argument had been in French and he hadn't understood much of what was being said. His instinct had been to stay hidden, but then she'd screamed and still he'd hesitated until the next scream. When he'd finally burst into the kitchen, Maria had been fatally wounded. John had had to fight for his own life and, somehow, he'd won. He wasn't sure how he'd managed to grab the knife and use it against his assailant, cutting deep into his palm as he'd wrested the blade from him, but John had caught the smell of strong drink on his dying breath as he thrust it into the man's belly again and again.

The memory of the stench of blood made his stomach turn. Sometimes he still felt that he could taste it on his tongue. There had been blood everywhere – his and the enemy's, as well as Maria's. Then the other nuns had arrived, looking scared and weeping, to carry Maria away and clean up the kitchen so that no trace of what had happened remained. He'd seen the nuns look at him with reproach. They couldn't wait to get rid of him after that and he'd been glad to go, even though his arm, shoulder and hand had been hurting, but not as much then as when the festering began after his fresh wounds had been untreated for long days and nights. He wondered if there had been further repercussions for the nuns and hoped they hadn't been punished because he'd killed that soldier. Would anyone have traced the man John had killed to the convent, or had he just followed an instinct?

He'd prayed that no further harm came to the women who had helped him, but he might never know. It was impossible to return there while a war raged and, when it finally was over, he wasn't sure he would want to go back.

Doing his best to push away the guilt and regret filling his head, John walked and walked; his limp was still there but it didn't trouble him as much now. It was peaceful here by the river, even the cattle were not yet put out to wander and graze, and only the cry of a wood pigeon disturbed the stillness. No one around to ask questions or intrude into his thoughts. For a while he could shut them all out...

* * *

Artie saw the man staring at the farm from the field across the road. He was standing by one of the huge horse chestnut trees in the gloom of a misty afternoon. It would be dark shortly, dusk falling faster because of the foggy weather. He wondered if it was an off-duty flier with nothing to do. Artie's parents had invited the men based locally to come for supper if they had nothing else to do and a couple of Australians had turned up once. Pam had made them welcome at her table, making the pie she'd cooked stretch a little further with mounds of mashed potatoes. The pilot and his gunner had been good company, but they hadn't returned. Artie didn't know why, as some of his friends regularly provided food and even a bed for men who wanted to get away from their base. He looked at his home critically. Did it look run-down or was it the smell of the farmyard that had prevented those two returning or others coming?

The man was still hesitating, smoking. Artie wondered if he should go over and ask him if he was looking for someone, but as he reached the farmyard gate, the man turned and walked off; he walked quickly, as if he had somewhere to be – or didn't want to speak to Artie.

A shiver went down Artie's spine. Had the man's behaviour been suspicious? He felt a prickle of unease. Everyone had assumed it was Ralph Harris who had killed Faith, but it had never been confirmed. Ralph's death had prevented any further investigation and the police considered the case closed.

Should he warn the girls to be careful? Artie considered the matter. If he told everyone about the man lingering opposite the farm and then walking off swiftly, he could frighten the girls, upset them – and it might just as easily have been air crew wondering if they should come to the farm and ask for supper. His father's invitation had been open-,ended but it wasn't easy for men from another country to just walk into a stranger's home and ask to stay to supper. It might be better to give a supper party and invite, say, six men – and then they could spread the word and bring friends. Artie decided he would speak to his father when he got the chance, but say nothing in front of the others...

As he was about to go in, he saw another figure loom out of the growing gloom.

'Artie?' John's voice reassured him. 'Everything all right?'

'Yeah, sure,' Artie said. 'Why wouldn't it be?'

'You seemed lost in thought...'

'Just because you joined the fly boys doesn't make you the only one capable of thought,' Artie said irritably. 'Don't you think it is time you pulled out of this mood, John? We're all tiptoeing round you like idiots, afraid of hurting your feelings. Grow up, brother. You aren't the only one who feels bad about Faith.'

And that's when John punched him in the mouth, hard.

Artie was rocked on his feet, but he didn't go down. John had hit him squarely and he tasted blood from a split lip. For a moment, in sudden anger, he almost threw a punch at John, but

Tom's warning was lingering at the back of his mind and it stopped him.

He wiped the blood off on his coat sleeve. 'Feel better now, do you?' he asked sarcastically.

John walked off without another word, towards the house.

Artie stood for a moment, torn between anger and remorse. Why did he always say the wrong thing to John? He shook his head in irritation and turned towards the dairy and ran some water into his hand from the tap there, washing the cut. It stung and would be noticeable. He grimaced as he dried his face on the towel they used to wash their hands. Everything had to be kept clean in this shed, because his mother made butter and little cheeses, she left to set on straw mats. Before the war she'd sold any surplus, but these days she used everything, wasting nothing, in an effort to feed them all.

* * *

When Artie entered the kitchen, John wasn't there. He'd obviously gone straight upstairs. Pam looked at him, noticed the red mark on his mouth and frowned but made no comment.

Jeanie came to him, looking up at him anxiously. 'Are you okay?' she said softly. 'John said you had an argument. He said he hit you?'

'I provoked him,' Artie admitted. 'I didn't hit him. I couldn't, not after all he's been through – besides, I was to blame.'

His mother looked at him but said nothing. She'd let John go upstairs and hadn't followed, so clearly, she felt it was best to let her sons sort out whatever they'd argued about between themselves.

Any thoughts Artie had held about telling his father or anyone about the stranger had vanished. He was torn between anger at his brother and concern for him at the same time. Never, in all the times they'd had words in the past, had John even tried to hit him. They'd jostled each other as youngsters, but they hadn't punched one another.

A rueful smile touched Artie's mouth. John packed quite a punch. It was a wonder Artie hadn't gone down. He sorted of respected him for having a go at him. Artie hadn't truly thought he had it in him.

* * *

Artie was preparing the tractor for work the next morning when John walked up to him. For a moment, they just looked at each other and then John said, 'I shouldn't have hit you. I'm sorry.'

'Lucky punch,' Artie shrugged. 'Maybe you needed to get something off your chest?'

'I did and do,' John said. 'I still shouldn't have hit you. Does it hurt much?'

Artie resisted the temptation to snarl back. 'A bit,' he replied in an even tone. 'I know we don't always get on, John, but I wish I'd heard or seen something... that I could have stopped what happened. I feel I let you down. I was here and I should have protected her.'

'I don't blame you for what happened to Faith,' John said. 'It just bloody hurts. She didn't deserve what happened to her, Artie. '

'No, she didn't,' Artie replied. 'Nor did you. We all feel terrible about it, John.'

'Didn't anyone see him hanging around?' John said, a look of such grief in his eyes that Artie felt his own chest tighten.

'None of us had any idea that he had sneaked into Lizzie's

house,' Artie confirmed. 'We didn't know he was there and had no reason to think anyone would hurt her.'

'If it was him...' John's face twisted with anguish. 'It's not knowing what happened...'

'The police were pretty sure it was him. Her father said he was acting oddly when he'd visited Faith's mother before his accident – and he said he thought it was him. The London police said he was suspected of murder – it all makes sense.' Artie hesitated, then, 'I haven't said anything in the house, because I don't want to alarm the women – but there was a bloke hanging around in the chestnut field opposite last night, just before you came back from your walk.'

'Is that why you were just standing there?' John frowned. 'Don't you think you should say – in case it was him – the one who hurt Faith? Supposing it wasn't her uncle?'

Artie looked at him. 'I think it was just one of the blokes from the airbase. Dad gave them a standing invitation to come for a. meal if they were at a loss...'

John's eyes were dark with anger and grief. 'I think you should tell Mum and let her decide what to say to the girls.'

'Maybe I will later,' Artie said. 'I need to start work. I'm harrowing the long bit in the fen this morning. I'll speak to you when I get back.'

19

Jeanie and Frances finished work in the milking shed and moved the full churns to the gate between them so that the lorry would pick them up. They returned the empty ones at the same time and those churns would need to be washed, ready for the evening milking session.

'I'm hungry,' Jeanie said as they turned towards the kitchen door. 'I hope there is more than toast for breakfast this morning.'

Frances laughed. 'You are always hungry,' she said. 'I don't know where you put it all. You never seem to put an ounce on.'

'No, thank goodness,' Jeanie replied with a smile. 'I don't want to put on weight before my wedding, because my dress won't fit. Pam is going to help me cut out your bridesmaid dress today. You haven't put any weight on, have you?'

'No. I used to watch my figure, but since I've been working here, it seems to be stable. I think it is all the fresh air and hard work.'

'You wait until harvest comes,' Jeanie told her. 'We have to work twice as long hours then – and hay time, too, is hard work...'

'It can't be worse than muck spreading,' Frances said ruefully.

'No, that is one of the worst jobs,' Jeanie agreed. 'Arthur is going to take another load this morning. I'll be going with him and I'll do the dress when I get back – but I want my breakfast first. Come on.'

Jeanie ran towards the kitchen door and went in.

Frances paused for a moment and looked over her shoulder. She had the oddest feeling that she was being watched but she couldn't see anyone. It was just her imagination. Had to be. Mrs Bates had told her someone was looking for her and it had given her a creepy feeling – but it couldn't have been Roy Bent. Surely, he wouldn't – couldn't – have seen that small piece in the daily newspaper? He wouldn't bother to come all this way to look for her even if he had... surely, he wouldn't?

* * *

Breakfast was scrambled eggs, bubble and squeak and toast with a scraping of marge and jam.

Jeanie ate three pieces of toast, before jumping up to pull on her coat as Arthur came looking for her. 'Give yourself time to get it down, love,' Pam told her, but Jeanie just laughed and went out with him. 'That girl will give herself indigestion,' Pam murmured and then looked at Frances. 'What are you going to do now, love?'

'I'll collect the churns and give them a scrub,' Frances told her. 'Then I've got the hens to feed, look for more eggs and the mucking out.'

'That will take you an hour or two then,' Pam said, nodding. 'When Jeanie gets back, we'll check your measurements again and start cutting your dress out for the wedding. I've done Angela's and Susan's. If we get them all cut and ready, we can have a clear run at putting them together. It shouldn't take too long, but it is surprising how the time goes. Before we know it, the wedding will be here; it's only six weeks or so.' She shook her head and sighed. 'I wish I could make them a proper wedding cake – but it will have to be a sponge. I'll try to get enough cream to make it a bit special.'

Frances nodded. 'I saw in the paper where someone had a cardboard cake so it looked nice for the photos...'

'Can't see the point in that,' Pam said. 'Food is food, and we'll get as much on the table as we can, but it might not be just what I'd like for them.'

The sun had crept out from behind the clouds for the first time in days and it felt warm on Frances' face as she emerged from the cowsheds, her work done for the moment. It was March and better weather was on its way. She stood with her face upturned to the warmth, reluctant to go in and leave it. It had been a long winter and now, at last, they had a foretaste of spring. She rinsed her hands and wellingtons under the outside tap and decided to go for a little walk in the fields across the road from the farm. Jeanie and Arthur hadn't come back yet, which meant Frances needn't go in for a few minutes. She would see them arrive from across the road and the trees would look so beautiful once they got their blossom later in the year.

Frances crossed the road, which was completely free of any traffic on this lovely morning. Only tractors and trailers, local cars, of which there were few, and the occasional lorry or bus, passed the farm gate. Pam had told her there used to be more before the road to Sutton was closed for the aerodrome. People from Sutton didn't bother to come this way much, preferring to go to the cathedral city of Ely rather than Chatteris or March.

There was no gate and she walked into the field, where the row of chestnut trees lined the road, and stood in the sun, feeling it almost hot on her back. How lovely it was after all the ice and snow the past two months.

Frances closed her eyes, lifting her face to the sky and enjoying the perfect peace of the countryside. Jeanie had told her how much nicer it was working on the land in nice weather and now she understood how pleasant it would be when they were just hoeing between the lines of potatoes or— Her thoughts were rudely interrupted by a hand on her shoulder. Her eyes flew open as she was spun round to face the man she had dreaded ever seeing again and she let out a scream of fear. He had found her!

'I knew it was you,' Roy sneered, his handsome face made ugly by the hate in his expression. 'Did you think a little thing like changing your name would keep you safe from me, Cathy?'

'Don't call me that,' Frances cried. 'I'm not that girl any more. She's gone. I'm someone else now.'

'You're still the little slut you always were,' Roy sneered. 'Don't imagine I came all this way for you to send me away, Cathy. You belong to me. You owe me and you're going to pay—'

'No! No, you can't make me go with you. I won't.' Frances screamed several times at the top of her voice. 'Help! Help me someone, please!'

Roy grabbed her by the throat and pushed her hard against the trunk of one of the huge trees. His face was close to hers, leering at her as she struggled against him. She could smell his breath. He'd been drinking alcohol and the look in his eyes terrified her. 'I told you, you owe me,' he said and squeezed her throat as she tried to scream again. 'I intend to make you pay and then I shall kill you, but not before you are longing for death.'

'No—' Frances struggled, desperately managing a small sound that was meant to be a scream but was cut off by his hand over her mouth. She brought her knee up sharply and caught him in the groin, making him gasp with pain, and let go of her. Frances started to run, but he was after her in an instant and threw her to the ground. She closed her eyes as he aimed a kick at her face – and then she saw a blur of something dark blue and Roy was suddenly jerked back and went staggering as a man punched him in the face and then the stomach. It flashed into her mind that it was John Talbot who had come to her rescue. She was surprised at how fierce he was as he pummelled Roy's body mercilessly, blow after blow, landing heavy punches.

She heard Roy gag and sat up, pulling her knees up to her chest as she watched the fight ensue. Roy had been taken by surprise at first, but now he tried to fight back and she saw the flash of metal in his hand.

'He's got a knife,' Frances cried and watched as John grabbed Roy's right wrist and twisted it. She saw the knife go flying and crawled after it, managing to grab it and throw it into the dyke, where it disappeared into lingering water and neither man could get it. Scrambling on to her knees and then her feet, she recovered her breath and watched as John speedily overcame his opponent. Roy was breathing heavily, clearly getting the worst of the fight as John delivered punch after punch to his guts and then, finally, he fell on to his knees, bending over, blood coming from his mouth.

'Don't hit me any more,' he whispered and was sick, bringing up blood. 'I've got a stomach ulcer... you'll kill me...'

'You deserve it, you scum,' John said. 'You were going to kill her the way you killed Faith...' His eyes were wild and he looked as if he would continue to attack Roy, but Frances caught his arm.

'It wasn't him who hurt Faith,' she croaked. 'He came here to get me, John. Don't kill him. He isn't worth it. They might imprison or hang you – it's him that needs prison, not you.'

John looked at her, dazed for a moment, as if his anger had temporarily made him lose his senses. 'He came here for you – you know him?'

'He's an evil man,' Frances told him. 'He did terrible things to me – made me his prisoner... made me work for him as a sex slave...'

Understanding came to John's eyes then and he nodded grimly. 'Get back to the farm,' he told her, then turned to look at Roy, who was still on his knees, a thin trickle of blood from the corner of his mouth. 'As for you, I'd kill you without turning a hair and say it was self-defence. Come near this farm again – touch anyone here, and I will. I killed a German soldier with the knife he tried to use on me – and I'll do it to you if you show your filthy face round here again. Now go before I decide you're not fit to live.'

Roy threw him a scared look, staggered to his feet, and began to walk off just as two tractors followed each other into the farmyard. One of the men spoke to Frances as she walked back to the house and then Artie raced across the road to join John; he was carrying the rifle that he often took in his tractor in case he saw a pheasant or rabbit to help his mother feed them all; it was loaded and he pointed it in the direction of Roy's back.

'Come here again and I'll shoot you...' he yelled after him and Roy ran off round the corner and disappeared from sight.

'I nearly killed him just now. I might have if Frances hadn't stopped me.'

Artie looked at him hard. 'Frances told me she was attacked,' he said. 'That is the bastard I saw hanging around yesterday. Who is he and what does he want?'

'He came for Frances. Tried to force her to go with him. He didn't succeed and I don't think he will be back in a hurry.'

'Well done, brother,' Artie said and grinned. 'You pack quite a punch. I didn't know you could fight like that...'

'I did some boxing after I joined up,' John said. 'Just to toughen me up. My instructor said I could have done it professionally.'

'You kept that quiet,' Artie remarked.

'It wasn't important,' John replied. 'It came in handy though. My instructor taught me a few dirty tricks as well.' He suddenly laughed. 'I don't think we'll see him here again. I went for the stomach and, apparently, he has a stomach ulcer...'

'Probably what kept him out of the army,' Artie said as they walked back to the yard together. 'He'll feel that for a while, I'll bet.'

* * *

Arthur, Jeanie and Frances were in the kitchen when they got there. Frances' blouse was ripped and she was sitting at the table, sipping a cup of tea, her hands a little unsteady.

She looked up as John entered. 'I haven't thanked you for what you did,' she said. 'If you hadn't come, he would have beaten me and he might have drugged me to force me to go with him.'

'Has he done that in the past?' Pam asked, shocked. 'You should have gone to the police...'

'I did after I escaped,' Frances told her, meeting her eyes at last. 'He kept me a prisoner for months and made me...' She lowered her head. 'I had to do things I am ashamed of. In the end, I was lucky; a man came who was from the police but working undercover. He helped me escape and I... I... testified in court to what he had done.' She raised her head. 'He went to prison and that is why he will never forgive me.'

'The wicked evil man!' Pam exclaimed. 'They should have hung him – or at least kept him locked up for much longer.'

'He was supposed to go down for three years, but he got out sooner. I don't know why or how – but he can be charming and persuasive. It's only when you won't do as he says that he gets nasty.'

'Well, he won't come here in a hurry,' Artie said. 'John gave him a thrashing. I don't think Tom could have done better.'

'Tom would have finished him with one blow,' John said. 'I don't have that power, but I know how to win.' He raised his head and looked at his mother. 'I would have killed him if I'd had to. I killed a soldier at the convent, because he had knifed a nun. I heard her scream, but I hesitated for a couple of minutes, because I knew what they would do to me if they caught me – and she died from her wounds – but he died too. After that, the nuns couldn't wait to get rid of me.'

Everyone was staring at John. He felt sick with shame, but he went on, 'If I hadn't hesitated, she might still be alive... I was a coward. I knew that if they found me, I'd probably be killed or tortured and imprisoned, so I hesitated and Maria died.'

'That doesn't make you a coward,' Artie and Pam spoke almost simultaneously.

'Is that what has been eating at you, son?' Arthur asked, but John didn't need to answer. They all knew.

'You hesitated,' Pam said. 'Any man in your situation would have done the same. You had been ill for a long while. You knew it might mean your life – but you still went and you fought him. I don't think that makes you a coward...'

'You were a hero just now,' Frances said. 'I think you are very brave and I can't thank you enough for what you did.'

'I think he was a bloody hero for killing that bugger who murdered the nun,' Artie said. 'To be honest, in your position I'd have been messing myself, John. I'm not sure I would have even gone...'

'Yes, you would,' John said. 'You would've had to – just as I did. I bitterly regretted that I hadn't gone instantly, but I couldn't understand what they were arguing about, because it was in French. He had got wind that I was being hidden there and Maria wouldn't give me up, so he killed her.'

'I understand you feel guilty over her death, but it wasn't your fault,' Pam told him. 'Maria could have told him what he wanted to know and he would probably still have killed her.'

'Yes, I know you're right,' John said and sat down as the tension suddenly left his body. 'I think I've got a split lip to match yours now, Artie...' He grinned at his brother and wiped the blood from his mouth. 'You're lucky I didn't use the low blows on you.'

Pam made a clucking noise and went to damp a cloth for him to hold to his mouth. He smiled up at her as his brother retorted: 'I'd have thrashed you then, brother,' but he was laughing as the atmosphere lightened.

Frances stood up. She hesitated, then, 'Do you want me to leave now, Pam – now you know everything...'

'Don't be silly,' Pam said and smiled at her. 'It was a terrible experience for you, love, but it wasn't your fault. Men like that exist, more's the pity. I want you to try to put it from your mind. Go up and change into some different clothes – we've got a wedding to prepare for and I want you men out of my kitchen. This is girls' stuff!'

'Right, I'm back to work,' Arthur said and looked at John. 'If you're well enough to fight, you can give me a hand loading the tractor with muck.'

'All right, just this once,' John agreed. 'Just give me a moment to change my clothes – I don't think I should be muck spreading in air-force blue...'

* * *

John left the kitchen seconds after Frances. He went to the bathroom and washed his face, looking ruefully at his lip. That devil had caught him once, but after that John had used the low blows and that had soon taken the fight out of his opponent. He nodded his satisfaction to himself. It had felt good. He felt better having got the maggot in his brain out into the open. No matter what anyone said, John would always feel that if he'd reacted more quickly that night at the convent, he might have saved Maria, but he knew that wasn't definite. It was probable that she would have died from the first wound and he could never have stopped that even if he'd gone when she first screamed.

John looked himself in the face. His grief for Faith hadn't gone away. He doubted it ever would, but he could begin to accept it now; a part of her lived on in his son and for that he would be eternally grateful. He knew that he'd been impossible to live with these past weeks, but now, yes, perhaps now, he could start to put the past behind him. Maria had died and he couldn't change that – but he'd saved Frances from something almost worse than death and that was good.

Changing into his oldest clothes, John went downstairs and out into the yard to join his father. Muck spreading was the worst job in his opinion, but he would do it with a good heart. He had some harsh words to make up for to his family and this would be a start...

20

'That was well done, John,' Tom said when he and Lizzie came to the farm kitchen for their meal that evening; they had been over to March to visit Lizzie's mother. She'd wanted to see the baby and Lizzie hadn't felt up to driving. Artie had filled him in on what had happened and he looked at his brother with respect. 'You must teach me some of those low blows – my men need all the dirty tricks they can get.'

John grinned. 'I doubt I know anything you don't, Tom,' he said. 'I don't have your hammer fists, but I can win most fights. I wasn't supposed to box in a gentlemanly manner. I was taught self-defence to toughen me up. My instructor thought I was a jelly bag when he first met me, but I proved him wrong in the end.'

Lizzie looked across the table at Frances. 'How did that awful man discover you were living here?'

'The *Daily Mirror* printed a tiny piece about the rescue I did in Ely,' Frances said and John looked at her. She blushed. 'I went in the river after a young lad who fell in and couldn't swim.'

'She was so brave,' Jeanie said. 'I just stood there and

watched, my heart thumping. I couldn't have done it – I can't swim that well...'

'I'm not sure I would have jumped in icy water I didn't know,' Tom said. 'It was very brave, Frances. Bad luck the papers got hold of it.'

'I thought it wouldn't go any further than the local paper,' Jeanie said. 'It was a good thing you were here, John. We were all busy on the land – it might have been too late by the time we arrived.'

'I caught a glimpse of the fight as I was driving past the field,' Artie said, 'but Dad was right behind me so I drove into the yard before I came to help – not that any was needed. John gave him what for. The bugger won't come here again and if he does, I'll put a shot in his leg.'

'Do you think we should tell the police that he came here and attacked Frances?' Pam asked, but everyone shook their heads, including Frances.

'They would only lock him up for a night and John might get into trouble for thrashing him,' Frances said. 'I doubt he will come near me while I stay at the farm. If we ever met by accident in the future, he might try to harm me, but perhaps he will just forget me now.'

'Let's hope so,' Pam murmured. She hesitated, then, 'John, there's a letter for you – I think it is official...'

John took the envelope from the mantelpiece, opened and read what it had to say, nodding as he folded the single sheet. 'I've been ordered to report to my base for a medical consultation. It's for Friday next week and early in the morning, so I'll probably be best to go in on the train on Thursday and stay overnight in Cambridge.'

'Yes, that is better than getting up at the crack of dawn to get to Sutton and then get a train. It gives you plenty of time if there are any delays on the track, which happens quite a bit these days, mostly false alarms but not always.' Artie looked at him. 'I'll take you to the station. Do you think you'll be coming back home after your medical?'

'I suppose it depends what they decide,' John said, frowning. 'My physical wounds have healed. I may always have a bit of a limp, but that doesn't affect my job, so they will probably want me back.'

'Oh, John,' Pam said worriedly. 'Don't you think they might give you a bit more time if you explained things.'

'Perhaps, or perhaps they would think I was just malingering,' John replied and frowned. 'I'm not sure I want to be given more time, Mum. I know that Jonny is all right with you until I can look after him. It's not that I don't like being here – but I'd rather be busy doing something important. We've still got a war to win.'

* * *

On the following Thursday, John booked into a small hotel in central Cambridge for a night. The last time he'd stayed in Cambridge, it had been at a friend's little terraced house with Faith. They'd made love for the first time there and he'd felt truly happy when he'd returned to his unit, making plans, for marriage and a home with the girl he loved, but after that it had gone horribly wrong. Faith hadn't been happy in Portsmouth when they'd made love in a seedy little hotel. They hadn't quarrelled, but they'd parted with annoyance on both sides. How John wished he could go back in time and tell her how much he loved her again. If he hadn't made love to Faith, she might still be alive. No matter what anyone said, he knew he would always feel that grief and guilt.

John also knew that he couldn't dwell on his grief forever. He'd felt good as he'd thrashed that rotter who had attacked Frances. She was a nice enough girl and didn't deserve to be treated that way, whatever she'd done in the past. It wasn't his business to question it and he had seen for himself how scared she was of the man who had attacked her. At first, John had mistakenly believed that man might be the one who had killed Faith, but it had turned out to be an entirely separate matter. He might not have attacked so furiously if he'd known, but he would still have done it, because he'd had a point to prove to himself.

He wasn't a coward. He would most likely have been too late to save Maria even if he'd acted sooner, but he'd been tired, not fully recovered from his wounds, and he'd hesitated – but not, he realised now, out of cowardice. It hadn't worried him that Frances' attacker had a knife. He hadn't thought once of the consequences for himself, just of stopping a brutal attack on an innocent girl and, in that instant, he'd felt he was avenging Faith's death. He would always regret that he hadn't saved Maria, but he no longer felt the burning shame that had haunted him through months of recurrent fever in hospital as the infected wound in his arm refused to heal. John knew he was lucky he hadn't lost it as the doctors had considered amputation at one point before trying a poultice of live maggots, which had eaten away the putrid flesh. After that, he'd recovered slowly, but it had taken a while to regain the strength in his arm and it had still ached when he was plastering for Jack. He would have to work on his muscles, otherwise he would find it difficult to return to his old job after the war.

John hadn't expected to be called in for a medical quite so soon after his discharge from hospital; he'd expected longer at home, more time to get to know his son. The doctors at the military hospital had told him he should go home and get strong again, but he knew the RAF desperately needed experienced men. He was aware that the bombing raids over Germany were likely to increase in the next months. Now that they had another strong alliance to call on, they would increasingly take the attack to the enemy. Russia was fighting hard and the Allies were holding the line despite many reverses, but if this war was to end they had to go on the offensive in a big way. He fully expected to be flying daily missions again quite soon.

Having booked into his room, John had nothing much to do that evening so he decided to go out for a drink. He found himself walking towards the pub he'd been to a few times with Faith. It was popular with the nurses and the men on leave from the various armed forces.

He went in and ordered himself a beer and took it to a table in the corner, sitting down so that he had a view to the green that ran by the river. His thoughts were of the future and it was only when he heard a disturbance that he looked up and saw a young woman being harassed by a clearly inebriated young man in army uniform. Without thinking, John got up and went over to them.

'I suggest you leave this young lady alone,' he said in a calm flat tone. 'She obviously doesn't want your attentions.'

'What do you know about it?' the soldier said belligerently and threw a punch at him.

John was ready for him and the swing was wild. He put up his arm to counter the blow and then punched the soldier in the stomach. All the fight went out of him and he doubled over, vomiting on the ground. A couple of soldiers came over and grabbed their drunken companion by the arms, taking charge of him.

'Sorry, Miss,' one of them said. 'Tony had some bad news and he's got the devil in him tonight.' He looked at John. 'He didn't realise she was taken, mate.'

As they left the pub, taking the staggering and very drunk soldier with them, John looked at the girl and then did a double take. 'You're Lucy – the nurse...' he cried in surprise. 'I didn't recognise you with your cap off.' Her dark hair was released from the tight knot she wore for nursing and was curled softly on her shoulders. 'Are you okay? He didn't hurt you?'

'I think he bruised my arm,' Lucy said. 'How are you, Lieutenant Talbot?' She looked at his face and he knew that there was still a small scab on his lip. 'Did you have an accident?'

John smiled ruefully. 'It's nothing. Just a slight altercation with a door,' he prevaricated.

Lucy nodded, though he wasn't certain she believed him. 'What are you doing here?'

'I have a medical at my base tomorrow. I thought it would be quicker to get there from here than my home in Mepal.'

'It's a bit quick, isn't it? We only released you three weeks ago.'

'I've had a long time recovering already,' John reminded her. 'Months in hospitals of one kind or another. I suppose they either want me back or to kick me out.'

'They won't do that,' she said. 'My brother says we need all the trained men we can get. Too many youngsters are being killed. Some of them only last a few weeks once they finish training and start flying missions.'

John nodded. He recalled her telling him that her brother worked as ground crew for the RAF. 'Yes, I know. I am expecting to be recalled to duty.' He looked at her glass, which was empty. 'Can I buy you another?'

'No, thanks. I came to meet a friend, but she hasn't turned up.

You could walk me back to the nurses' home if you like. It shook me a little bit just now and I'd rather not walk home alone.'

'Of course I will,' John said at once. 'It was a nasty experience. Some men just think they can bully girls to get their own way. I doubt his friends will let him loose again this evening, but I'd like to see you safely home.'

It was in John's mind to tell her what had happened to Faith. In the hospital she'd told him she was always available if he wanted to talk, but he wasn't ready yet. One day perhaps, but not yet.

'Did you see your son?' she asked as they left the pub and began to stroll across the green. Men and women were walking arm-in-arm and students were cycling along the paths. It was dark and they rang their bells to let walkers know where they were because there were no street lights, though a bright moon made it light enough to see where they were going without the aid of the shaded torch Lucy carried.

'Yes. He is beautiful, like Faith,' John said. 'My mother, sisters and sister-in-law are looking after him. He will be fine – as much as any child can be without its mother.'

'I'm sorry you lost her,' Lucy said and he heard the sincerity in her voice. 'I can't imagine what it must feel like...'

'You don't have a boyfriend?' he asked.

'On and off,' she answered truthfully. 'I go out with a friend when he's home on leave, but we *are* just friends. I went out with someone I liked a lot for a few months, but he was stationed away and found someone else. I'm not sure if it broke my heart or not. I missed his letters for a while, but because of the war it is hard to get to know anyone well. I meet lots of men at work who want to date me, but I mostly say no. I'm not sure why.'

'Perhaps you just haven't found the right one,' John said. 'You might be sensible to wait until this is all over. It means separation and heartbreak if things go badly.'

'Yes, that's what I tell myself,' Lucy replied. 'I need to focus on my work for the moment. We can't afford to lose nurses. We never seem to have enough of them.'

'What about when it is over? Will you continue working then?'

'No. I'll get married and have lots of children,' Lucy said and laughed. 'What a daft question, Lieutenant Talbot! How do I know what I'll do. I think when it happens, love will just creep up and hit me and then who knows what I'll do. If it's anything like the romance stories my mum likes to read, I'll marry a rich man and go off to lead a merry life in his mansion...'

John laughed. 'That's the idea. You look for a millionaire, Lucy. At least you'll have comfort for the rest of your life.'

Lucy smiled and asked him if he'd seen Humphry Bogart in *The Maltese Falcon* and the subject was changed.

They walked in silence for a time and were at the nurses' home before John was ready. He hesitated for a moment, reluctant to let her go, but then he offered his hand and she looked up at him before giving him a quick kiss on the cheek.

'I think what you did deserves that,' she said. 'All you men are so brave.'

'You did so much more for me in the hospital,' he replied. 'Goodnight, Lucy. I might see you when I get leave. Would you like to go somewhere if I ring you here?'

'Why not?' she said breezily. 'I've always rather liked you, Lieutenant Talbot.'

'You could call me John now you're not on duty,' he pointed out with a half-smile.

'I could,' she agreed. 'Perhaps I will another time. Goodnight now and thank you.' She turned and went into the shadowy building without turning round.

John stood for a moment and then walked away. It was turning colder again after a few mild days. He hoped it wouldn't snow any more. Artie was worried enough about the land as it was. John considered for a moment what it must be like for his brother to have to stay at home and do his duty; his father would never manage it all despite the land girls.

Shrugging his shoulders, John walked back to his hotel. He'd enjoyed Lucy's company and he might ask her out one day – but merely because she'd told him she was only interested in casual friends. He wouldn't want to rouse false ideas, because he didn't think he could love again, not the way he'd loved Faith. As he'd stood by her grave, before he left Mepal, he'd promised her that he would never let their son forget his mother. One day he might marry, as much for his son's sake as his own, but that wouldn't be until the war was over...

* * *

Lucy stood at the top of the stairs, looking out of the window. In the moonlight, she could see John as he stood for a moment and then walked away. She didn't think he'd guessed how she felt about him. She had been very careful to hide it all the time she'd been his nurse and she wasn't about to let him see it now.

Lucy had first fallen in love with the handsome young airman when he injured his ankle in 1940 in a crash landing at his base. She'd hoped then that he might like her enough to ask her out, but he'd told her he had a girlfriend and she'd tried to put him out of her mind, though she'd never managed to get him out of her heart.

Lucy had carried on working and meeting friends. She'd

hoped it was just a crush and that she might find someone else, and then he'd been sent to her hospital again and she'd known her feelings for him weren't going anywhere. She'd never felt this way about anyone else, but she also knew that John was grieving for the girl who had died having his baby. Lucy's heart ached for him, but she'd never let him see how much she cared and she wouldn't now. John wasn't ready to love again. If she really cared, she had to give him time.

Making her way along the corridor to her room, Lucy smiled. It was probably an impossible dream, but she was no worse off than the girls whose lovers and husbands had been snatched from them by the war. She would hold her head high and go on with the work she knew was so desperately important. However, she could dream and she would keep doing so.

21

'Who is this young lad Mum wants me to fetch from Ely station?'
Tom asked Lizzie the following Monday morning. 'I mean, I
knew Mum had sisters and a brother – but she hasn't had
anything to do with them for years.'

'I know. Some of them were horrible to her when she had
you. I'm not sure I would have taken George on if I'd been her. I
mean, why should she? She already has more than enough
to do.'

'I'm surprised Dad didn't put his foot down and say no,' Tom
remarked thoughtfully.

'I doubt Arthur ever says no when Pam really wants something,' Lizzie said and laughed as he nodded. 'I know she agrees
with him most of the time, but if he thinks she wants something,
it's hers.'

'Yes, I suppose you are right,' Tom said, 'but a boy of that age
will be more difficult to control than she imagines. She isn't his
mother and he may not take kindly to being sent off to people he
doesn't know.'

'Well, I think she told Arthur it will be a trial period. If he isn't happy and her sister won't have him, he might have to go to an orphanage. Pam doesn't want that to happen,' Lizzie suggested.

'No, I'm sure she doesn't. I wouldn't either – but surely there is someone he knows who would take him?'

'Not according to Pam's letter from her sister. It was made clear that she either took him in or he would be given to the children's welfare people to be sent wherever they chose. Poor kid. It's rotten for him.'

'Yes, it is,' Tom agreed. 'He doesn't even have a grandmother like the young lad Frances rescued...' Tom frowned. 'What do you reckon to Frances' story about that bloke who attacked her? Do you think she was telling the truth?'

'Oh yes, I believe so,' Lizzie said. 'I think she told a few fibs when she first came, but I believe the truth came out this time. Pam seemed to know something about it, though she hadn't told me.'

'Mum probably felt sorry for her. If what she says is true, she's had a lucky escape.'

'I'm sure she was young and lonely, didn't know what she was getting into,' Lizzie said. She heard a wail from upstairs. 'That is Master Archie. Ready for his feed by the sound of it.'

Tom smiled. 'I'll fetch him for you, Lizzie, and if he is wet, I'll change him.'

Lizzie smiled as he left the room. It melted her heart to see Tom's gentleness with his baby son. He had big strong hands, capable of giving hard blows, but he was so careful and tender with Archie that she was overwhelmed with love for them both. Tom was making the most of his leave, spending his time with her and their child, though he'd helped Artie prepare the bottom field for the spring planting. She was going to miss having him around once he left for his camp again, not for the first time cursing the war that had kept them apart so often.

Tom returned with the baby in his arms, his crying miraculously ceased. Tom changed the wet nappy expertly and then gave him to Lizzie to feed. She was breastfeeding because she could and it was easier than preparing bottles of feed that were less nourishing than her milk. It meant she couldn't go far until he was weaned, but Lizzie didn't particularly want to as yet. Her business would do well enough without her for a few months and she enjoyed having her quiet time with Archie.

Now she was in her own home again, Lizzie might find the house a bit empty when Tom had gone back to base, but she was lucky in having Pam just a short distance away, Jeanie and the others too. Vera and Jeanie's father were coming to stay with her in another week's time, so she would have guests in her home again. Lizzie had never forgotten Vera's kindness to her when she was in London and always felt pleased to see her. They were officially coming to meet their prospective son-in-law, though Vera already knew him. They would all make plans for the wedding. Although the dresses were nearly made, there were still more details to arrange. Pam and Arthur would host the wedding reception, though it ought to have been Mr and Mrs Salmons. They would no doubt wish to contribute to the expense and perhaps find some food rationing coupons to help make sure there was plenty of fare on the table.

Tom was watching her, a fond smile on his face. 'A penny for them,' he said. 'You looked far away.'

'I was just content, thinking of your brother's wedding and the future...'

'Yes. I'll try to get home, but I can't guarantee it...' Tom hesitated. 'I might be sent on another mission. It isn't certain yet, Lizzie. When I started training others, I never thought it would happen. I still limp a bit, but it has improved lately and wouldn't really be a problem.' He sighed. 'They desperately need all the trained men now – which is why John has been called for a medical, even though he might need more rest.'

'I know,' Lizzie said. 'I guessed there was something you didn't want to tell me and it had to be that you may be in danger again.' She gently held Archie to her shoulder, rubbing him on the back so that his wind came up. 'I'd rather you didn't have to go, Tom, but I know you will if they want you.'

'I couldn't refuse,' he said, 'but I shan't volunteer. I promise you that, Lizzie.'

She smiled at him as she placed Archie in his carrycot. 'You'd better walk up to the farm and get your instructions from Pam. You don't want to leave that poor boy standing waiting on the station.'

'No, I don't,' he said. 'Poor lad will feel lost as it is. I still don't see why the aunt he knows won't have him.'

'She says she's too ill,' Lizzie said and he frowned. 'I know – but she won't have him and you know your mum's soft heart... he's only eight after all.'

Tom nodded, then drew her into his arms and kissed her. 'I wonder why I love you so much,' he said, grinned and then left her to stare after him with a smile in her eyes.

* * *

Tom parked his father's car outside the station, bought a platform ticket and walked on to the allotted destination for the next London train. It was due in any moment and he was pleased he'd managed to get here in time. He felt his mother was being taken advantage of by a sister who had treated her abominably when she needed help, but he also knew the young lad would be scared and anxious about his new home.

He glanced at the headlines on a newspaper stall nearby. Someone called Sir Arthur Harris had taken over as head of Bomber Command at the RAF. To Tom that sounded as if the Allies were planning to boost their raids over Germany and he frowned as he wondered if John would be flying such missions again soon; he was bound to if he passed the medical. About to buy a paper to read more, he saw the train pull into the station and turned his attention towards it as the passengers began to alight.

It was only a moment or two before he saw the boy he thought must be George, standing alone with one small parcel in brown paper tied with string, The boy wasn't looking his way. His hair was a bit long and looked in need of both a wash and a cut, one sock clung to his right shin, but the other was down around his left ankle. His trousers were far too short and he wore a jacket that had been patched at the elbows. As he turned, Tom saw a face that was almost cherubic in expression with wide innocent blue-grey eyes, his hair dark and waving back from his forehead.

He moved towards him, and saw the lad's eyes open as he approached. 'I'm Tom Gilbert,' he said, offering his hand. 'Are you George Sawyer? My mother is Mrs Pam Talbot – your aunt.'

'Yeah, I know,' the lad said. 'Yer a soldier. Ma told me afore she died. She said that me Aunt Pam would take me in – said the others were too mean...'

'You will be welcome in our family, like one of us,' Tom said, sensing the underlying tension in his young cousin. 'I've got the car waiting outside.'

'Cor, are yer rich?' George asked, trotting beside Tom's long stride as they left the station, handing over both their tickets to the inspector. George saw Tom take a last puff of his cigarette before casting it on the ground and grinding it out with his heavy boots. 'You didn't finish it. Yer must be stinkin' rich, like me aunt said. I would've finished it fer yer, mate.'

Tom looked down at him, hiding his smile. 'You're too young to smoke yet, George. Don't you know it will stunt your growth?'

'Nah, that's old wives' tales,' George said stoutly. 'I've smoked fer ages and I'm still shootin' up. Look at me trousers. Me aunt in London said I would be too expensive fer her to keep; she reckons she's ill, but Ma said she's a hypercondriak or somefin like that. Me other aunt says Aunt Pam fell on her feet and married a rich farmer so she can have me.'

'Did she now?' Tom observed him in silence for a moment. George seemed to be sure of himself and yet he couldn't mistake that hint of fear lurking in his eyes. He'd used bravado himself at school when some lads had taunted him about being a bastard born out of wedlock.

'Your father ain't Mr Talbot,' they'd mocked. 'He run off and left your ma with a bun in the oven – that's what my ma says.'

Tom had given the bully a black eye and been caned for it, but he'd always felt it was worth it. The other bullies at school had left him alone after that – but he'd been upset until he'd asked Arthur about it and he'd put a hand on his shoulder and nodded in his bluff way.

'It's true that I'm not your father by blood, but I love you – and I'm proud of you, Tom. You stood up to the bully and that's the way to be. Show them what you think of them – but next time just laugh and tell them your dad loves you and you know the truth. You can't use your fists on every bully with a nasty tongue, lad.'

Tom had grown a hard skin.Though he had resorted to a swift punch from time to time, he tried to hold his temper, unless it was a slight against someone he cared for.

He grinned down at the lad. 'I dare say Mum has a few pairs of long trousers that might fit you. She had three of us boys, so I bet she'll find some. If not, we'll have to see if we can find something in the shops.'

'Long trousers? Honest?' Suddenly, George's face lit up with an unholy smile. Tom suspected he might look like an angel but was far from it in reality. 'Cor that's aright that is, mate.' He looked Tom up and down. 'Are yer a bleedin' hero? Me aunt said yer was...' He jerked his head as if to indicate where he'd come from.

'I don't think so,' Tom replied with a chuckle. 'I've seen a bit of action, but now I'm training others for the moment.'

'I wish I was old enough to fight,' George said fiercely, 'I'd shoot all the buggers.'

'I don't know if your mum let you use language like that, but I shouldn't in front of your Aunt Pam if I were you,' Tom said mildly. 'She might wash your mouth out with salt.'

'She never would?' George stared at him.

'She did mine when I was your age,' Tom told him solemnly. 'I said something far less rude and I was made to drink a glass of brine. It made me sick. I never did it again.'

'Bu— blow me,' George said, looking at him in awe. 'Ma threatened me but she never done it. Your mum must be fierce.'

'She doesn't look it and she's generally nice and kind – but I wouldn't upset her if I were you.' Tom kept a straight face, though he didn't know how. He would laugh about it with Lizzie later.

'Cor – if you have ter do as yer told she must be a dragon lady.'

Tom wisely said no more, merely opening the car door for George to hop in.

'This is a bit of aright,' George said. 'What's that smell?'

'It's leather covers on the seats. It's your Uncle Arthur's car, not mine.'

'He's the rich farmer,' George said, nodding wisely. 'You ain't got the same name though, 'ave yer?'

'No. I had a different father – but Arthur is just like a proper father to me. I think you will like him, but he'll clip your ear if you swear.'

'Cor blimey,' George said. 'I don't remember me dad much. Mum said he used to swear. He was a soldier in the last war. She reckoned it was what he went through that was the reason they had me late in life – took him years to get over it. Gassed he were and that's why he died young...'

'I didn't know that,' Tom said as he started the car. 'I am sorry you lost your dad and now your mum, George. It isn't very nice having to come to strangers to live, but I hope you'll be happy with us.'

'Yeah...' A cloud passed across George's face. 'Me ma was aright. She said she was sorry she'd fallen out with her sister Pam, but it wasn't her fault. She was told she had to ignore her, so she did for years, but when she were desperate, Aunt Pam was the only one that helped her.'

'That's when she made contact,' Tom said, nodding. 'I think they've been exchanging cards since soon after you were born.'

'Yeah, I reckon,' George replied, looking out of the window of the car as they left the small market town and pulled onto a country road. 'There's a lot of trees and fields 'ere ain't there?'

'It is the countryside,' Tom told him. 'You've lived in London all your life I think?'

'Yeah. Houses and big buildings and noise,' George said. 'It is quieter 'ere. I ain't sure I like it.'

'You'll get used to it.' Tom smiled. 'Once you start school and make friends. Do you like paying sport, George?'

'We played footie in the street where I lived,' he said. 'My mate had a proper football an' all.'

'I've got a real leather football,' Tom confirmed. 'I'll give it to you if you promise to look after it.'

'Cor – really?' George looked at him. 'Thanks, mate. I promise I'll keep it proper.'

'Good. We can play together sometimes when I'm home – but I have to go back to my unit soon.'

'That's a shame,' George said. 'I reckon I like yer aright, mate.'

'You can call me Tom when you're ready.' Tom smiled at him. 'I reckon you are all right, too, George.'

* * *

Pam had a meal ready when they got home. She'd kept her rabbit pie, mashed potatoes and cabbage chopped up with marge and salt and pepper warm in the range oven and both Tom and George sat down to eat. George stared at it in surprise for a moment, but as Tom tucked in, he tried it and the look on his face made Pam smile.

'Cor, this is good,' he told her. 'I ain't tasted anythin' this good for ages. Ma used to cook lovely afore she was ill, but me other aunt only gave me dripping on toast or a pie made of vegetables – and her pastry is like cardboard. This crumbles in your mouth and it has got chicken in it...'

'It is rabbit actually,' Pam told him. 'My son Artie and my husband catch them in the fields and so we have meat more often than people can in town these days. We've always had a lot of rabbits and they've been driven away from the airfields, so we get more than we used to on our land. If we didn't kill them for food, they would be a nuisance, eating the crops and making too many burrows in the land.'

George stared at her in awe. 'Will I kill them too?'

'Perhaps one day, if you want to and if you decide to stay with us when you're older. It's not something you have to do. This is your home while you need it, George, but you don't have to be a farmer. My son John is in the RAF now, but before the war he was a plasterer. You could be a builder or an engineer or anything you wanted, if you work hard at school and learn what you need to learn.'

'I ain't much good at sums,' George told her frankly. 'I can read and add up just about, but I reckon I'm good wiv me hands. I like woodwork.'

'You could be a carpenter,' Tom said. 'If you learn to drive, one day you could drive a tractor on the farm. I like farm work; it is always interesting and, in the summer, you can't beat working outside.'

'Maybe I'll drive a tractor then,' George said. 'I reckon I could do that – would you let me learn to drive now?'

'You'll have to ask Tom or your uncle or Artie,' Pam told him, smiling at his enthusiasm. It was clear he'd taken to Tom. 'They all learned to drive tractors on the farm when they weren't much older than you. It isn't lawful to go on the road until you're seventeen and you must pass a test for that – but you can drive on private land. I'm sure someone will let you drive with them down the Fen when the weather warms up a bit.'

'I don't mind the cold,' George said. 'I'd do what they told me and not play up, Aunt Pam.'

'We'll see,' she promised. 'Now, if you've finished that pie – what do you say to a slice of treacle tart?'

'Cor, really?' George stared in amazement. 'Afters as well? I 'ad a bit of treacle tart once at school and it was smashing.'

'Then it's a good thing I made one,' Pam replied. 'We usually have custard on it, but I am afraid there isn't any today. I will try to make some when I can get what I need from the shops.'

'What is custard?' George asked. 'I don't think we had that at school.'

'You're in for a treat then,' Tom told him with a grin. 'I hope you've got a bit of that tart for me, Mum?'

'Of course I have,' she said and put a plate in front of each of them, with exactly the same size slice of her delicious tart.

'You'll never eat all that,' Tom teased George. 'I'll race you and if I finish before you, you have to give me your last piece.'

'Okay,' George grinned. 'But you have to do the same.' He took a huge bite of his tart and swallowed, finishing it in three bites, then looked expectantly at Tom who had cut a small piece off his, which was still on the plate.

'You win,' he said and chuckled as George's hand reached for it. The lad hovered and then drew back.

'Nah, it's yours and you let me win,' he said. 'You eat it, Tom. I've had enough.' He rubbed his tummy and grinned. 'I ain't never had a meal as good as that, Aunt Pam.'

'I am glad you enjoyed it, love,' she murmured as she turned away with a smile.

It was like having her boys back as lads again and she was glad George had come to stay at the farm. Pam had no doubts he would cause more work – and she doubted it would all be plain sailing, but when was it ever? George couldn't be more trouble than Tom and Artie when they were small, always joshing each other and fighting over silly things. John had been quieter, but her eldest two had been little imps, and if she wasn't mistaken, George would be much the same once he'd got settled in as part of the family.

22

John hadn't expected anything different. He'd been passed as physically fit and told to report to his old unit immediately. As he'd walked into the mess room at his base later that evening, there had been silence and then a round of spontaneous cheers and welcoming cries.

'Couldn't do without us, old chap?' one of his former crew stood up and came to greet him, hand outstretched in welcome. 'Glad to see you back again, John. We thought we'd lost you.'

'What the hell happened?' another man asked. 'I saw your crate go down and then flames. We thought you were dead – and then they told us you were in hospital fighting for your life?'

'All true,' John replied with a casual nod. 'How are you, Pete – Sam? I thought I was finished too. It's a long story and not worth repeating. I was lucky and that is all there is to it.'

'You always were a lucky bugger,' Sam said. 'I hope I get to fly with you this time round.'

'Ah, John,' a quiet but authoritative voice spoke from behind him and he turned to see the face of his wing commander,

Captain Dave Carson. 'Come and have a drink and a chat with me.

It was an invitation but also an order.

John followed him to a secluded corner and sat down. Captain Carson signalled for a waiter to bring them drinks. Two beers were produced and sipped before his senior officer got down to business.

'How are you, John?' he asked. 'I thought we'd lost you when your plane went down. I was told you were lucky, but we all thought your luck had run out. I've been told more or less what happened and we'll leave it there – but I want to know if you think you are fit to fly?'

'Yes, sir,' John replied. 'I passed my medical with a good report. Bit of a limp, but that shouldn't bother me in the cockpit.'

'We've lost too many good men these past months. Do you consider yourself ready? Have you got the stomach for it? I need men who can hold their nerve. Honestly, after what happened, are you prepared to fly again – or would you prefer to be transferred to training headquarters and give us the benefit of your experience there?'

John hesitated for the briefest time. 'I haven't been in a good place, sir – but I want to fly. I think I still have something to give.'

Captain Carson nodded. 'Then you will be flying with me in future. I lost my navigator last week. We went through some heavy flak and he was badly wounded. He managed to see us home despite heavy cloud near the coast, though God knows how – but he died before they could get him to hospital.' He frowned. 'It's going to get even rougher in the near future. There's a lot of missions coming up, John. We've been in intensive talks with the Americans and we have agreed to step up our bombing raids. So if you change your mind...'

'I shan't do that, sir,' John told him. 'It's my duty and it is what I want to do for as long as I can, Captain.'

'Good.' Captain Carson smiled at him. 'I am sure I told you to call me Dave. I'm glad to have you with me – and I think your fabled luck may be needed in the next few months.' He sipped his beer. 'I don't want to know anything I haven't been told. I understand you have personal issues, but I trust you not to bring them along when we're on business.'

'Understood,' John said. 'May I get you another?' Dave had almost finished his beer.

He glanced at his watch. 'Better not. I'm off duty for a couple of days now and I promised my wife I would be home in time for her dinner party. Relax and get used to things – spend some time in the gym and get rid of that tension.'

Rising, he nodded and walked off, leaving John alone at the table. He finished his drink and wandered over to the bar. A game of darts was in progress and he watched as one of the players scored a treble in the twenties twice but failed to score the maximum one hundred and eighty.

John smiled and shook his head as he was offered the darts. 'My brother Tom is the one for darts,' he said. 'I'll give you a game of skittles if you like...' The old pub game was popular in the mess and John smiled as he was taken up on his offer, not by the darts player but another fresh-faced young airman who introduced himself as Ross Addington.

'I like a game of table skittles,' he said, grinning. 'I saw you chatting to the old man. I'm his rear gunner. Someone said you're a lucky devil to fly with – said you should be dead.'

John gave a shout of laughter. The air crew seemed even younger than he'd been when he'd joined nearly two years before, or perhaps, he'd grown up on the way. 'Well, let's hope my luck holds,' he said cheerfully. 'You will probably be cursing it when I wipe the floor with you at skittles.'

Ross grinned. 'We'll see about that,' he challenged. 'I am a pretty mean player myself.'

* * *

John lay on his bunk that night, listening to the sounds all around him. Men breathing, some snoring. He was glad he was with others and not alone. At home in his room, he had sometimes given way to his emotions and wept; he couldn't do that here and it was good. John had given his word to his captain that he was fit to fly and that meant he needed to keep his mind on the job. He couldn't be weak and give into his emotions or torture himself with thoughts of Faith or Maria. John needed to move on. The lives of other men would depend on him and he wasn't about to let them down.

He was a good navigator, one of the best. It wasn't luck that had got him and his crew home on several occasions when it might have been otherwise. John was stubborn and he'd got them through by sticking to what he knew and believing in his own judgement. He had to continue to believe. For a while after Maria's terrible death, he had lost his belief, but he'd better get it back ASAP or he would let men down who were relying on him.

He grinned as he remembered the battle between himself and Ross on the skittle board. The young man had done everything to win, but John had wiped him off the board every time.

'Sorry,' he'd apologised afterwards. 'I get carried away. My brothers could nearly always beat me at everything else, so I like to win where I can.'

'I'm glad,' Ross had told him with a broad grin. 'It was luck –

and that means you've still got it, old chap. I'm glad to be flying with you.'

John had just smiled. If they all wanted to believe in the myth of his luck, then let them. He would do his best to see them through, though at times he'd felt that his luck had run out. His smile faded now as he whispered her name, 'Faith...'

What was he going to do with the rest of his life without her? Yet a part of her lived on in his son; he would build a new life around little Jonny, but he would never forget the girl he'd loved.

23

Frances heard George chattering as she walked down to the kitchen that morning in early April. The sun had peeped out from behind the dark clouds, she noticed from the landing window, and was shining into the kitchen, making her feel that life was moving on for the better. She heard George laughing and smiled. He was full of it these days as he'd begun to settle into life at the farm, always asking questions and seeming to relish his new world. He followed Arthur about the yard whenever he got the chance, wanting to know about the animals and the tractors. Until he started school, he was spending most of his time with his uncle, and Arthur patiently answered his questions, even taking him with him when he went harrowing, letting him sit on the tractor with him and help to steer down the rows.

'I like the lad, he's no bother,' Arthur had said gruffly when Pam had suggested he should leave George with her one wet and windy morning at the beginning of the month. 'He'll be off to school after Easter, but I hope he'll still take an interest in the farm once he starts his lessons.'

Pam had nodded and said no more.

The mild, even springlike sunshine that had drawn Frances to the chestnut field had given way to rough winds that could be piercingly cold and then rain throughout much of March. She and Jeanie did their work and hurried inside to get warm whenever they had the chance, but George was out as often as the men and thrived on it. Thankfully, it looked to be warmer again that morning and perhaps spring was truly here at last.

'I don't need ter go to school,' George was telling his aunt when Frances entered the kitchen. He took a long drink of the milk she'd given him with his toast and strawberry jam. 'I can work on the farm wiv Uncle Arfur...'

'I am afraid you do,' Pam said. 'You can help at the weekends just the same and continue learning to drive on our land – but just like the law that says you can't drive on the road until you are seventeen, you must go to school until you are fourteen or fifteen at least. Tom went until he was sixteen. John did the same. Artie left at fifteen, but he passed the exams he took that year and his father decided he could leave if he wanted to, because he intended to work on the farm.'

'That's ages away,' George said. 'Why do they make silly laws, Aunt Pam? I don't see what's the good of school...'

'You learn all sorts of things and you have fun, playing football and cricket – and you learn to read.'

'I like reading,' George conceded. 'Not silly books about pretend things. I like the newspaper. Read about the war – the bloomin' Japs are at it again. They bombed another two of our ships, HMS *Hermes* and can't remember the name of the other, but it was an Australian destroyer. I like to know what is going on, like Uncle Arfur...'

'Arthur,' Pam said patiently. She glanced at Frances. 'Did you sleep all right, love? I'm afraid there isn't much choice this morning. You can have a poached egg on toast or toast and jam.'

'I'd love a poached egg if that is all right,' Frances replied. 'Lizzie was saying her friend Vera would do anything for fresh eggs. They can't get them in London, unless they know someone who keeps a few hens. It is all the powdered stuff and that isn't a bit nice.'

'We are very lucky to have our own hens. Arthur brought those little ducklings from the market last week. If we manage to rear them, we'll have duck eggs and perhaps a nice roast out of them, too.'

'They are almost too sweet to think of eating,' Frances said and George gave her a strange look.

'That's soft,' he said. 'Uncle Arfur said we can't afford to be soft. We 'ave ter be practical, 'cos farming is a business.'

'He is right,' Pam said. 'Sometimes when we kill a chicken or a pig, I feel a bit uncomfortable with it, but folk need to eat after all.'

George nodded wisely.

Frances smiled and accepted a piece of buttered toast to eat while her egg was poaching. She was down before Jeanie or the two Talbot girls, but they came clattering down the stairs as she started to eat her breakfast.

'I don't want to go to school,' Angela announced as she sat at the table. 'I feel sick.'

'You don't want any breakfast then,' Pam said. 'I started the strawberry jam this morning, but if you don't want any...'

'I'm hungry,' Angela began and then pouted as her mother looked at her. 'I've got an arithmetic test and I don't know how to do the sums. We were supposed to learn them, but they are too hard...'

'Show me,' Pam demanded. Angela handed over an exercise book and Pam looked at the sums written down. 'You have to work them out bit by bit,' she told her daughter. 'They look harder than they are. You add these three numbers together and then multiply them by four and then divide them by two and that is your answer.'

'Oh...' Angela sighed. 'No one told me that...'

'Or you weren't paying attention.'

'George doesn't go to school...'

'He will after the Easter holidays. They couldn't find a place for him until then, but some of the older children are moving on then and George will go every day, just like you.'

Susan munched her toast and then picked up the exercise book. 'I'll help you with these if you like,' she offered. 'Come over to the fire and I'll show you.'

The pair of them settled on the floor by the range, their heads bent over the book.

Frances finished her breakfast and took her plate to the sink and then slipped her feet into wellingtons and pulled on her coat.

'I'll be in the milking shed,' she told Jeanie, who was just starting her toast. 'Arthur said I could have a few hours off later if I got my work done. I thought I might go into Ely on the bus.'

'It is market day,' Pam said. 'You might do a bit of shopping for me if there's anything decent going. I'll give you a list.'

Frances smiled and nodded. Pam always had a list because it took a lot of food to look after her big extended family.

It felt quite mild when Frances went out into the fresh air. She'd thought it might rain and spoil her plans, but the dark clouds she'd seen earlier from the landing window had completely rolled away now. It would probably be intermittent sunshine and clouds all day – April showers bring May flowers – but it looked as if the threat of rain had gone for the moment.

Frances was looking forward to a few hours away from work. Since Roy had attacked her, she had stayed close to the farm for weeks, not wanting to go anywhere in case he was still lurking around. She didn't mind working on the land down the Fen, because Artie or Arthur would be there and Frances was pretty sure he wouldn't dare to come near any of the men again. Artie always had his rifle with him in the tractor in case there was any game to be shot and she thought that was enough to frighten Roy off.

For a few weeks, she had avoided going anywhere alone, but she knew she couldn't spend the rest of her life hiding and had made up her mind that she would go to Ely alone and risk it. She had to learn to stand up for herself and Arthur had given her a whistle. He said it was a police whistle and that if she blew it, people would notice and any policeman in the vicinity would come running.

Frances wasn't sure if she believed him, but it couldn't hurt to carry it with her. Anyway, she wasn't going to let Roy ruin the rest of her life. It was time she put the past behind her. She'd heard most of John Talbot's story now and reckoned that if he could put his grief and pain to one side, then so could she. She would always be grateful to him for what he'd done. Artie too had told her that he wouldn't allow anyone to bully her. Being a part of a big, normal and happy family was a new experience for Frances and she was beginning to feel truly at ease amongst them. Just listening to the children trying to get out of school and their laughter made Frances feel alive again. Something inside her had died after Derek was killed and she'd felt it was all she deserved for letting Roy use her the way he had. She'd felt unworthy, though she'd put on a show of confidence like a suit of armour, pretending to be something she wasn't feeling – but now she thought she knew what contentment truly was.

It was to be a family. To be loved and love in return.

Would Frances ever find that again? She thought it unlikely, but for now she could be a part of the warm, loving family at Blackberry Farm.

* * *

Frances caught the bus at ten minutes past eleven. There were always more buses into Ely on a Thursday because it was market day. She had Pam's list and money in her pocket and part of the wages she'd saved in her purse. Her purpose in going to Ely on her own was to buy a nice wedding gift for Jeanie and Artie. Their wedding was only a few weeks away now. She wasn't sure what she would find or what she could afford. Her wages were more than she'd earned before she came to the farm, because she paid nothing for food and lodgings, and she had brought five pounds with her, which was more than she'd ever spent on anything her whole life, but she liked Jeanie and still felt a bit guilty for flirting with Artie when she'd first arrived – not that he'd been interested.

Frances smiled wryly to herself. None of the Talbot men had shown interest in her as anything but a girl who worked for their father. Tom was happily married to Lizzie; Artie was in love with Jeanie – and John was grieving for the girl he'd loved and lost. There was no chance of her finding a husband and becoming a permanent member of the family, which meant that at the end of the war, when Tom returned to his job, she would need to move on.

Descending from the bus as it pulled into Market Street, Frances made her way past the various shops to the square where the stalls had set up. She looked for food first and was able to buy several things on Pam's list, none of them so far needing the coupons required for things like red meat, ham and sugar. Wandering on to a stall selling materials and sheets and pillowcases in sets, Frances lingered. Everyone needed sheets and towels – but these weren't as special as she wanted, so she moved on.

A stall further into the market was selling second-hand goods, old tea sets and crystal glasses – and a very pretty silver teapot. Even as Frances reached for the pot, a woman behind her snatched it up.

'How much is it?' a sharp voice demanded of the stallholder.

'Seven pounds, two shillings and sixpence,' he replied. 'Cheap at half the price, missis.'

'Ridiculous!' she said. 'I'll give you four pounds for it.'

'Sorry, can't sell it for less than seven,' the man replied and the woman let it fall carelessly from her hands as she snorted her disgust and stalked off. Frances caught it before it fell to the ground. She stroked it lovingly with her fingertips before restoring it to its place. It was just what she would like to give Jeanie as a gift but too expensive.

'Like it, do you, miss?' the stallholder asked with a grin.

'I like it very much,' Frances told him ruefully. 'I was hoping to buy it as a gift for a friend's wedding – but I can't afford it. I only have five pounds to spend.'

'It's yours if you want it,' the man told her. 'Five pounds and I'll wrap it nice in its own box for you.'

'Really? You just told that woman you couldn't sell it to her for less than seven pounds...'

He laughed. 'I wouldn't sell her anything. She comes here every week trying to beat me down on the good stuff – but you can have it for a fiver. I always ask her more than I want. Don't like her.'

Frances laughed and made up her mind. 'Thank you,' she said and took out her purse. 'I'm really pleased. I wasn't sure I could afford anything this nice for my friend.'

'She'll like it,' he said and handed Frances the teapot wrapped in tissue and in its own box and a paper bag. 'You come and see me again one day, love. I often have something nice – and it will be the right price to you...' He winked at her and Frances smiled. His cheerful kindness had lifted her spirits. There were nice people in the world. Perhaps she might find someone to love her again one day.

24

'Did you have a nice time?' Jeanie asked that evening when Frances had returned and, having changed, came into the sheds to help with the milking. 'Did you get what you wanted?'

'Yes, mostly,' Frances said vaguely. 'I went to see Mrs Bates too. She was telling me that she has unofficially adopted Billy. His grandmother had to go into hospital and, according to Mrs Bates, she may not come out.'

'That is sad,' Jeanie said. 'I suppose in a way it is better for Billy, because it sounds as if his grandmother was always on to him, but it is sad when someone is so ill.'

'Yes, it is,' Frances agreed. 'I was thinking how lucky George is that Pam took him in. He has a home for as long as he needs it, whereas Billy might be whisked off to an orphanage by the authorities. Mrs Bates doesn't know if she will be allowed to keep him.'

'That is stupid,' Jeanie said crossly. 'He has a perfectly good home with her. You could tell how kind she is and she obviously likes him. Why would they think of taking him away?'

'I don't know.' Frances frowned. 'I said she should try to

contact Billy's father. If he gave permission for Billy to stay with her, it would probably be all right.'

'Yes, it would.' Jeanie looked up as George appeared in the doorway of the milking shed.

'Aunt Pam says will you bring a jug of milk when you've finished,' he said. 'And I've got to look for some eggs. She says the hens lay them anywhere and not just in their house...'

'Yes, they're not always particular,' Frances replied with a laugh. 'That was one of my first jobs when I came, George. I found some under the haystack at the far end of the yard – and I noticed one of them scratching around where the muck heap is. You might find some there.'

'Righto,' George said. He looked speculatively at Jeanie, who was milking their one Jersey cow. 'She's a pretty one – what do you call her?'

'Henriette,' Jeanie told him with a smile. 'Henriette is special so she has a special name. Her milk is so creamy. She doesn't give as much as the Friesians, but it makes it all taste better. When Pam makes butter or wants cream, we always keep Henriette's milk separate.'

George nodded. 'Will you teach me to milk her?' He was looking at Jeanie, who was stroking the full teats with practised hands. 'Arthur says you're the best milker he's had – and I want to do it proper. I want ter be the best...'

'I'll teach you to milk, but we'll start with Dolly,' Jeanie told him. 'She is the most patient and gives her milk more easily. You will have to wash your hands first – and for now, you'd best do as Pam asked. I'll give you a lesson on Saturday morning, if you like?'

'Yeah.' George grinned at her and ran off. They heard a hen squawking as they scattered before him.

'If he scares the hens like that, they will stop laying again,'

Frances said with a laugh. 'You're brave teaching him to milk; he will probably knock the pails over or frighten the cows...'

'Oh, I don't know, he's not that bad and he's keen to learn,' Jeanie said. 'I feel sorry for him sometimes.'

'He seems happy enough?'

'Yes, he has settled in well – but I've seen a look in his eyes when he thinks no one is noticing him. He's lost his mother and father and he's not sure where he belongs yet – even though he likes the farm. He must wonder if this will always be his home.'

Frances nodded. 'I think he can be pretty sure it is. He would have to do something awful for Pam to send him away – he's a lot luckier than some.'

There was a note in her voice that made Jeanie look at her. Frances' situation was different from Jeanie's, because she would always belong here as Artie's wife – but after the war Frances might no longer be needed on the farm. Was she wondering where she would go then? Jeanie would have liked to reassure her, but it wasn't her place to say that she would always have a home here. Jeanie couldn't imagine what it must feel like, to not have a home nor a family – no one to love you. It wasn't surprising that Frances had behaved oddly when she first arrived.

* * *

George had been successful in finding several eggs and Pam was baking when they got in from the milking that evening. She looked at them and smiled. 'Frances found some almond essence and some vanilla today. I thought I'd make an almond Madeira for a nice change. Then, after supper, we can finish your bridesmaid's dress, Frances. I've finished Susan's and Angela's.' There were only a few weeks to go to the wedding and Pam wanted to finish the dresses so she could concentrate on the food for the party afterwards. She was hoarding coupons, and had promised a friend some fresh eggs in return for some of her sugar ration.

'I'm looking forward to wearing it,' Frances told her. 'You're a good seamstress, Pam.'

'I learned the basics at school, we all did when I was a girl – sewing and cooking was thought more important for us then than the rest of it. I've always made my own curtains and clothes for the girls.'

Frances and Jeanie went upstairs to change for the evening and when they returned, everyone was gathered at the table and Pam had started to dish up their dinner.

When they were all served, Jeanie told them what Frances had heard in Ely about Billy.

Pam nodded, looking pensive for a moment. 'Billy comes from London, too,' she told George, looking across the table at him as he ate his way steadily through a mound of potatoes and carrots. She'd made a stew with onions, carrots, turnips and only a small amount of meat but lots of gravy and everyone was filling up with the vegetables and a slice or two of bread. 'Do you think you'd like to invite him over for tea one Sunday, Billy?'

George stared at her. 'Dunno. What's he like?'

'He's a bit younger than you,' Frances said. 'And his mother died last year.'

George was silent for a moment, then shrugged. 'Might be aright,' he said indifferently, but swallowed hard.

'Artie could fetch him over now and then,' Pam said. 'Or Mrs Bates might put him on the bus once he gets used to coming – that's if you like him, George.'

'Does he like playin' footie?'

'I should think so,' Pam replied. 'You'll make friends locally once you've been to school.'

George shrugged but didn't reply. He hadn't made any friends in the village yet, preferring to stay close to the farm most of the time, but he would start school the next week and was sure to meet some boys of his own age then. 'Mebbe,' George agreed. 'He's the one you was talkin' about in the shed – his gran was took bad.' He looked at Frances, who nodded. Neither she nor Jeanie had realised he'd heard their discussion. 'Let 'im come then, Aunt Pam. See if he's aright.'

'You've got her address, Frances? I'll write and ask Mrs Bates if she will let him come.'

After that, the conversation turned to the farm and the war, the prices of everything, which seemed to have increased recently – traders making a profit, so Pam reckoned – and then everyone helped to clear the table and Jeanie and Frances did the dishes. Jeanie and Artie then went off together, for a walk down to the pub, but really for a chance to be alone.

Pam was busy with her dressmaking and George and Angela had been sent to bed with instructions to read their comic books for no more than half an hour. Susan asked her mother if it was all right to go and visit a friend and was told she could stay out until nine and no later.

'It is still chilly out and you have been out three times this week already, Susan. You should be revising...'

'I've been revising all day, Mum,' Susan said. 'Please – I promise I've done my work.'

'Go on then,' Pam said without looking up. 'Don't be late or you won't go again.'

Susan muttered something, grabbed her coat and went out quickly before her mother could change her mind. Frances watched her go and Pam glanced up at that moment.

'I'm not too strict with her, am I?' Pam said. 'I know she isn't a child any longer, but I worry about her being out in the dark. It wouldn't be so bad if it wasn't for this wretched blackout.'

'She is very lucky to have a mum like you,' Frances said and Pam nodded.

'I just love my children – and I get fond of other people, too. You do know that you will always have a place to stay if you need it, Frances?'

'Oh, Pam, that's such a nice thing to say.' Frances felt a lump in her throat. 'You've got such a big family...'

'The more, the better,' Pam told her. 'Before the war, I always had room at my table for anyone who came to call. We often used to have friends to supper, because they just came round for a chat with Arthur. He gave the lads at the airfield an open invitation, but we haven't seen many. Perhaps it is too far for them to walk at night...'

'I doubt it,' Frances said. 'Perhaps they didn't get the message. If you wrote a little note, I could walk up one day and take it?'

'Perhaps you should,' Pam agreed. 'I have a friend in Sutton who regularly gives the airmen supper. They are farmers too and share whatever they get with the lads. I feel as if I'm not doing my bit...'

Frances laughed and shook her head. 'Oh, Pam, you do a wonderful job feeding us all, but I know what you mean. You write a note and I'll deliver it for you. I'll bet they didn't get the message, because I'm sure they would all like to be invited into someone's home. It must be lonely being so far from home – especially for the Australians and New Zealanders.'

'Yes, that's what we thought. Arthur asked once, he's not the sort to ask again – but if you go, I'm sure we might get a few.'

'Why don't you suggest a Sunday afternoon?' Frances said. 'Perhaps it's better than just an open invitation. You could bake as much as you can manage and I'll help – and it will keep in tins if no one comes.'

'I've got George's ration book, too, now,' Pam said, smiling and nodding. 'The more books we have, the easier it is to make things stretch. Yes, I'll do that, Frances, and thank you for offering.'

'Thank you for making me feel so welcome,' Frances said. 'I think I'll go up now and read my new library book.'

'You do that, love.' Pam looked at her work. 'This is finished, so you can take it up and try it on – and then pop down and show me, but I think it will fit you well.'

* * *

The next morning was a Saturday and Frances went down to the kitchen to a shocked silence instead of the usual chatter. Pam looked thunderous and, as Frances saw what they were all staring at in horror, she realised what Susan had done the previous evening. Her hair was green and she was in tears.

'My friend said it would be blonde,' she said as Frances stared at her. 'I know it looks a mess, but I thought it would look nice like the picture on the label of the bottle.'

'You're not the only one to make a mistake like that,' Frances said, feeling sorry for her. 'A girl at the munitions factory where I worked had it done by a friend and hers went green too. It was ages before it all grew out and she had it cut as short as she could to get rid of it.'

Just at that moment, Lizzie walked in carrying Archie in a portable cot. 'Pam, I wondered—' she broke off as she saw Susan's hair. 'I was going to ask if you would have Archie this afternoon, Pam – but I think what I had in mind can wait. Susan, why don't you come home with me and we'll see what we can do to sort it out?'

'She is a very silly girl to let a friend practise on her hair,' Pam said. 'Are you sure you can do it, Lizzie – are you feeling up to it?' Lizzie hadn't been into the salon since Archie's birth but looked and felt perfectly well. She was thinking of popping over to her hairdressing shop in a day or so, but wouldn't be starting work for another few weeks.

'I'm fine,' Lizzie assured her. 'If you don't mind, Pam, I'll leave Archie with you now so I can concentrate on Susan's hair for a while.'

Susan grabbed her coat and followed Lizzie out swiftly.

Pam shook her head but said no more and Jeanie leaned over Archie as he lay in his carrycot. 'He is so beautiful,' she said and Pam smiled.

'Yes, at that age they are. Wait until he grows up and starts flouting his parents...'

Frances realised that Pam was still angry with her daughter and wisely said nothing. She finished her toast and jam and went out to the cowsheds, working solidly for two hours. When she returned to the kitchen for her morning break, she saw that Pam was smiling, and then did a double take as she looked at Susan. Her hair was now a glossy red that shone and waved around her face in the latest style, the tips just a lighter shade that made it sparkle with highlights.

'That looks fabulous, Susan,' she said and then looking at Lizzie with respect, 'I didn't know you could do hair like that?'

'Yes, I don't always do set waves and curls,' Lizzie told her with a smile. 'I won a few competitions when I worked in London – and tinting was one of my special things. This flame-red is rather nice on Susan.'

'It is gorgeous,' Frances said. 'Could you do something like that with mine, Lizzie?'

Lizzie looked at her and nodded. 'I think a deep auburn would suit your hair, Frances. What do you think, Pam?'

'I dare say,' Pam replied in a non-committal tone. 'Thank you for repairing the damage, Lizzie – but it makes her look... very grown-up. I am not sure I like Susan growing up too fast.'

'I'll be going to college in the autumn,' Susan said. 'I'm not a child now, Mum. Two of the girls from my class are already married and one of them is having a baby.'

Pam frowned at her. 'Perhaps they are, but they're not my daughters. I want you to pass your exams so that you have a better future, Susan. I don't want you to marry too young and have no chance to see life – I'd say see the world, but there's no chance of that these days with that wretched war going on.'

'Oh, I don't know,' Lizzie said. 'One of my old customers wrote to me last week. She is with an official touring group and has been all over the place entertaining the troops. Tilly reckons she's seen more because of the war than she would have without it.'

'Susan isn't likely to entertain troops,' Pam objected.

Lizzie was silent. Pam didn't often get a bee in her bonnet, but she'd been upset over Susan's hair and it was clear she hadn't quite forgiven her yet.

Frances went upstairs and changed into a simple skirt, jumper, warm jacket and walking shoes. It was warmer now, but the wind could be chilly, especially if you had quite a long way to walk.

She returned to the kitchen to find that Lizzie had gone and Susan had her nose in her schoolbooks. She glanced at Frances who gave her a sympathetic smile. Seeing the letter on the table, she turned to Pam, who was changing Jonny's napkin and smiling as he gurgled up at her. 'Is that for me to take to the airfield?'

'Yes, it is,' Pam agreed. 'Thank you, Frances. I've done as you suggested and invited up to six men for Sunday next week. I think that is as many as we can manage in one go...'

Frances nodded and left. Outside, the sun was shining, but the wind had risen since earlier and she was glad of her sensible attire. It would be a pleasant enough walk to Sutton, even though she had to go the long way round via Witcham, but she was in no hurry. She would be back by lunch and ready for the afternoon shift. The men were already out on the land, but for the moment neither she nor Jeanie were needed other than in the yard. They would have plenty of work to do once the hoeing and spraying and then harvesting was in full swing. If the weather kept dry, they might be haymaking in a few weeks. Frances was looking forward to that.

25

Jeanie and Pam spent an hour or so in the dairy that morning, making cheeses and butter from the cream they had managed to skim from the milk. Henriette's milk had been set aside, because that always gave the best results, and after some arm-aching churning, that they both took turns at, a nice pat of fresh farm butter was borne back to the kitchen in triumph. The cheeses were far more complicated and would need to be strained and squeezed a few times before being shaped into little rounds and set out to drain on tiny mats of straw. It was an old-fashioned way of making cheese at home and quite a few farmers' wives did it, but they all seemed to have their own particular taste. Pam added a few herbs to hers during the long process, which gave them a whole different flavour.

Both babies were still asleep in their soft carrycots, watched over by a penitent Susan; Lizzie had popped up to Sutton in Tom's truck. She'd wanted to see a friend but returned soon after the two women were back in the kitchen and accepted an invitation to stay to docky. Neither of the men were expected back. They had taken a packed lunch and bottles of cold tea with them and would probably get in just before dinner that evening. The work of harrowing and preparing land for planting was skilled and father and son were a good team. One of the girls might be asked to sit on the drill when the potato seed was set the following week, but for now they were allowed to have more free time than would be theirs once the growing season was under way.

Jeanie thought it was probably easier work than that of the newly formed Timber Corps – the Lumber Jills as they were already being called. Princess Elizabeth – one day to be Queen Elizabeth – had registered for war service and the papers had photographs of her wearing a uniform. Women were working harder than ever as the need for more and more fighting men at the Front increased.

It was a companionable meal. Frances had not yet returned, which caused Pam to look at the clock and wonder where she was, but she arrived just as they were having a cup of tea after eating and apologised for being late.

'I posted the letter to Mrs Bates and I took your note to the airfield,' Frances said, a little blush in her cheeks. 'The Military Police wouldn't let me on site, but one of them took the note when I explained what it was. He said he'd met Artie Talbot and he was a brave man.'

'Artie?' Pam looked at her in surprise.

'He saw Artie pull that German out of the plane that crashed,' Frances said. 'He said it was already burning and a few seconds later there was an explosion. Arthur made him come away or he would have tried to get another. Apparently, he made to wrench free of Arthur to try to rescue the last one from the soaring flames, but Arthur wouldn't let him go.'

'No!' Susan looked at her. 'He never told us – did he, Mum?'

'He didn't tell me, but his dad knew and told us later, but you were at school that day,' Pam said and looked at Jeanie for confirmation. She nodded but said nothing.

'I thought he hated Germans,' Susan blurted.

'He does,' Pam agreed. 'Especially since John was so badly injured. I suppose he just acted on impulse. I don't think he wanted us to know.'

'Well, Frank might say something...' Frances said and blushed as Pam looked at her. 'Frank Simmons. He is the MP I told you about – Military Police. He was one of the first from the airfield to arrive when that plane crashed the morning I got here.'

'It seems ages ago,' Pam said, looking at her. 'It is only a few months, but you seem to have been here always, Frances.'

Frances laughed and looked happy – happier than any of them remembered seeing her. 'Thanks, Pam. Frank says that he will bring a couple of friends with him. He says to expect four of them at most. He's got a car and he will bring them – he gave me a lift back...' She flushed a delicate pink. 'We sat talking. I didn't realise the time...'

'It didn't matter. We only had a cold lunch this morning,' Pam assured her. 'Hard-boiled egg sandwiches with some watercress Arthur got me on the market in Ely yesterday. I saved some for you. They are in the pantry with a damp tea cloth over them.'

Frances went off to fetch her lunch and Pam looked at Jeanie, her eyebrows raised. Jeanie nodded and smiled but said nothing as Frances returned.

'I'd better take Archie home,' Lizzie said. 'He has been sleeping so well lately and when he wakes, he'll be ready for his feed, so I'll get him home.' She looked at Frances. 'If you would like a new hairstyle, let me know. I'll sort something out for you.'

'Thanks,' Frances said and smiled vaguely. 'I'll go up and get changed – make a start on the milking.'

'No rush, finish your sandwich,' Pam said, but Frances only nodded, picked up her last sandwich and walked out, munching it. 'Well, then,' Pam said to Jeanie when the sound of her footsteps had retreated up the stairs. 'That's what I'd call a result. I'd better see what I can scrounge from our butcher and come up with some ideas for next Sunday's tea.' Her eyes gleamed with the plans she was making. 'Fancy that...'

Jeanie nodded. She knew exactly what Pam wasn't putting into words. Frances had clearly taken to this young officer and it sounded as if he might rather like her, too.

* * *

Frances sat down on the edge of her bed and smiled to herself. Frank was so nice – tall and strong, but with a gentle manner, at least towards her. He'd seemed to have an air of authority when he'd arrived at the gate. The other two guards had been quizzing her, making out they thought she was a spy and refusing to either let her in or take her letter. They might have done so in the end, but then Frank had arrived and they'd saluted him smartly and told him what she'd come for. He'd said he was sorry she couldn't be admitted for security reasons, but he'd come through the gate, read the letter and told her that he would let people know, but then he'd walked her down the road, where they'd stopped, still talking and smiling at each other. When he'd suggested driving her back to the farm, she'd tried to refuse, but he'd insisted it was no trouble and so she'd let him take her. His car was a small roadster with no top to it, so it was breezy and noisy, but it had been fun.

Frances didn't know how long they'd sat talking across the road from the farm. He'd asked her about the family at the farm, and then how long she'd been there. She'd told him that she'd arrived on the day of the plane crash in the top field and that's when he'd told her about Artie's heroic deed. It had all seemed so natural and pleasant and Frances had allowed herself to enjoy the obvious look of admiration in his eyes.

Now that she sat on her bed, the warm glow of excitement faded. Frank was a lovely person, but he wouldn't want her if he knew of her background – of the way Roy had soiled her forever. Yes, Derek had told her he loved her and she believed he'd meant it, but he came from the dirty back streets of London like her and he understood that things like that happened. He'd told her things about his own life and she'd known that he could accept her, because he too had known pain and failure and hurt.

Frank was an educated man. Frances had seen that instinctively. He probably came from a good family and he would expect any girl he courted to be pure and demure.

Frances swallowed the lump in her throat. She didn't want to deceive Frank. She wouldn't allow him to fall in love with her, only to suffer disappointment when he discovered what she truly was – and Pam's kindness and sympathy could never disguise what Frances knew to be true in her heart. She was a fallen woman and could never be good enough for a man like Frank.

Blinking back tears of regret, Frances decided that she would take herself off somewhere when the airmen came to tea. Better to cut any romantic notions off swiftly than be drawn into more pain and regret. Despite the air of confidence she put on sometimes, Roy had taken advantage of her innocence and vulnerability; it wasn't her fault, but it had ruined her forever. For a while, Frances had thought she might find love again, but now she knew she never could. What decent man would want her when they knew the truth? It wouldn't be right. Her new-found peace had shattered all because of the look of near adoration in a young man's eyes. Frank had looked at her as if she were special

– so how could she let him get to like her, and perhaps love her, knowing that it would end in grief or disgust for him?

Going back down to the kitchen, Frances saw that Jeanie was ready for work and they went out together.

Jeanie glanced at her as they entered the cowsheds. 'Was this MP nice then?' she asked conversationally.

'He was all right,' Frances said in a flat tone. 'Good-looking but I don't really know him.'

'Well, you can get to know him better next week,' Jeanie said.

'Yes, I expect so,' Frances replied, then, to change the subject, 'When are you going to start George's lessons in milking?'

'He's already had one, but he's going to have another tomorrow. He went with the men today, so I said he could help me in the morning.'

Their conversation ceased then as they got on with their work. Jeanie did most of the milking, while Frances mucked out the stalls and brought in fresh hay and straw. She filled the feeding troughs with the special mixture of foodstuffs that they called cake, of all things, though it was nothing of the sort, being made up of mangles, other vegetables, ground maize and minerals and vitamins the vets advised them would improve the limited diet through the winter months. In the summer months, the cows would feed on the long rich grass in a meadow halfway to Witcham, where they would need to be driven each morning after being brought back to the yard in the evening for milking. It made a lot of extra work, but the fields closer to home had been taken over by the ministry for the airfield and were unavailable for grazing.

Frances reflected again that it was a pleasant life. One she knew would almost certainly end for her when the war was over, but which she must enjoy for as long as she could. The future, when she would probably have to return to London, wasn't something she cared to think about much. She had no idea what she would do with her life then. For a pleasant hour or so she'd let herself dream of a different life, but that was foolish when she knew it could never be.

* * *

Something was wrong with Frances. It was as if she'd gone back to the prickly, uncertain girl she'd been when she arrived. Pam sensed it and Jeanie confirmed it when they had a little time alone that evening. Frances had gone up to have the one bath a week they were allowed. Pam hadn't drawn the Plimsoll line on her bathtub, though she knew hotels were doing it and so were many others. She trusted her family to obey the rules and did so scrupulously herself. Everyone had to be as honest as they could these days because things were getting tight in a lot of way. It wasn't just rationing, it was shortages, too, and Pam knew that living in the country on their own farm they were privileged. She'd told Arthur that he mustn't hold back a pig every so often, as he had at the start of the war.

'It isn't fair for us to have more than others, love,' she'd told him. 'We have the eggs and the vegetables you grow and we're lucky to be given apples and pears in autumn when friends have spare – but we mustn't abuse it, and not just because it is against the law.'

Arthur had grudgingly agreed, though she knew he resented having to account for every animal on the farm. Like many other families, Pam kept her own chickens and she had a few ducks now, but that was allowed if it was personal. She didn't sell the eggs or the poultry and many others kept hens caged in back-yards simply for the eggs so that never made her feel guilty. The rabbits Arthur and Artie trapped and the game they occasionally shot were always welcome. Neither were rationed, though not in general supply, but if you lived in the country or had your own land, you had the option of adding meat to your table if you were willing to take the trouble. Some of the river fish were edible, too, though not to Pam's taste and she didn't encourage the men to catch them; eels were considered a delicacy by some country folk and there were plenty of those in certain spots along the river-bank. Arthur quite liked them jellied, but Pam hated preparing and cooking them, so on the rare occasions he went eel fishing, he prepared them himself. The only one of Pam's family to like them besides Arthur was Jeanie, who had eaten them in London; she said Arthur's were even better.

Pam's thoughts were busy as she ironed her family's freshly washed clothes. She looked at Jeanie when she came back down-stairs after changing.

'Did you argue with Frances, love?'

'No – but something is bothering her,' Jeanie said. 'She seemed happy when she came home after her walk this morning – but, when we did the milking and feeding, she hardly spoke to me. I don't think I said anything to upset her.'

'It must be something to do with the officer who brought her home,' Pam said thoughtfully.

'But she was smiling and happy until she went upstairs to change...'

'Yes,' Pam agreed. 'As if her own thoughts had upset her...'

'She seems more like she did after she arrived – making out she's cheerful and friendly, but holding back inside.'

Pam mused and then nodded. 'Maybe I can think why – the silly girl.'

'What do you mean?' Jeanie asked curiously.

Pam was mindful that Jeanie only knew a part of Frances' past. She hadn't revealed all the unhappy details to everyone, just that Roy had hurt her. 'Oh, it doesn't matter, I'm just thinking aloud,' she said and smiled. 'Is Artie taking you out this evening?'

'We might go to the pictures in Ely,' Jeanie said. 'Artie hasn't got much petrol left – but if Arthur will give him some...'

'I expect he will,' Pam said. 'You ask him, Jeanie. He hardly ever uses his private ration himself, though he saves a bit for Tom and John when they are home.'

Jeanie nodded. 'Have you heard from John yet?'

'He rang me after his medical and told me he was going back to his base. I had a very short letter to say he was happy and I wasn't to worry. He promised to come home when he could, but I've had nothing since.'

'You do worry, though,' Jeanie said. 'I saw you reading the headlines about plans to increase the bombing raids in the paper the other day. This Bomber Harris, as they are calling him, seems determined to fling everything we've got at them.'

Pam sighed. 'Yes, I do worry, Jeanie. Tom seems to be settled in a safe job now, but John is exposed to danger every time he flies...'

26

The briefing was direct and to the point. Their mission was to cause as much havoc and pain over enemy cities as possible to try to bring a halt to the relentless progress of the enemy. The Americans were concentrating much of their effort against the Japanese for the moment, wanting to wipe out the awful pain and humiliation of being caught off guard at Pearl Harbour. British war planes would constantly bomb Germany and the Allies would combine in a big push they hoped would end this war sooner rather than later.

John listened attentively. The attack was planned for that night. They expected some cloud cover at first, but it was likely to be clear once they were over the Channel and it was a bomber's moon. That meant the target would be easier to find, but so would they and the ground fire from the ack-ack as well as enemy fighter planes would be busy. It made everything that much more dangerous.

'Do you think they were telling us we are expendable?' Ross asked him as he walked beside John to the mess hall. 'All that talk about our efforts helping to turn the tide and the need for sacrifice for the sake of others...'

John looked at him. He could see the youngster was nervous, tiny beads of sweat along his upper lip and apprehension in his eyes.

'It was an unfortunate choice of words,' John said. 'But we all know that some of us might not come back when we go on a mission like this one – it will be rough, I imagine. No worse than some others I've been on though.' For John nothing could ever be as bad as learning Faith was dead but he understood the young airman's fear. 'You'll be fine.'

Ross grinned. 'You're still here, though,' he said and the slight look of fear disappeared. 'That's proof enough that some of us make it whatever the risk.'

'It's war.' John shrugged. 'We do what we must, don't think about it too much and get the hell out as quickly as we can afterwards. I think that's the best way, don't you?'

'My cousin is a fighter pilot,' Ross said. 'He is six years older than me. He laughs about it all as though it is a game. They have bets on about who will shoot down the most bandits – and a chart on the wall. The prize each month is a bottle of old malt whisky.'

John nodded. 'I doubt any of them really think it a game,' he said. 'We all get scared sometimes. Mostly, for me, after it is all over, and it hits how close we came to not making it.'

Ross looked relieved. 'It's the waiting before we go,' he confessed. 'I'm fine once we're in the air – but I hate the time between the briefing and when we go.'

'I expect most of us feel the same,' John agreed. 'Don't go thinking you're a coward because you get the jitters. Everyone does at some time or other. We do it anyway, because we have no choice.'

'Yeah.' Ross stopped to light a cigarette and then quickened his steps to catch up. The weather was dull with a hint of rain in the air and a slight curling mist over the flat land that surrounded the airfield. 'Don't know where the warm weather has gone.'

'April showers,' John said dismissively. 'Back home in the Fens we get a lot of mist early mornings even when it comes out sunny later.'

'We get that on the east coast where I live,' Ross agreed. 'It comes off the sea and then it suddenly lifts.'

'We'd better get something to eat,' John said as they entered the dining room, where several men were already queuing. 'I hope it is something better than Woolton pie today. That doesn't fill me up for longer than an hour. I could do with a nice suet pudding...'

* * *

John wrote a letter to his mother and then lay down on his bed and closed his eyes. He wouldn't sleep, but he wanted to think. It hadn't occurred to him to make a will, but he realised now that he probably should have done so. He had a son now and ought to make some kind of provision for him. John didn't have a lot, but even a few mementoes might mean something to Jonny one day. Of course he would be all right. John knew his mother would look after the boy and no doubt anything that might come to John in due course would go to his son. He smiled at the thought of the boy. He was a bonny little lad and John had felt affection for him when he'd held him.

His thoughts moved on to Faith as they always did. There was an emptiness in his chest as he felt the familiar grief and longing for her. How he wished she was still alive, still nursing and enjoying her life. She hadn't died because she gave birth to his child. It was a small consolation, but he still believed that if she hadn't been pregnant, she would not have died. He couldn't know why her uncle had attacked her so viciously, but suspected it was partly caused by the fact her mother was upset over what she'd done.

John picked up a paperback of one of Raymond Chandler's novels, but the words just ran into one another. He sat up and took out his cigarette packet, lighting one. All the men smoked. It was something to do with your hands when you couldn't rest. He glanced at his watch. Another half an hour and they would be off. He would be better employed getting ready and sitting with the rest of the crew.

Throwing the book carelessly aside, he got up, collected his flying jacket and other gear, and set off for the mess room. It wouldn't be long before they were in the air and then he could relax and just be a navigator, his mind honed in on one thing and that was to get them there and back, preferably all in one piece.

Glancing up at the night sky, he saw that the moon was bright, no clouds to obscure it or them. It might be different over the Channel, but John knew they would catch it from the flak and enemy planes that night. He was glad he'd written to his mother. The letter would be amongst his things if he didn't make it this time.

John shook his head. It was stupid to let such thoughts into his head. He needed to keep his mind alert. He wasn't the only one who would suffer if he didn't.

* * *

Ross was cock-a-hoop when they touched down safely despite sustaining damage to the undercarriage and the loss of one engine. He downed two glasses of whisky in the mess later and slapped John on the back. 'I got three of the buggers,' he bragged. 'I know I did. I saw two go down and the third was hit.'

'Well done,' John said but felt none of the euphoria of his younger colleague. The night had been clear and they'd had to dodge both the flak and enemy attack, before dropping their bombs. John had made the mistake of looking out of the plane's window. On a night like the one they'd just survived, the destruction below was only too clear, flames lighting the sky over the city below. How many lives and homes had they destroyed?

He drank the whisky someone had brought him and then left, seeking solitude. In the grey of early dawn, he walked back to his barracks. All he wanted to do was sleep and forget. War was a dirty, rotten business and it made him feel sick to know the pain and grief he'd helped deal out to others that night. Like his mother always said, each death was personal to someone and revenge wasn't sweet. It was needed, he knew that.

The war would drag on forever unless the combined efforts of the Allies could stop the aggression of Hitler's lust for power and domination. He was a madman. He must be, John thought. Why start a war that would lead to so much pain, grief and loss? Surely no sane man would do it?

He squared his shoulders as he reached his sleeping quarters. John hadn't started this war. He hadn't wanted it, but he would do his duty, even though it turned his stomach. Realising that he was tired, he lay down on his bed and closed his eyes. John wasn't sure he would sleep, but withing minutes, he was gently snoring.

* * *

In the morning when John woke, his self-recrimination and revulsion had gone. He was a member of a team and he'd done what was expected of him, no more nor less. John didn't plan the missions and he didn't make decisions; he just did as he was ordered.

The raid over the Ruhr had been deemed a result. Ross was still exultant as he came in for breakfast – or an early lunch, as he'd slept a long time. John listened to his chatter and claims to have shot down enemy planes, making no comment.

'I'm going for a spin on my motorbike,' Ross told him as they both prepared to leave the dining room. 'Do you want to come?'

'Thanks, but no,' John replied. 'I'm going to make a phone call and then I might catch a train into Cambridge.'

'Going to meet someone?' Ross asked and John nodded.

'Perhaps – if she has time,' he agreed.

Ignoring the look in the younger man's eyes, John turned off towards the telephone booth. He had to wait for a while, but then his turn came and he dialled the number Lucy had given him.

She wasn't at the nursing accommodation but the girl who answered told him she would be off duty from four onwards that afternoon.

'Will you give her a message – say John is coming in on the four-fifteen train and I'll call for her if she's free. If she isn't, I can have a meal somewhere and catch the seven-fifteen back...'

The girl sounded confident when she said she didn't think Lucy was busy that evening. 'She doesn't go out much. She's got someone she likes and she's waiting for him to ring – if that's you, she'll be happy.'

John just laughed. He didn't think Lucy would stay home to wait for his call, but if she had nothing else to do, they could go somewhere together – and he was free for the rest of the day. He wouldn't be asked to fly again for a couple of nights, though the Government directive to Bomber Command had been to prioritise the destruction of the cities within range all along the German coast, and when the weather was clear more central targets were to be attempted.

* * *

Lucy was dressed in a navy-blue dress with a white jacket when she came down to meet him that afternoon. The early-morning dullness had cleared and it was a pleasant afternoon.

She smiled at John brightly. 'I was surprised to get your call,' she told him. 'I didn't think you would ring me.'

'I said I would,' John reminded her. 'I know it was short notice but we've been busy. I've got a few hours free now.'

'That's nice. I'm on morning shifts at the moment – I start at six and finish around three. Next week I'll be on nights.'

'At least you know when you're working. We don't get briefed until a few hours before...' He stopped abruptly. 'Don't know if that is classified. Shouldn't talk about work.'

'I'm not a spy in disguise,' Lucy said, laughing. 'I know what you do, of course I do.'

'Your brother talks about it?'

'Sometimes, if I ask him,' Lucy replied, serious now. 'He doesn't give me details about the raids, but I can read the papers.'

'Yes.' John grinned. 'If we're successful, it usually gets blasted across the front page.'

'The disasters get relegated to inside the paper,' Lucy said. 'Normally that's land battles or sea, though. You fly boys are doing a wonderful job, everyone says so.'

John smiled. 'Glad you think so. It doesn't always feel that way.'

'You shouldn't feel guilty,' Lucy said, reading it in his face. 'If it hadn't been for your lot, we might be in the same boat as France now, under the German heel. I don't fancy that much.'

'No, nor I,' John said ruefully. 'Take no notice of me – it's just stress or something.'

'I know. I'm a nurse. I see it all the time,' Lucy replied. 'So what are we going to do then?'

'Shall we have something to eat?'

'I could murder a bag of chips and a pie,' Lucy said. 'Why don't we take them to the river and then have a drink in the pub after?'

'Sounds good to me,' John agreed. He hesitated, then, 'It's just friends, Lucy. You don't mind that, do you?'

'Not one bit,' she said cheerfully. 'I like you, John. It doesn't have to be more.'

'Good, because I'm not sure I'll ever be ready for more.' It had taken him a lot of soul-searching to ring her that morning.

'Come on,' she said and took him by the arm, her face alight with a smile of encouragement. 'Let's grab those chips. I'm starving.'

* * *

John caught the last train back that evening. It should just get him through the gate before his pass ran out, providing there were no hold-ups. He didn't want to be late, because although train delays were accepted as an excuse, they could carry a reprimand; it was a man's duty to make sure he got back on time and John didn't want to lose his next pass. He'd enjoyed his evening with Lucy, but he would pop home and see his son and his family as soon as he could.

It was good that Lucy could be happy with friendship and

not expect more. She'd kissed him on the cheek when they had said goodnight with no sign of embarrassment or coyness and told him to give her a ring the next time he was free.

'I enjoyed myself,' she'd told him. 'I'll come out again when you ring if I'm able, but I won't always be. Sometimes I am working and sometimes I go out with other friends.'

John had assured her he was happy with that, and he was. It was nice to get away from his base and the company of men for a while, but he didn't want Lucy to sit at home waiting for his call. He wasn't ready for anything more than casual friends and he wouldn't want to hurt her.

27

'Where is Frances?' Pam asked as Jeanie came downstairs wearing a pretty, blue, full-skirted dress. It was the day they had arranged to entertain the airmen and she'd been busy all morning with Lizzie's help, baking and preparing for their guests. Lizzie had gone home to get changed and would return shortly with Archie.

'She will be down in a moment, I expect,' Jeanie said and frowned. 'She has been a bit moody all morning.'

'I hope she isn't coming down with anything,' Pam said. 'I thought she was looking forward to today. She took the letter for me and seemed happy when she met that young man – Frank Simmons.'

'I like her, Pam, but—' Whatever Jeanie was about to say was lost as Frances entered the kitchen. She was wearing clean working trousers and a jumper with flat shoes.

'You haven't forgotten what today is?' Pam asked. 'Why don't you put something pretty on, love – like that polka dot dress we made together?'

'I thought I might go for a walk,' Frances said. 'You don't really need me, do you, Pam? I'll help clear up later.'

Pam glanced at Jeanie. 'Will you pop down to Lizzie's for me, love? Ask her if I can borrow her crystal bowl for the fruit salad?'

'What...?' Jeanie began and then nodded. 'I shan't be long.'

After she'd put her coat on and gone out, Pam gave Frances a straight look. 'Now, what is all this nonsense?' she asked. 'This is a special afternoon, Frances, and I think you would be foolish to miss out on the fun. That young military policeman you told us about sounds nice. Don't you want to see him?'

Frances blinked hard. 'He wouldn't like me if he knew what I'd done. I don't want to get to like him too much... he is not like me. He comes from a good family and I...' She swallowed hard. 'I'm from the slums of London and you know...' She finished in an anguished tone.

'I know you've been torturing yourself for no good reason,' Pam told her sternly. 'What you were forced to do doesn't make you a bad person, Frances. You must put all that behind you and live for yourself, dear. If you wish to be honest with Frank, then choose a moment to tell him, when the time is right, but if he is as nice as you think, it won't make any difference – and besides, neither of you may wish to go beyond friendship. You can't shut yourself away forever.'

'I'm frightened of getting to like him and then...' Frances wiped a tear from her cheek. 'There was someone who loved me despite what I'd done – but he was killed. I don't want to feel like that again – so alone and empty.'

Pam nodded her understanding. 'We all go through terrible grief when we lose someone, Frances, but we can't stop living. We must walk through the pain, and sometimes we love again.' She smiled at Frances. 'Go back upstairs and put on a nice dress and dry your eyes and then come back, my love. You aren't alone now; you have me and my family. We are all your friends.'

'Thank you.' Frances sniffed. She hesitated, then, 'I'll do as you say...'

Pam nodded as she ran back up the stairs.

Jeanie returned a few minutes later. 'Lizzie says she doesn't have a crystal bowl, Pam.'

'No? Oh, I thought she did,' Pam said. 'Never mind, I expect I can find something.'

'Where is Frances?'

'She went upstairs to change,' Pam replied. 'Open that tin of fruit salad for me, Jeanie. It is the last of the tinned fruit Arthur put by at the start of the war. I've been saving it for a special occasion.' She went to the sideboard, took out a large crystal bowl and washed it in the sink. 'There – if you tip that in the bowl, I think we are ready.'

Frances changed into the dress Pam had suggested. She looked at herself in the mirror. Would anyone notice she'd been crying? Frances rarely used anything much but a touch of lipstick these days, but perhaps she should just powder her nose to take away the slight redness? She fluffed up her hair, wondering why she had let Pam talk her into staying for the tea party. It was bound to end badly, but her kind hostess had been to so much trouble for this afternoon. Pam wanted her there so she would attend and she'd put on a smile and talk to their guests, even though she was scared.

Frances went back downstairs just as Lizzie arrived. She'd brought a porcelain bowl which Pam accepted with a smile and placed on the sideboard. Neither of the men had appeared yet.

Arthur had tried to wriggle out of it but had been sent up to change. Artie had gone up while Frances had still been changing. She'd heard him speak to his father before they went to their own rooms.

'It's only for an hour or two, Dad. Mum has been to a lot of trouble and it was your suggestion in the first place.' Artie's voice had carried clearly up to Frances in the attic bedroom above, though Arthur's reply had been monosyllabic and muted.

Frances smiled inwardly. It seemed she wasn't the only one reluctant about the little party.

* * *

The airmen arrived just on three o'clock and Pam greeted them all, smiling as the introductions were made.

'Sergeant Frank Simmons, Lieutenants John Collins, Bill Franklin and Keith Tyler,' Frank introduced them all. They were all in uniform and fresh-faced young men, none of them over twenty-five years.

Pam introduced herself, her husband and son, Lizzie, Jeanie and Frances. Jonny and Archie were upstairs sleeping and George had gone out to play with his new friend, Billy, who had also been invited to tea, but they had both promised faithfully to come back in time.

'We want you to come to us whenever you feel like having a break from life on the base,' she told them. 'If you are hungry, I'll find you something to eat and if you just want to sit quietly for a while in warmth and comfort, that is all right, too.'

'Thank you, that's right nice of you,' Bill Franklin said and shook her hand heartily. 'I'm from New Zealand and you folks round here have made us all feel at ease, inviting us to your homes. I've made some good friends in Sutton, but they always seem to have a houseful.'

'Our house is pretty busy sometimes,' Pam said. 'I have two more sons serving in the forces, one with the RAF and one the army, and two younger daughters. The girls are both out with friends, but they will be back later. My nephew George will turn up when he's ready.'

'It will be nice to meet them, ma'am,' Bill said politely. He looked at Arthur. 'I think I saw you on land near the airfield the other day? You were mending a piece on the back of your tractor?'

'I broke the link that fixes the trailer,' Arthur replied. 'It is old and I can't get a new one these days. I keep fixing it up with wire.'

'I think we took over some of your land when the airfield was built?'

'Yes, quite a few acres, but I wasn't the only one,' Arthur replied. 'A lot of small farmers lost land then – but it was needed for a good cause.' Airfields had sprung up all over the place at the start of the war; there was another one between Sutton and Ely, at Witchford.

Artie was chatting to Keith Tyler about football and Lizzie, having taken a moment to fetch Archie down, was showing her son to John Collins, who had told her his wife had recently had a little girl. She was telling him about Jonny, who was still asleep in his cot upstairs.

Angela, Susan, George and Billy came in then, which led to more introductions.

'Cor, that's a proper spread that is, Aunt Pam,' George said. 'Can I have one of them egg sandwiches?'

'Of course you can, George, and you, Billy. Help yourself, love – and then George will show you his favourite cow later,' she replied, then, nodding at the airmen. 'These are the gentlemen from the airfield – say hello, both of you.'

George looked around at them. 'You fly them planes then,' he said. 'What's it like in the air when them bug— Germans are firing at you?'

'Come and talk to me and I'll tell you,' Lieutenant Tyler invited and George went to squat down on the floor next to his chair. Billy followed, munching his sandwich and sitting next to George, he looked rapt as the airman told them stories of how they attacked from the air.

'Cor blimey,' he said. 'Me Dad's in the army but I'd like to do what you do...' He held an imaginary gun and fired off round the room, making the company smile at his enthusiasm.

'We'll enrol you and we'll soon win the war,' Lieutenant Tyler said with a grin.

Pam shook her head over them but she was smiling. Angela was sitting close to her dad on his chair, but Susan had found a seat on the sofa and was soon talking to one of the airmen.

* * *

Frances looked at Frank, hesitating before asking if he would like a cup of tea. 'Why don't you come and talk to me for a moment first?' he asked. He had chosen to sit on the couch a little apart from the others. 'I've been looking forward to seeing you, Frances. How are you?' His eyes seemed to search her face. 'I ought to have asked you out, but I wasn't sure when I would get a night off – we've had a lot going on recently.'

Frances nodded. 'Someone told me you'd lost nine planes this past week. That sounds an awful lot?'

'We had an incident the other night,' he said, lowering his voice. 'One of our Lancaster bombers spun off the runaway as it was preparing for take-off and ended up close to a lot of houses behind York Road. It was loaded with bombs and it smoked all night. We had to evacuate the folk living nearby just in case. It was the night I was supposed to be off duty, but I stayed behind to help.'

'That could have been nasty,' Frances said. 'What happened to make it spin off?'

'That is being investigated,' he told her with a frown. 'It could have been a fault in the undercarriage or a pilot error. Some of the crews are working non-stop and they don't always get enough sleep. But I don't know the official verdict and I may never be told. These things are sometimes pushed under the carpet.'

'We hear the planes going over,' Frances told him. 'We listen for them to come back and try to count them, but we always wonder how many made it back.'

'Sometimes they all do,' Frank said, 'but sometimes we lose a plane and that isn't a good day – when it's more than one, it gets a bit tense at times.'

'It must do,' Frances replied. 'You don't fly, do you?'

'No. I am military police – but I am also a gunner. If the airfield is attacked, I'd be out there shooting at the beggars with the rest of them.'

Frances smiled, relaxing. He was pleasant to talk to. 'What made you join the military police?'

He laughed. 'I sometimes wonder. We are not the most popular chaps. I suppose I fell into it. I got involved trying to stop a fight soon after I was recruited. I was arrested with the other men involved, but then an officer spoke up for me and told them I was trying to stop it – and, a few weeks later, I was asked if I wanted to do that officially and I agreed.'

'What did you really want to do?'

Frank looked at her thoughtfully. 'Before the war, I was

training to be a vet. I'll go back to it one day, to Yorkshire. I had no desire to fight a war, but I couldn't just carry on with my job, so I volunteered for the army and ended up helping to guard this airfield as an MP.'

'That sounds interesting,' Frances said a little wistfully. 'Will you live in the countryside when you go back to being a vet?'

'Yes. I'll be a country vet,' he said and smiled at her. 'Perhaps one day you'd show me round the farm – you have cows here, don't you?'

'I help milk them, but I'm not very good.'

'I have a day off next Thursday,' Frank said. 'Unless there is an emergency, I'd like to visit the farm and then take you out to tea somewhere – if you'd like that?'

'Thank you, I'd like that,' she said, forgetting her fears as she looked into his smiling eyes. He was so easy to talk to – and perhaps Pam was right. Perhaps she ought to let go of the past and make a new life for herself...

* * *

'Well, that went well,' Pam remarked after the young men had gone. They'd stayed more than two hours, talking and eating their way through the mounds of fresh bread, farm butter, hard-boiled eggs, soft cheese, pasties and cakes Pam had baked. 'Everyone seemed to enjoy the food.'

'They loved it, especially those egg and watercress sandwiches and the mushroom and streaky bacon pasties,' Jeanie confirmed.

Pam nodded. 'It was lucky that Artie went out early and picked those mushrooms. They make tasty fillings mixed with some bubble and squeak and a little bacon. I'm afraid it means no bacon for the rest of us for a few days, but those pasties were delicious hot.'

'Frank loved his and I gave him half of mine,' Frances said. 'He says they get fed quite well at the canteen, but none of it tastes as good as your food, Pam.'

'Then it was all worthwhile,' she said. 'Perhaps we'll do another tea later in the summer, but the next thing is Jeanie and Artie's wedding – only a couple of weeks now. I invited them all, but, of course, they may not be able to get a pass that day.'

'Frank wants to come if he can. He liked it here.'

'I am hoping they will feel able to treat our home as theirs now,' Pam said. 'Sometimes I might only be able to give them some hot toast and marge with a little jam, but there is somewhere for them to sit and plenty of hot drinks of one kind and another.'

'I think Bill will come sometimes,' Jeanie said. 'He got on well with Arthur and Keith was talking to Artie for ages. John Collins was a bit quieter, but he sat and talked to Lizzie and, also Susan, about her college and teaching for half an hour or so. She told me that his sister is a teacher and he is thinking of returning to college after the war to train as a sports master.'

'Yes, I noticed that,' Pam said. 'He was the older of them, I think.'

'Yes, but not much more than twenty-four,' Jeanie agreed. She yawned and stretched. 'I'd better go and give Artie a hand with the milking. I know he said he would do it, but that isn't fair on him. I'll just pop up and change.'

Pam nodded, turning to Frances as the sound of her footsteps up the stairs died away. 'Well then, was it all right?'

'Yes.' Frances smiled at her. 'Thank you for making me see it was silly to run away, Pam. I do like him – and, as you said, everyone needs to make friends.'

'I am glad you stayed and enjoyed yourself. Did he ask you out?'

'He is coming here next Thursday. He would like to look at the cows – he's training to be a vet in civilian life – and then he will take me out to tea after he looks round the farm.'

'If Arthur knows he's a vet, he'll be asking him about Daisy,' Pam said with a laugh. 'He was worried about her again this morning. She seems off her food, so he says.'

'Yes, I know,' Frances agreed. 'She is getting on a bit – perhaps...' She shook her head. 'Mr Talbot really is fond of Daisy, isn't he?'

'Yes. Normally, he's businesslike when it comes to the animals being sold but not that one.'

'Do you think I should change my clothes and go out to help?' Frances asked. She'd just dried the last plate and stacked them back on the oak dresser.

'No, leave Artie and Jeanie to get on with it; they probably want to be alone to talk,' Pam said and smiled. 'It's not long until the wedding...'

'You are excited about it, aren't you?'

'Yes, I am,' Pam agreed. 'I wasn't sure Artie would settle down with a wife. He seemed restless since... well, since his brothers joined up. I knew he felt he wanted to do the same but couldn't leave his father in the lurch. Arthur isn't young any more. However, Artie has been happier since he made up his mind to ask Jeanie to marry him.'

'Everyone thinks the men who volunteer straight off are the brave ones, and they are, of course – but it must be hard for those who are forced stay at home. The Government made it illegal for the miners to join up – they are in necessary jobs and women can't take over, as they have in many other situations.'

'Yes, that's true,' Pam confirmed. 'Some jobs are essential and the men who are employed in them just can't be spared. Like the firemen and the police – the country needs them to continue.'

'Yes,' Frances agreed. 'The firemen are as much in danger of being hurt in the terrible fires that happen after an air raid. I saw them battling to put out the flames on a factory near where I worked when it was hit. It was like a nightmare, the sky lit with flames and men seared by the fierce heat – and trying to catch a woman and child as they jumped from an upstairs window in a house that had been caught by the blast and was blazing.'

'It must be horrendous,' Pam closed her eyes. 'I thank God we've been spared anything like that here.'

'Frank told me they had a heavily laden bomber spin off the third runaway a short time ago. He said it smoked all night and they thought it might explode and demolish some houses in Sutton. They had to evacuate the people living nearby.'

'Artie heard something about it, but thought it might worry us so only told his father.'

'Well—' Frances began, but a wail from Jonny cut her off short. He'd woken up after a long sleep. 'I'll go and get him,' she said with a smile. 'He probably needs changing – and it must be time for a feed?'

'Look at the time,' Pam cried. 'Yes, fetch him down, love and I'll warm some milk. And I'll have to think what to do for supper...'

'I shan't be hungry after all that tea,' Frances said and Pam laughed.

'I'll bet Artie and Arthur will, even if it is only toast and marmalade.'

Frances smiled and went off to fetch the baby. It was true the men on the farm always seemed hungry. She thought it must be all the fresh air.

28

Tom read Lizzie's letter before folding it and placing it with others in his locker. She'd asked him if he thought he would get leave for his brother's wedding. Artie had already asked him to stand up with him as his best man and he'd said he would be pleased to, if he could get leave, and at that time he'd still had hopes that he might, but he'd been told he was needed elsewhere.

Because of his injury, which had left him with a permanent if slight limp, Tom had expected that he would spend the rest of the war training younger, fitter men to do the job he'd done at the start of the war. It had certainly looked that way for a while, but now he'd been told he was being transferred to active duty once more.

'You've done excellent work with this latest batch of men,' his superior officer had informed him at their meeting. 'Now I'm going to ask you to go further, Captain Gilbert. I don't need to tell you that you can refuse this mission if you wish, but we hope that you will take up the challenge. We need men like you where the action is. We have been forming an elite band of men, as you know, highly trained and ready to go anywhere. However, none of them have your leadership qualities and so we would like you to accompany them to their first destination.'

'May I ask where this action is, sir?' Tom had asked. He'd promised Lizzie he wouldn't volunteer but he could hardly turn down this request.

'You will be part of a supply chain to a very brave set of men in the desert,' Colonel Royce had told him. 'They are taking on the enemy, outsmarting them – one of our code names is Desert Rats, but they are a secret division, and they live hand-to-mouth existences out there in the desert. We need good men to keep them supplied with food and ammunition.'

'Not to join them, sir?' Tom had asked. He'd been aware of what was happening but had never expected to become part of a group that was considered ruthless as well as brave.

'No, Captain Talbot. We wouldn't ask you to do that. Perhaps had you not been injured previously, you would have been sent to join them, but the supply chain is vitally important. It isn't like popping down to the local bazaar to get what you need; you must take convoys through the desert to reach their secret hideaways and you may be subject to air attacks, as well as other dangers.' Colonel Royce had raised his eyebrows, waiting for Tom's reply.

'Yes, sir,' Tom had saluted. 'When do we leave?'

'Good man. I thought you would take it on. You will be shipping out in ten days. In the meantime, you must prepare the men – but you will all be given a forty-eight-hour pass three days before you go.'

'Yes, sir. Thank you, sir.'

Tom decided he would telephone so that Lizzie knew to expect him. Because of the travelling involved, he would get only one night at home, but since it wasn't long since his last leave, his intuitive wife would sense something different was happening.

He would tell her as much as he could, which was only that he was being moved abroad to help with a supply chain. He wouldn't be fighting but he couldn't promise her he would not be in danger, because the supply chains were vital and if they were spotted from the air, they would be sitting ducks in the middle of the desert.

* * *

Lizzie knew instantly that something was changing for Tom when Pam told her that he had rung to say he was coming home soon for a short visit. He'd hinted that he might be due for a change of scenery, but she'd prayed it wouldn't happen. She knew Pam was worried, too, though neither of them said a word. Both John and Tom were fighting men and they had to accept that things could happen; though both women felt that their family had already given enough, they knew others had given more. Some men from the village would never return.

It was the Monday after the young airmen came to tea when Tom telephoned to say he'd be home the following Thursday just for one night. Lizzie was in the kitchen, drinking tea and chatting with Pam when he rang, so she was able to speak to him herself.

'I'll look forward to it, my love,' she told Tom quietly.

'I can't wait,' he said. 'I'd better go, my darling. There is a queue waiting behind me for the phone.'

'I love you, Tom.'

'Love you too...'

* * *

Tom replaced the receiver. He was smiling as he walked away from the phone booth and another man took his place. All the men wanted to phone home. They were all excited because they knew a mission was coming up, but they didn't yet know where they were going, though most of them had nodded as though they could guess when he'd briefed them. He'd told them it was warm and dry and they were an intelligent bunch, all of them eager to prove themselves and get at the enemy.

'Are you coming with us, sir?' one fresh recruit waiting in line for the phone asked.

Tom nodded. 'Someone has to keep you in order – were you hoping to be rid of me?'

'No, sir,' Robert Youngs saluted smartly. 'I'm glad you're our officer. You've had experience, not like some of the desk johnnies that walk around the parade ground.'

'Mind your words, corporal,' Tom said. 'Disrespect towards your superior officers can result in being put on latrine duty.'

'Righto, sir,' the young soldier replied, but he knew Tom was relaxed, smiling. 'I'll remember that.'

Tom held his laugh inside. He liked Robert; just eighteen and fresh-faced, he reminded Tom of his youngest brother before the war, with his blond hair and wide blue eyes that held a deceiving air of innocence. He wondered how long that innocence would survive under the hot sun of Tobruk.

A frown creased his brow as he thought of John. His eyes no longer held that innocence or look of delight in the world. They'd talked a great deal when Tom was last home and he understood that his brother was battling with both grief and guilt. He'd done his best to understand and offer comfort, but how could anyone take away the kind of pain John was carrying? He just hoped his brother would be able to put it out of his mind when he was in the air and that he would see him again.

Bloody war! Tom thought, scowling as he thought about what John had lost. If anything happened to Lizzie and his son – it didn't bear thinking about. He knew that Lizzie would feel the same if anything happened to him. Tom wished they hadn't asked him to return to active service, but he couldn't refuse – there were men relying on him and he had to do his duty.

* * *

Tom greeted his wife with a bear hug that Thursday afternoon, holding her tight and then kissing her passionately. She looked up into his face and he saw the brief flicker of fear in her eyes that she swiftly controlled.

'It's wonderful to have you home,' she whispered against his ear. 'I love you so much, Tom. When are they sending you overseas? I won't ask where, because I know you can't tell me.'

Just as he'd known, Lizzie had sensed his feelings. He smiled down at her, touching her beloved face with his fingertips. 'We go on Sunday,' he told her. 'I was going to tell you – but I knew you would guess.'

'I always know when something is on your mind,' Lizzie said. They were standing in the kitchen of their house. 'Shall we stay here for a while? Your mum said to come for supper this evening – but I'd like to be alone with you for now. Would you like to look at Archie? He's sleeping in his cot.'

Tom bent and kissed her tenderly on the lips. 'That is just what I'd like,' he agreed and the look in her eyes told her what was in his heart. Taking her hand in his, they walked up the stairs together.

29

Frank arrived at the farm promptly on his day off and Frances took him to see the cows who had been brought into the milking shed by Jeanie and Artie. Arthur was there too and the vet, Mr Johnson, had been called to see Daisy, who had a tummy upset. Frank joined in the conversation as to why the old cow was suffering runny excretions and made a suggestion that had the others turning to look at him.

'I don't know, but my father had a cow like that,' he told Arthur. 'The vet was puzzled because she seemed fit – and he suggested there might be something in the hay that was upsetting her stomach. Sometimes, when you cut, you get a poisonous plant with the grass and that can produce symptoms like Daisy has. It isn't enough to kill the cow, but it upsets their tummy. Try feeding her other things for a while.'

'Wouldn't it affect the other cows as well?' Arthur asked.

'There probably wasn't that much of whatever it was,' Frank replied. 'And some cows don't seem to be affected. Only one of Dad's cows had it – but changing her feed worked for us.'

'Training to be a vet, are you?' Mr Johnson offered his hand to

Frank and they shook. 'I agree with this young man. I believe it is something Daisy ate. Remove the hay from her feeding stall and don't give her any more for a few days. If that doesn't work, we'll have to think of something else.'

Arthur looked doubtful but then nodded. 'Yes, it is worth a try. Any idea what it was that caused it so we can look out for it when we are next haymaking?'

Frank shook his head regretfully. 'We never knew either – but the change of diet worked for our cow.'

Arthur thanked him and they chatted some more and then Frances and Frank left, changing their shoes before getting into Frank's car. He turned to smile at Frances before starting the engine. 'Where shall we go?'

'Let's go to Ely,' she suggested. 'It is a pretty market town and the cathedral is lovely. There is a river we can walk by and somewhere to have tea...'

'Sounds ideal,' Frank said and smiled at he started the car. 'I've been a couple of times, but to the cinema in the evening. We could go there later if you wished?'

'Let's see what we feel like doing,' Frances cautioned. 'The time flies and I'm not sure we can fit it all in. I mustn't be too late back or Pam will worry.'

'Lovely lady. You get on well with her, don't you?'

'The whole family is kind,' Frances said. 'But I am very fond of Pam. She understands things. I can talk to her.'

Frank turned his head to look at her for an instant. 'You can talk to me, too,' he said. 'I'd like us to be friends, Frances.'

'I'd like that, too,' she told him. 'And perhaps one day I'll tell you all about myself.'

'When and if you want,' Frank said. 'But I know all I need to just by looking in your eyes, Frances. I know you've been hurt and I want you to believe that I will never hurt you – and I wouldn't let anyone else if I could prevent it.'

Frances smiled. 'Thank you,' she said. She was beginning to like and trust him, but there were things she just couldn't tell him – not yet anyway.

* * *

After visiting the beautiful old cathedral, they walked from the high street, where Frank had parked his car, down to the river and along the path that led from the quayside to the Cutter Inn. Frank remarked on some of the old buildings. He thought Ely a pleasant place and it was very peaceful away from the market-place, where busy traders were selling their wares. They stood watching the swans glide gracefully by and laughed at a young child feeding crusts of bread to some noisy ducks.

As they stood there for a moment, Mrs Bates came out of her front door and waved to them. 'Bring your young man in for a few minutes and have a cup of tea with me, Frances.'

Frances looked at Frank and he nodded, so they crossed the narrow street and followed her into her neat kitchen. She bustled about making tea and offered them scones with jam.

'I'm glad I've seen you, Frances,' she said. 'Young Billy's father was home on leave from the army last week and he came to see his son. He took him off for a few days, but he says he'll be grateful if I keep him until after the war and offered to pay for his new clothes. When I told him about you, he said to be sure to tell you how grateful he was.' She smiled at Frank. 'Did you know Frances was a heroine?'

He shook his head and she proceeded to tell him how Frances had jumped in after Billy when he fell in the river.

'That was brave of you,' he said, looking at Frances. 'I'm not sure many young women would do the same.'

'I never even thought about it,' she said. 'It wasn't really very brave. I can swim perfectly well and he wasn't difficult to grab and drag out. The water is very shallow in that bit where the ducks are.'

Frank nodded and said no more on the subject but looked impressed. After they left Mrs Bates' home, he asked if she wanted to go to the matinee of a film that would be starting soon.

'I'd rather go and get some fish and chips in the café,' Frances said. 'We can drive back slowly afterwards and just sit and talk.'

He grinned and nodded. 'The smell *was* enticing as we passed.'

'They open most of the day on a Thursday,' Frances told him. 'I'm hungry, even after that scone Mrs Bates gave us.'

'Me too...' Frank agreed, looking at her with an amused smile in his eyes. 'Are you always so easy to please?'

She laughed. 'I don't know. But it is hard work on the farm so it is lovely to just get out for a while.'

'You don't come from here, though?'

'No. I was born in London, and not in a nice area at all,' she admitted. 'It is so different here – peaceful and nice.'

'Yes, it is a nice town – very busy on market day, and the centre of the district; I suppose, because of the cathedral. I live in a village. Our nearest town is York. That's where we go when we want to enjoy a day at the shops or go to the cinema. It's quiet in our village, but I like it.'

'When I first arrived, I wasn't sure I'd like country life,' Frances confessed. 'But I do. Living at the farm, there is always something going on and I'm usually tired at the end of a working day, ready to just flop into bed and sleep. It's nice to help Pam or sit talking to her and the others. I go to bed early and read a magazine or a novel if I've been to the library. Very different to what I knew before...' She broke off in confusion as Frank directed an enquiring gaze at her.

'I wondered what made you volunteer for the land work rather than one of the other services?'

'I wanted to get away from London,' she admitted. 'I wasn't happy there. I've been much happier since I came here.'

His eyes held hers for a moment, then he nodded thoughtfully. 'Maybe you'll tell me one day what made you unhappy there?'

'Perhaps,' she agreed. 'When we know each other better.'

Frank reached for her hand. 'I think I already know you, Frances,' he said, gazing into her eyes. 'I like what I know very much. One day I hope you will like me enough to trust me.'

Frances nodded; the tears very close. 'There are things I'm not proud of,' she told him. 'Bad things. There was a man who hurt me – and another who loved me. I cared for him, too, because he helped me through a bad time. He... he was killed on active service. I had too many unhappy memories in London – and I was afraid of the man who hurt me.'

'Yes, I understand,' Frank said softly. 'I knew you had been badly hurt. Thank you for telling me, Frances.' He looked deep into her eyes. 'Please believe that I will never hurt you.' He smiled and offered his arm. 'Shall we go and get our fish and chips?'

30

Pam thought Frances looked happier when she came back at around eight o'clock that evening, but she didn't ask questions. Frances would tell her anything she wanted her to know. She accepted Pam's offer of a cup of tea, but refused supper, telling her that she'd had fish and chips at the café in Ely. After chatting to Jeanie for a few minutes about the wedding, she went up to her room.

Artie and Arthur came in then and wanted supper, so Pam was busy for the rest of the evening before everyone went up. The talk had mostly been of the farm and the wedding. It wasn't long now and they were all looking forward to it. A family wedding was something to celebrate in dark times and helped to occupy Pam's mind and stop her thinking about her sons who were involved in this dreadful war.

It was when Pam lay in bed in that time between letting go and the comfort of sleep that she sometimes became wakeful and anxious about John and Tom. She'd thought Tom was in a safe job, training new recruits after the wound that had left him with a slight limp, but he'd told her privately in a quiet moment that he was returning to active service.

'Lizzie knows and so must you, Mum,' Tom had told her. 'I'm not going to be at the forefront, but there is always a chance that I won't make it back. I know Lizzie will always have a family if I'm unlucky, but it is only fair that you know.'

'I'll look after her,' Pam had promised, refusing to show the fear his words engendered in her mind. 'But she needs you back, Tom, and so do I. Arthur too. You know that...'

'Yes, of course, and I'll do my damnedest to get back,' he'd assured her.

Pam would have known instinctively if he hadn't told her, but she was glad he had. She wished with all her heart that he could remain in his safe job until the end of the war and then come home, but nothing she could do or say would change that, and so she would let him go with a smile of acceptance rather than making the violent protest that was in her heart. Silently, she cursed this war and she prayed every night for its swift end, but knew there was at present no end in sight. Men like Tom and John were needed to fight and keep on fighting until the might and will of the enemy was broken.

All the bombing of towns and cities like Exeter, named the Baedeker Blitz, because of a series of German tourist guides of that title, which gave detailed maps of towns and cities in Britain, were said to be in retaliation for the British bombing of Lubeck in Germany. So many raids on military bases, the sinking of ships in the Atlantic, the deaths of so many young men in Europe and else-where, the devastating attack on Pearl Harbour, all took a toll on the minds and hearts of good, decent people. Pam felt like weeping for all the mothers who had lost sons, brothers and husbands. So far, she had been lucky – but how long would her luck last?

Arthur's arm went round her as she lay thinking. His head rested against hers on the pillow. 'I know, love,' he whispered. 'I know how you feel – but he will come home to us one day; they both will.'

'If only I could be so sure,' she said, a half-sob in her voice.

'I feel it inside,' Arthur said. 'I believe it, Pam. You must, too.'

She swallowed a sob. 'I know. I'm being stupid. I sensed it when he said he was coming home again so soon after his last leave. I'd hoped he would be safe... and John too.'

'They are both brave lads,' Arthur said. 'Neither of them would want you to make yourself sick with worry, love.'

'I know – and I won't,' she replied. 'Thank God Artie didn't join up as well...'

'I just hope he doesn't resent it too much,' Arthur said. 'I think I've found him and Jeanie a decent house at last. They had hopes of another, but it was let before they could see it. The one I found belonged to old Mrs Grant, but she's gone to live with her daughter-in-law because she can't manage any more on her own. I'll take them to look at it tomorrow afternoon. It will probably need a lot of work, so it will be a while before they can move in.'

Pam nodded and snuggled into him. 'I don't mind how long they stay here, Arthur. I suppose they'll be in and out most of the time even after they move....'

'Jeanie wants to carry on with her work for as long as she's needed,' Arthur said. 'She is the ideal wife for Artie. She'll be around whenever he needs her to help on the farm, even when the land girls are no longer necessary.'

'Until they have a family,' Pam reminded him. 'She won't carry on then surely?'

'Not as she does now, but I dare say she'll help when she can. She won't be the first young woman to take her baby into the fields while she works. Frances is a good worker, but I wouldn't say she enjoys it as Jeanie does.'

'No, perhaps not. She isn't keen on the cows. Prefers being in the fields, when the weather is nice anyway.'

'Do you think she likes that young chap she was out with today?' Arthur asked. 'If she goes off and gets married, I'll have to find another one to take her place – and it takes time to train them. Some of them don't settle to it. I was told last time I applied that there aren't enough of them to go round.'

'They volunteer but don't realise what the work is like,' Pam said. 'I suppose if it is a choice between the factories or the land... but the other women's services are more glamorous, especially now Princess Elizabeth has joined up. I read a lot of young women have followed her example.'

'I dare say,' Arthur grunted. 'Well, I just hope Frances doesn't up and leave too soon. I don't want to start another girl all over again – though young George is shaping up well. I reckon it won't be long before he's a big help – though ten to one when he's old enough, he'll want to be a train driver or something.'

'Stop being grumpy,' Pam said. 'George is only a boy – and if Frances is happy and wants to get married, I'd wish her good luck.'

He muttered something and she snuggled into his warmth. Arthur only knew some of Frances' story. Pam hoped that she would find happiness with her new friend, but it was bound to take time she thought as she drifted into sleep.

* * *

A letter came from John the next day. He'd had a few hours' leave and had gone into Cambridge to meet a friend – a nurse who had looked after him in hospital. He'd written a cheerful letter, but told his mother he didn't think he could get time off for the wedding. Artie had asked him to be his best man when he knew Tom wouldn't be around for the wedding. Pam thought Artie might have been trying to mend fences between himself and John, but John couldn't be there either, according to his letter.

We are busy at the moment and I had a long time off to recuperate. Tell Artie I am sorry, but he should get someone else as his best man. I've managed to buy a present and it will arrive the day before the wedding, through a mate of mine who has some leave coming. Pete is a nice chap so if Artie is stuck, he could ask him...

Pam shook her head over the letter. It told her nothing she needed to know – except that he'd been to see a friend in Cambridge. She was glad he had a friend he liked to visit but sad that he didn't think he would get home for the wedding. With John being in the RAF and stationed not too far away, she'd hoped he might get home more often than men serving overseas could, but it seemed that for now that was out of the question. It occurred to her that perhaps John didn't want to come home and that upset her, but she tried to put it out of her head. No point in worrying. Arthur was right; the boys were men now and had their own lives to lead.

Susan entered the kitchen as she was putting the letter on the mantelpiece. 'Is that from John?' she asked. 'May I read it?'

'Yes, of course. It doesn't say much,' Pam told her. 'You're home early?'

'My headmaster told me I could work at home. Several teachers are off sick, so they sent all the older pupils home with work to do. We're short of teachers at the best of times – we've had to double up the classes for ages, since three of the masters joined up. I can work here just as easily.' She read the letter and nodded. 'John doesn't want to come for the wedding, does he?'

'I don't know. Perhaps he can't get leave.'

'I was talking to Bill and he said they all get leave sometimes, especially the aircrew, because they would just burn out if they didn't – John could wangle it if he wanted to. I expect it is just too painful to see Artie getting married when he can't marry Faith.'

'Don't say that to Artie,' Pam warned. 'Who is this Bill? Oh, you mean that young man who came to tea with the others. When did he tell you that?'

'I saw him yesterday,' Susan said, a faint blush in her cheeks. 'He was on his cycle when I got off the bus from Chatteris and we talked for a while.'

Pam looked at her. 'He's a little bit old for you, isn't he?'

'I like older men,' Susan said. 'Not that I'm interested in anything but friends, no involved stuff – but he has asked to take me to the cinema.'

Pam looked at her. 'Shall you go?'

'I think so,' Susan laughed. 'Don't worry, Mum. You won't have another wedding to cater for just yet.'

'Good,' Pam said and smiled. 'I'm glad you've got some sense in that head of yours, love. There's that stupid law that says you can't teach if you're married – mind you, by the time you've done college, it will probably be repealed. I read somewhere that it is likely to happen.'

'I'm going to my room to study – unless you need me to do anything?'

'No, you go, love,' Pam said, smiling. 'You're getting very grown-up, aren't you?'

'So you've noticed at last,' Susan retorted and laughed as her mother aimed a tea towel at her; it fell short of hitting her. 'You'll have to do better than that...' She escaped, laughing, and clattered up the stairs to her room, where she put a jazz record on her wind-up gramophone. Pam wondered how she could work like that, but she did.

31

A few days before the wedding, Frances asked if Frank could come. Pam said it was fine if he had a day off. Artie heard her speaking to Jeanie about it later and said that if Frank were willing, he might stand up with him as his best man.

'Neither of my brothers will be here,' he said. 'Most of my mates are in the army and can't come. I had asked a friend who lives in Chatteris, but last week he broke his ankle and he's stuck in hospital, so I was wondering who I could ask.'

'It's a shame one of your brothers couldn't get leave,' Frances said, 'but I am sure Frank would love it. He's a nice person.'

Artie nodded. 'Yeah. He was right about that feed too. The cow is fine now. It was something in the hay.'

'I'm seeing him this evening,' Frances said. 'We're just going to the Chequers for a drink. I'll ask him, but I know he will be pleased.'

'Serious about him?' Artie asked with a lift of his brow and Frances blushed.

'I... might be,' Frances replied. 'I haven't known him long enough to be sure...'

'Does he know about that bloke that came after you?'

'Sort of...' Frances said and looked down, her cheeks hot now.

'I'd tell him it all if I were you,' Artie advised.

'I may – after the wedding...'

'None of my business. I'd want to know if it were me – but up to you.' As usual, Artie was brusque, but she knew he'd advised her for her own good and nodded.

Artie walked off, leaving Frances to ponder. Did she care about Frank and if she did, could she risk telling him the whole story? He had the right to know before either of them was too involved. She wouldn't do it before the wedding, though. That was only a few days away and if they quarrelled it might spoil things.

* * *

'You look beautiful,' Frances said that sunny May morning as she helped Jeanie with her coronet of wax flowers and the short bridal veil. Lizzie had trimmed and set her hair the previous day and it shone like silk. 'That dress is perfect for your figure, Jeanie.'

'Yes, I liked it as soon as I tried it on,' Jeanie told her with a happy smile. 'I had almost given up and thought I might have to go to London for it, but the moment I put it on, I knew it was the one.'

'You were so lucky to get it,' Frances told her. 'I don't think there are many wedding dresses about these days.'

With all the new regulations, rationing and restrictions on what the shops could sell, wedding dresses were likely to be plainer than in peacetime and many shops had hardly anything in stock.

Jeanie nodded. 'At least my sister has got leave from the hospital and is coming for the wedding and so is my brother Terry. Artie's brothers can't get leave – and nor can most of his friends. Susan has asked that airman she has been seeing, but he isn't sure he will be able to come.'

'Your mum and dad are coming too.'

'Oh yes, of course,' Jeanie brightened. 'They stayed in a hotel in Cambridge last night and took Annie out to dinner. Dad is driving them all here this morning...' A smile lit her pretty face. 'I just heard a car and I think that's Mum's voice.'

Sure enough, voices were heard downstairs and then footsteps on the steps leading up to their room. The door opened and Vera and Annie entered. Introductions were made, because Frances hadn't met Jeanie's sister before or her Mother.

'I'd better go and finish getting ready,' Frances said, leaving the family together. Because there wasn't much room in their attic bedroom, Jeanie was using John's room to get ready. Artie had been banished to Lizzie's house early that morning so that they didn't meet before the wedding. Neither of them had been allowed to do their usual work, although Artie had argued that he could perfectly well milk a few cows. His father would hear none of it and he'd been bustled out of the house with his suitcase and told that Lizzie would give him his breakfast, long before the girls were stirring upstairs.

Frances smiled as she heard the chattering in Jeanie's room as she went up to the attic room she would no longer share with her friend. The young couple would sleep in Artie's room until their own house was ready for them.

She would miss Jeanie, Frances realised. When she'd first arrived, she hadn't been too keen on sharing, but then she'd begun to like Jeanie and they'd laughed a lot. Yes, she would miss that...

Her thoughts ran on to the future, leading her to wonder if she really could have a life full of love and the happiness of having her own family. The memory of her past shame still hung like a dark cloud at the back of her mind, though she managed to push it away most of the time. Artie was right, though, when he'd said she should tell Frank the whole truth. It was the honest thing to do and she would – but just not today...

* * *

Jeanie looked radiant as she walked down the aisle on her father's arm that morning in May. The expression on Artie's face as he turned to look at her told it all. Normally not one for showing his feelings, they were plain enough to read as he looked at his bride – love, tenderness, and pride. It was obvious that Artie thought the world of his Jeanie and Frances felt a pang of envy. She wished that one day a man would look at her like that...

The ceremony brought tears to Frances' eyes and Pam was sniffing into her handkerchief. Arthur looked pleased and Lizzie was smiling as she took Jeanie's bouquet. Sunshine suddenly flooded in through the windows, lighting up the tiny church. The ring was placed on Jeanie's finger and then the two of them went to sign the register. A few minutes later, the bells rang as the newly wedded pair walked out into the warmth of a late spring morning. Confetti was thrown, good-luck charms and trinkets offered to the bride and Artie was told to kiss her, which he did to the sound of cheers and laughter.

It was a small gathering of family members and a few friends. Arthur's cousin, Alf, was there with his wife and daughter, Jeanie's entire family, Lizzie, Susan, Angela and George and Frances and Frank, and, at the last minute, Artie's mate from

Chatteris had come limping in, the sound of his plaster cast loud on the church flagstones.

Some of the villagers had joined the congregation at the back of the church but melted away after confetti was thrown and some photographs taken. Arthur drove the bride and groom back to the farm, Cousin Alf took Pam as well as his family, and Jeanie's father took Annie, Vera and Artie's friend in his car as he naturally couldn't ride his motorbike in a plaster cast and had been dropped off by a neighbour on his way to Ely. Frank took Frances, Terry and George with him in his car, but Lizzie, Susan and Angela said they would walk home. They were saved from having to do so by the late arrival of Susan's friend Bill. He'd managed to wangle a couple of hours off, though hadn't been able to make it in time for the ceremony.

Pam's kitchen and sitting room were crowded with the guests, all talking and laughing, congratulating the happy pair. Presents were piled on the sideboard in the sitting room; everyone had managed to find something even with the strict rationing, but Frances' silver teapot was one of the nicest things they'd been given.

Arthur produced a bottle of champagne and popped the cork. He'd had it stood in a pail of cold water in the dairy and it was lovely and cold. Even Pam was surprised but didn't ask him where it had come from until much later. They all toasted the bride and groom and then tucked into the spread Pam had managed to put on. Another of Arthur's surprises earlier that morning had been a whole ham and some tinned peaches. Pam hadn't even questioned the ham; she was just too delighted to add it to her table. She'd saved what rations she could for weeks and had produced sausage rolls as well as cold roasted chicken, flans made with egg, bacon and cheese, and hot jacket potatoes, tomatoes, pickles and a variety of pastries and cakes, even a wedding sponge filled with fresh cream from their Jersey cow. She regretted there was no traditional iced fruit cake, but as Vera said, she could rightly be proud of her table that day.

'Your friend looked lovely,' Frank whispered to Frances as they watched the pair greet guests and thank them for coming. 'I'd like to think we might do this one day... when you know me better.'

'Frank...' Frances' heart missed a beat. 'You don't know me either...'

'Yes, I do,' he said and kissed her cheek. 'I knew the first moment I saw you.'

Frances smiled, but her heart was racing. She was going to have to tell him the whole story and she dreaded seeing that look of love in his eyes turn to disgust, but she knew now that she had to tell him everything.

32

'Happy, darling?' Artie asked later that evening. They'd left their friends at the farm and Arthur had driven them to the railway station in Sutton. From there, they had taken the train to their hotel in Cambridge for their wedding night. Their honeymoon was to be in Clacton, a resort on the east coast, and he'd booked a posh hotel on the seafront there. In other circumstances, he might have considered going to Devon or Cornwall, but he felt it was too far in these restricted times. Jeanie had agreed and Artie had promised that when the war was over, he would take her somewhere nice for a long holiday.

'I don't really mind where we go,' Jeanie had told him. 'Mum and Dad never had a honeymoon. They just had a few days off to settle into their own home before they both went back to work. Dad didn't own his business then.' It was often the case for ordinary working folk. Long extended honeymoons were usually only for the wealthy, and Artie's family were better off than most.

Artie was determined to get on in life. There wasn't much he could do with a war raging. He couldn't see any opportunities for making money however hard he worked. His father had helped him by buying the house on Witcham Road for him, and John's boss was renovating it for him. It was a start. Artie had always looked after his money and he had a bit saved. As yet, he wasn't sure what he wanted to do. Working on the farm was fine for the moment, but he intended to make a better life for him and Jeanie. He already hired five acres that he cropped each year, and would have several acres of his own one day but was in no hurry for it.

Maybe Artie would find a way to buy and sell after the war – perhaps property. He thought the house they were intending to live in could be sold in a few years and a better one bought; he might think of buying a plot of land and building the house he wanted. It was an idea that had appealed to him for a while. His father's cousin was a builder, too, and Alf had spoken about the opportunities after the war. It was something to keep in mind for the future.

Jeanie snuggled up to him on the train. They'd been lucky to get a first-class carriage to themselves, which made it worthwhile paying the extra for the tickets.

'You seem thoughtful?' she asked, looking up at him enquiringly. 'Not regretting it already?'

Artie laughed at the mischief in her face. 'Never,' he told her and bent to kiss her. 'I was just thinking of the future. I shan't be just a worker on Dad's farm forever, Jeanie. I've got plans for us. I want to make a good life for us – to give you a good life, all the nice things that money can buy.'

Jeanie squeezed his hand. 'Just love me always,' she said. 'Yes, it is nice to have special things and perhaps we shall one day – but I want you and a family to love most of all.'

'You've got that already,' he told her and looked down at her. 'I'm not much with words, Jeanie, and sometimes I'm an awkward bugger.' She gave a gurgle of laughter. 'But I do love you and you must know that I always will.'

'Then I'm happy,' she said. 'What is the hotel like in Clacton?'

'It's the Carlton – the biggest, poshest one I could find,' he said and grinned. 'It is right on the front, nearly opposite the pier. I don't know if they'll have any shows on the pier because of the danger of air raids, but the theatres and cinemas in the town itself will be open.' He smiled at her. 'We both work hard, Jeanie – but this week we are going to have as much fun as we possibly can.'

* * *

It was a lovely week and the mild weather held for six of the seven days, fine and sunny despite a sea breeze, but they hardly noticed the weather, because they were having too much fun. They breakfasted late in their room, which was a wonderful treat, for they were normally up at the crack of dawn and out in the sheds. After that, they spent their mornings walking on the beach or the long promenade, enjoying the sights, smells and sounds of the seaside. Sometimes, they shopped, though because of the war there wasn't always much choice on the shelves, but on the third day, they discovered a lovely antique shop tucked away in a side street.

It was run by an elderly man with a beard and when he discovered they were on their honeymoon, he insisted on showing them all his treasures. Amongst the important pieces of furniture, like Chippendale mahogany cabinets and imposing partners' desks, were pretty chairs with cabriole legs and bird-cage tables of dark wood, also little display cabinets filled with beautiful porcelain. Locked away in cabinets in dark corners, were small enamel patch boxes, silver trinkets like snuff boxes and pincushions in the shape of pigs and other animals. Jeanie exclaimed over one of the pigs and Artie asked the price.

'I don't normally sell these,' the shop owner said hesitantly, but when Artie told him they worked on a farm together, he smiled. 'Then this has been waiting for you. I only let my treasures go to the right people.'

He then made Jeanie a present of the pig, refusing any payment. Artie had seen a pair of vases he thought Lizzie would like and a copper kettle on a stand for his mother. He was allowed to buy them and they carried off their treasures with smiles on their faces.

'Come back again and have a cup of tea with me,' the shop owner invited. 'I don't often get nice young folk in my shop.'

Jeanie promised they would. 'I might find something for Mum and Annie,' she told Artie. He laughed at her enthusiasm.

He indicated the kettle and vases. 'I bought these, but I think we'll need another suitcase to carry them home, if we can find one.'

'We can get a brown paper carrier bag,' Jeanie suggested. 'I noticed a small cabinet of sparkly things on my way out so I might buy them something small.'

'Most people take home a stick of rock or some fudge,' Artie said, teasing her.

'Oh, no, not for Mum and Annie,' she said. 'I've only been to the sea at Southend before this. Mum used to take us there for the day when we were kids. When Annie and I went on our own once, we bought some pretty silver earrings for Mum.'

'What about your dad?'

'Oh, he might get some fudge,' Jeanie said and giggled. 'Men don't appreciate earrings as a gift...'

Artie grinned. 'Mine would ask me why I'd wasted my money

if I bought him anything – but he nods his approval if I take something for Mum.'

'Men are funny like that,' Jeanie said. She'd bought him some new shoes as his wedding gift as it was what he'd wanted, and he'd bought her a new suitcase because they'd agreed on practical gifts, but then he'd given her a pretty, silver bangle on their wedding night.

They ate lunch at their hotel and then went to the cinemas for the early-evening show most days, because the streets were dark at night due to the blackout and they didn't know the town well. One evening it was almost dark when they left after enjoying a concert at one of the theatres in the town and were walking back to their hotel when the sudden roar of planes overhead made them look up, startled. There were so many and they came from the direction of the sea, the noise so intense that for a few minutes they were frightened and unsure what to do in case it was an air raid. Several people were running on the street, others took shelter in doorways, but Artie pulled Jeanie down some steps leading to the beach and they crouched behind the sea wall until the planes had passed over. Despite the panic the fly-over had caused, no bombs had been dropped.

'Do you think they were ours or theirs?' Jeanie asked once the noise had gone and she'd stopped feeling trembly inside. Artie had his arm about her and he kissed the top of her head.

'I think they were German,' he told her. 'I don't know where they are headed, but I pity whoever is on the receiving end of the load they carried. I'm glad it wasn't us, though.'

'Let's hope they were intercepted before they got there,' Jeanie said with a little shiver. 'Mum told me how bad it was in London during the Blitz, but I didn't realise how terrifying it must be to suffer an air raid before.' She bit her lip. 'I hope Mum and Dad will be all right.'

Artie squeezed her hand. 'Don't be frightened, love. You can ring your mum when we get back to the hotel – and I doubt they're headed for London. They seem to have turned their attention to places like Bath these days.'

'It's horrid for whoever it is. I was scared just now.'

'Me too, but we were lucky,' Artie said, putting a protective arm about her. 'If they'd been sent to bomb us, we'd have been caught on the street. I've no idea where the nearest shelter is...'

'I think I saw a poster the other day,' Jeanie remarked, 'but I didn't take much notice at the time.'

'Well, they're probably after the factories or the big cities. But it makes you realise how lucky we are to live in the country. We hear a few bangs from the aerodrome now and then when planes crash on landing, as they sometimes do, but as yet we haven't suffered a raid.'

Jeanie shivered. 'Don't tempt fate,' she begged him.

'Let's get back to the hotel. I could do with a drink.'

* * *

Artie made it his business to enquire where the nearest shelters were after that and was given a little map of streets with flags to mark the shelters. The hotel had its own arrangement for guests.

'We've had a few scares,' the receptionist told him. 'However, most of the attacks are on the industrial towns.'

'It makes me feel I ought to be fighting when something like that happens,' Artie told Jeanie later that day. 'I'm not a coward. I knew one of us had to stay and help Dad, and Tom wanted to join the army. He's probably far more use than I am – but sometimes—'

'Don't,' she begged him, putting her arms about him. 'Don't feel guilty or restless, Artie. If the authorities thought you could be spared, you would get your papers regardless of how you felt about it.'

'I suppose,' he admitted. 'Well, I shan't let it spoil our honeymoon...'

'Good.' She leaned up to kiss him. 'It was a bit of a shock and I didn't like it either, Artie, but I know I'm doing a good job.'

Artie agreed to it, but he brooded on the incident, even though he tried not to let Jeanie see, but it had set him wondering again. Jeanie and Frances could manage most of the work on the farm with his father to help them. Perhaps it *was* time he went along to the recruiting office and asked if he was needed. After all, they could take on another land girl to help his father.

He knew that the feeling of guilt had been there at the back of his mind ever since first, Tom, and then, John had been injured and he made up his mind to speak to his father about it when he got home. Artie wouldn't say any more about it to Jeanie, but if his father thought they could manage with an extra land girl, he might do what his conscience had been telling him he ought for some time.

33

Pam heard Arthur grunt beside her and felt him move. He pushed himself up the bed, propped up against the pillows but he was obviously trying not to disturb her. However, she was awake and snapped on the table lamp beside her.

'What is it, love?' she asked. 'Can't you sleep?'

'I think it's a bit of indigestion,' he said and rubbed at his chest. 'Had it a couple of times lately.'

'Why didn't you say?' Pam asked, looking at him in concern. She knew her Arthur and he would never complain unless it was bad. 'Shall I get you some Milk of Magnesia?'

'I had some before I came to bed,' he told her. 'It's been hanging around for a while. I might go up to the doctor in the morning.'

Pam felt a chill at her nape. Arthur never went to the doctor unless he was forced. 'How long have you had pain in your chest?' she asked, her voice calmer than she felt inside.

'A week or so before the wedding,' Arthur replied vaguely. 'I didn't want to say anything – it's probably only a bit of indigestion, love. Nothing to worry over.'

'You should see the doctor though,' Pam said. 'He might give you something stronger than I buy from the chemist.'

'Yeah, I dare say.' Arthur turned his head to look at her. 'I think I'll go down. You go back to sleep, love.'

'I'll come down and make some tea.' Pam put back her covers and got out of bed, shrugging her dressing gown on. 'Don't argue, Arthur. I shouldn't sleep thinking of you down there in pain.'

He said no more but dressed for the day as she went ahead of him out of their bedroom and down to the kitchen. The range was still warm, but she poked it and made it up so that the kettle would boil quicker. Arthur came down a few minutes later. She gave him a large spoonful of the Milk of Magnesia, which he swallowed without complaint. If it was indigestion bothering him that should ease it for a while. Though it was unusual for him to suffer it; he always said he had an iron constitution and it was Pam who knew it if she ate too much rich food.

'Time flies – nearly a week since the wedding; they will be home tomorrow, Artie and Jeanie,' Arthur said as she sat in the chair opposite him and sipped her tea. 'I was that proud of him in church. He looked so smart in that suit. I think he'll make her a good husband – and he'll look after you, love. Artie isn't always good with words; he takes after me in that way – but he's honest and I can trust him. You can rely on him to see things are right, Pam.'

She felt that coldness at her nape again. 'Arthur... Why are you saying this now? I've got you to take care of me. You always have.'

'I've done my best, love,' he told her with a smile of affection. 'I just thought it should be said in case. I'm quite a few years older than you, Pam. It's reasonable to think I'll go afore you – I'm just saying Artie is here and he'll see to things. Tom is the one I always thought would hold the fort if the worst happened, but they've sent him off again and he may not be around for a while if you need him. I reckon marriage will settle Artie. I know he's been restless since John was hurt. I thought he might go off and join up, but he didn't, thank God.'

Pam looked at him in silence. She had a horrid notion that Arthur wasn't telling her everything. Surely he wouldn't talk like this if he thought it was just a bit of indigestion?

'Artie cares a lot for you,' Pam said. 'I know he'll do whatever he thinks right – but I don't want you to leave me, Arthur. Is there something you haven't told me?'

'I'm not sure,' he replied and his eyes met hers briefly. 'I've had a few warnings lately – bit of breathlessness and pain – a lot of pain. I'll see what the doctor says later... but it's best to be prepared.'

'No!' Pam spoke sharply. 'I won't have you just accepting things, Arthur. If you're ill, then I'm coming to the doctor with you. I want to know what they can do to help you.'

'Nay, lass, don't upset yourself,' Arthur said. 'You can come if you wish, but don't fret over me. You know I don't like a fuss.'

Pam looked at him mutinously. She was frightened and angry. Why hadn't he told her he was feeling ill? With Artie and Jeanie away for a week, he'd had too much to do, but he hadn't said a word. She knew he hadn't wanted to worry her but feared he must be in more pain than she knew or he wouldn't have said what he had. Her throat caught in a moment of grief. She didn't want to lose him!

* * *

'It's your heart, Mr Talbot,' Doctor Price told him. 'I can hear the irregular beat and that will cause the breathlessness you've experienced. I can't say without further tests at the hospital, but I believe you have an enlarged heart, probably due to it being overworked. It may be that some arteries are blocked. We can't do very much yet for this kind of thing, I am afraid, but my advice is to rest as much as possible – and I can give you something for the pain. There are some drops to put under your tongue that may ease the condition, if I am right, and we won't really know that until you see a consultant at the hospital.'

'But there is no cure for it?' Arthur asked. 'My uncle had something similar and he died in his fifties.'

'We are learning a lot about these things,' Doctor Price said. 'One day I am sure we'll have more medicines available and perhaps even treatment for blocked arteries, but it doesn't exist yet, I'm afraid.'

'That's it then,' Arthur said. 'I can't see the point of being prodded and pulled about if there is no cure – but I'll take the painkillers and thank you, sir.'

Doctor Price looked grave. 'I'm sorry to give you such news, Mr Talbot... I could be wrong. Won't you let me send you for X-rays and further tests?'

'There was nothing they could do for my uncle,' Arthur replied. 'I doubt there's anything to be done. I'll take the pills and let it take its course – and now I'll bid you good day.'

'Won't you do as the doctor says?' Pam asked him, but she could see by his face that it was useless to argue. She'd insisted on going with him into the doctor's surgery, because she knew he wouldn't tell her everything if the news was bad. He would just shut it out of his mind and get on with things. Arthur had made up his mind and he wouldn't change it. She would need to use gentle persuasion, because she wasn't ready to lose her Arthur. She couldn't even bear to think about it.

* * *

'You knew what he was going to say before you went, didn't you?' Pam accused as they drove home. 'I never knew your uncle had a bad heart, Arthur.'

'He was an invalid for years with it,' Arthur told her. 'I spoke to my cousin about his father after the wedding, and from what he told me, I guessed it might be the same trouble – our grandfather had it, too, so he told me.'

Pam was silenced. He'd obviously been brooding over this since the wedding. Now he'd made up his mind to it that there was no hope.

'How long did your uncle live with it?'

'A couple of years or so, I think,' Arthur replied as they drew into the yard. 'If there's nothing to be done, there's no point in upsetting yourself, Pam. I'll take the pills and I'll leave the hard work to Artie and the girls. Now don't go saying anything to anyone. I'll speak to Artie about it myself – and perhaps we'll get another land girl to help if they will let us.'

'Couldn't we get Tom home?' Pam asked. 'If we need him on the land... I know it is what he would want.'

'Tom is doing what he has to do and I won't have him told,' Arthur said firmly. 'I don't want John or the girls to know either – not yet anyway. I will tell Artie and we'll carry on as always, but I'll spend more time in the house. You'll soon be sick of me being under your feet all the time.'

'Don't be daft!' Pam's voice was harsh, but it was hurting her because she could not accept that Arthur was so ill. She had suspected nothing and what anger she had was at herself. She'd been so wrapped up in the wedding and looking after them all – and she'd taken on young George. His pranks in the yard were no trouble, but Arthur could have done without his yelling and rushing around. 'I'm sorry. I shouldn't have taken my sister's boy...' Her throat caught with the tears she was fighting.

Arthur turned to look at her and smiled in his gentle way. 'I'm glad you did, love. He's a decent lad and will be a help to you one day. Artie says he keeps pestering him to let him learn more about milking the cows. I'm not going to die tomorrow. I'll fight it, I promise, but in my own way.'

Pam sniffed, refusing to cry, though she knew she would when she was alone. 'You always were too stubborn for your own good,' she told him as she got out of the car and went into the house. Frances was there with George. Pam frowned at him. 'What are you doing home? Why aren't you at school?'

'It's Saturday,' George said indignantly. 'Blimey, it's bad enough 'avin' ter go five days a week, Aunt Pam.'

'Oh, in that case where are Susan and Angela?' Pam swallowed hard; she'd forgotten it was a Saturday. Her head went up as she fought the emotion that threatened to undo her; she mustn't let anyone see what she was suffering.

'They went to Lizzie's house to have their hair done,' Frances supplied the answer. 'George helped me with the chores this morning. He did most of the mucking out while I milked the cows and then we fed them together.'

'That was a good boy,' Pam said and forced a smile. 'I think it deserves sixpence for sweets, don't you?'

'Yeah. Cor, you're a smasher, Aunt Pam, thanks,' George said. 'You ain't forgotten that Billy is comin' over fer his tea today on the bus, 'ave yer?' It was Billy's second visit; they'd got on well the first time and George was looking forward to him coming.

'Yes, I had,' Pam said and decided to pull herself together. Arthur hadn't followed her in and she knew he'd gone for a walk to sort his own thoughts out. Her distress had upset him and that wouldn't do. Arthur needed her to be strong and carry on as she always had. The house couldn't run without her and the workers needed to be fed. She had too much to do to let her own worries intrude into her thoughts all the time. 'I'll bake some jam tarts and make egg sandwiches,' she promised George. 'Why don't you go for a ride on the bike Artie did up for you?'

'I was thinking he'd be home soon,' George said hopefully.

'Not until late today,' Pam said, holding back a sigh. She wanted Artie back too. Perhaps he could persuade Arthur to have the tests the doctor had suggested...

* * *

The homecoming was noisy and happy, everyone chattering and laughing as gifts were distributed. Pam received her copper kettle with a hug for her son and Jeanie, and George was delighted with his sticks of peppermint rock. Frances liked the big bag of fudge she was given and Arthur put his on the mantel with a grunt.

Jeanie showed them the silver pincushion she'd been given, explaining it was a gift from the elderly shop owner. 'He told us his name was Mr Sylvester, and he has no family. His only son was killed at the start of the war and his wife died a few years ago. He was so nice, and lonely, I think. We went to see him again and had tea with him – and Artie bought this for me.' She showed them a beautiful Victorian gold brooch in the form of a love knot.

'He almost gave it to us,' Artie said. 'He knew you liked it. Jeanie bought two pieces of silver jewellery for her mum and Annie, but the brooch was nearly five pounds. I said I'd buy it and he said we could have it for two, so we did.'

'That was nice of him,' Pam said. 'It sounds as if you had a lovely time?'

'It was wonderful,' Jeanie said. 'We bought something for Lizzie, too. I'll take it down later.'

'She will be here for supper,' Pam said. 'I think she has asked a friend to look after Archie for a while so she doesn't have to wake him if he is sleeping – he's been keeping her awake a lot just lately.'

'Is he all right?' Jeanie said at once. 'Not ill?'

'No, just a bit of a tummy upset, so Lizzie says...'

'Oh, good,' Jeanie said and then looked at Pam. 'Are you upset over something?'

'No,' Pam lied. 'Nothing at all, love. I'm glad you had such a lovely time.' She gave her a quick hug. It wouldn't do to let anyone see that inside her heart was breaking.

34

Artie stood looking out across the land as a slight summer mist curled away and was gone. It had rained all night and the moisture had just made the haze hang because it was already warming again in the spring sunshine. He frowned, wondering how he would approach the subject of his leaving to join the army. Jeanie wouldn't be happy and his father might feel he was deserting him.

'Ah, there you are son,' his father's voice behind him made him turn. He threw his half-finished cigarette down and ground it beneath his boot. 'I wanted to talk to you.'

'Something wrong?' Artie asked, because he hadn't often seen that desperate look in his father's eyes. 'It isn't John...?'

'No, lad, it's not your brothers or your mother or your sisters,' Arthur said heavily. 'But it's not good news...'

Artie's heart sank as he looked at him and something triggered in his brain. 'You're ill, Dad. I've seen you rubbing your chest a few times, but you said it was indigestion?' He'd noticed his father taking it easy now and then but assumed it was just the natural slowing down that came with age.

'Aye, I hoped it might be,' Arthur said, 'but it's my heart, lad. If I take it easy, I might get a few years yet. I shan't be able to do much in future – driving the tractor is about all I can manage... so you are going to have to do a lot more.'

'What does the doctor say?' Artie pushed away the torrent of protest and rage at the unfairness of life that flared up in his head. He wasn't a man to speak of feelings, but he'd always thought the world of his father, looked up to him and respected him.

'Oh, he wants me to have tests and things – but it's what my uncle died of, and I don't see the point of being mauled about if they can't do anything for me. They will tell me to rest and not to get upset and that's about it. Nothing much they can do – Doctor Price told us...'

'So that is what is upsetting Mum,' Artie said. 'Jeanie said there was something.' He looked at his father. His own hopes of joining the army had vanished like the mist. 'Don't you think you owe it to her to at least try, Dad? I'll take you into the hospital – and don't worry about the work, we'll get through. We might get another land girl if they will let us, but I can manage and I'll look after everyone if anything happens to you – but Mum loves you and needs you. It's only fair to try.'

'I suppose you are right,' Arthur acknowledged, giving in with a sigh. 'I'll leave it to you to arrange then, lad.' He smiled. 'I'm glad you're back. I told your mother she could rely on you.'

Artie grinned. 'I wondered for a few minutes if we'd get back,' he said. 'A fleet of planes went over one evening, heading in from the sea. They raided somewhere else along the coast that night, but it could have been us – this is a bastard war, Dad! I wish it was done.'

'Aye, so do I, lad,' Arthur replied. 'And don't think I don't know what it is costing you to stay here when you're itching to fight – but you *are* doing your bit, Artie. If we can't feed our people, then the buggers will win because we'll have to capitulate.'

Artie met his eyes and nodded. 'I'm glad to be here,' he told his father. 'I'll be around when you need me, don't you fret.'

'I know,' Arthur said. 'Now, tell me, what are we planning for today?'

* * *

So that was it then. Artie knew he had no choice now. His father wasn't one to make a fuss. He'd been putting up with the pain for a while, saying nothing, hoping it would go. Artie had wondered, seeing him rubbing at his chest a few times, but his father hadn't complained. Well, he wouldn't. It must have been bad for him to let on to his wife, because he'd known it would worry her.

Artie shrugged off his own disappointment. He'd always known his place was here on the farm, that one day he and Tom would have to run it between them for the sake of the family; he just hadn't expected it to be any time soon. His father wasn't sixty yet.

Maybe the hospital would have another opinion; Artie sincerely hoped so, for everyone's sake, but particularly his mother's. Pam Talbot was a very capable woman and she ran the house as Arthur had always run the farm, but she would miss him terribly if the worst happened. She was some years younger than Arthur – young enough to marry again, though Artie couldn't see her doing that. She was too young to be a widow!

Artie frowned and shook his head. It wasn't something he wanted to think about. For now, he would just try to make sure his father didn't do more than he ought. No more loading trailers with muck and spreading it on the fields, and no milking or carrying heavy bales. It was going to make more work for Artie, but he'd never shirked from his duty. Had young George been a few years older, he could have helped more. He was a willing lad and it was a good thing they'd taken him on. There were plenty of jobs he could do, like carrying in the coal and helping with the easier jobs in the yard when he wasn't at school – he'd be company for Angela too, when Susan went off to college and he and Jeanie moved into their own home.

His father's illness had cast a bit of a cloud over things. The wedding and honeymoon had lifted life, making Artie feel freer and happier than he had for a long time. He loved Jeanie and wanted to make a good life for her, but some of his plans would have to be put aside for the moment. He was going to be too busy on the farm for anything else. It wasn't likely they would get another land girl. They were in demand these days, with so many men either in the forces or dead in some foreign land; a lot of men would never come back to their families or their jobs.

Artie felt a chill at the nape of his neck. If Tom or John were killed... But no, he couldn't allow himself to think of such a bleak future. It was bad enough that his father was ill. Shaking off his mood, he straightened his back. Time to stop brooding and get on with it. His long hours were going to be even longer in future...

35

Frances got off the bus that sunny Thursday and started to walk towards the farm. She was smiling, thinking about her successful morning; she'd managed to buy quite a few things Pam needed. Feeling happy and relaxed, she didn't notice anything amiss until the man suddenly appeared from behind the trees. He looked at her for a moment and then sneered.

'Thought I'd gone for good, did you, Frances?' Roy asked, leering at her as she looked about for help. 'Your friends aren't around. The one with the gun went off on his tractor – so now you and me are going to have a little chat...'

'No...' Frances stared at him, feeling anger well up inside her.. Who the hell did he think he was? He had no right to follow her or interfere in her life. 'I don't need anyone to protect me. I can cope with a little worm like you on my own.'

Roy gave a cry of fury and launched at her. Frances dropped her parcels and was ready. She struck at his face as he grabbed for her arm, pressing her fingers into his right eye, and then kneed him hard in the stomach. He reeled back, shrieking and clearly in pain, and she saw he had a dribble of blood running from the side of his mouth. She must have really hurt him.

'Bitch...' he muttered. 'I'll kill you for this...'

'No you won't,' Frances said, suddenly her fear of him had gone. She looked at him in disgust. 'You won't kill me because my friends know all about you – and I've written it all down. If anything happens to me, you will be a suspect – and when they get you, you'll hang.' She smiled. 'I'm no good to you if I won't work, Roy. Kill me and you'll be the one who suffers most...'

'Bitch...' Roy stared at her for a long moment, obviously puzzled. 'You've changed...'

'Yes, I have,' she said, meeting his wary gaze. 'I'm not afraid of you any more. Roy stood there staring her at her, his right eye watering, one hand holding his stomach, looking wary and indecisive. Frances guessed he was considering another attack but she just stared at him fiercely and he looked down. Frances knew that she'd won.

Just as she bent to pick up her parcels, a military car pulled up beside her on the road and the driver opened his door. 'Are you all right, Frances?' he asked giving Roy a sharp stare.

She turned her head to look at him. 'Yes, thank you, Frank. Were you coming to see us?'

Frank got out of the car. He looked from her to Roy who was standing uncomfortably a few feet away from her. 'Was this bloke bothering you, Frances?' He was tall and strong and his uniform gave him an air of authority. She saw the flash of fear in Roy's eyes and knew he was fearful of any kind of police.

'Oh no,' she said and smiled at Frank. 'He doesn't bother me at all.' She walked to his side. 'Have you got time to come for a cup of tea? I am sure Pam has the kettle on.'

'I was hoping you might let me take you for a drink?' Frank said and opened his car door for her.

Frances watched as Roy turned and walked off. She got into the car and let Roy drive her away.

'Are you sure you're all right?' he asked, giving her a sideways glance. 'It's not my business, but if someone was upsetting you, I'd deal with him...'

'Thank you,' she replied with a little smile. 'But I think *I* just did.'

She had a feeling that Roy wouldn't bother her again. He must realise now that she had friends, more than he'd known, but most important of all, she had stood up to him herself. She'd hurt him. He might hate her and want revenge, but he would no longer think of her as being weak and easy to manipulate. He'd realise that it wasn't worth the effort to pursue her. She smiled at Frank. Frances was going to forget about the unpleasant incident and enjoy herself with Frank.

* * *

After a week of pondering over it, Frances had decided she would tell Frank everything. It was her day off and he was taking her out for a meal at a small pub near the River Ouse in Ely, and it was to be a celebration of her birthday. She had an idea he might be going to say something important to her, so when he came to the farm to collect her in his car, she turned to look at him.

'I want you to know the truth about me,' she told him and, before he could protest: 'No, you *have* to know Frank. I don't want you to find out one day and hate me because of what I did.'

'I could never do that,' he said and looked at her in such a loving way that her courage almost failed her. 'I think you know I am in love with you, Frances.'

Her eyes stung with unshed tears, but she lifted her head and began her story.

Frank let her go until the end, perhaps judging that she needed to tell him all of her shame and her pain at what Roy had forced her to do. He sat in silence for a moment, then, 'Look at me, my darling...'

Frances raised her eyes to his; the tenderness hadn't gone from his gaze and she caught back a sob. 'You can't still love me...'

'What you told me just makes me more protective of you,' he said softly. 'I want to look after you for the rest of our lives – I want you to be my wife, Frances. I love you – more than I ever thought possible.'

'I'm not worthy of you...' she choked, eyes wet.

'Say that again and I'll be cross,' Frank murmured and then leaned in to kiss her on the mouth. 'I love you and you have nothing to be ashamed of. If I ever meet the man who harmed you again, I'll kill him. It was him the other day when I stopped, wasn't it?' She gave a little nod. 'If I'd known, I would have dealt with him in a way that he wouldn't have liked, but you sent him away and that's the end of it – and that's all you'll hear from me on the subject.'

Frances felt suddenly cold, because she knew he meant what he'd just said. If Roy ever bothered her again, Frank would kill him. She prayed they would never meet. She didn't want Frank to be punished for murder – however just it might be, it was against the law and she couldn't lose Frank for such a reason.

'I pray he will never be foolish enough to return,' she said and reached for his hand. 'He came looking for me once. I changed my name from Cathy Bristow to Frances Grant to hide from him, but after he read about my rescuing Billy from the river, he recognised me. John Talbot saw him attack me and went for him and then Artie arrived and threatened him with a gun. He went off as fast as he could...' Frances knew that the Talbot brothers would fight Roy if he came, but they wouldn't kill him – Frank would if he dared to attempt anything like that again.

'Now we are going to forget him and have a lovely day,' Frank said and took a small leather box from his pocket. 'I was going to propose over champagne at lunch if I could get some – but I'll say it now. Will you marry me, Frances? I should be proud to make you my wife.'

'Yes, please, Frank! I do love you. I had to tell you because I love—' Her words were cut off as he drew her into his arms and kissed her passionately.

'We'll visit my home together if we can both get leave,' Frank said. 'We might get a special licence and get married there. I'm expecting to be stationed at the airfield in Sutton for the rest of the war. It must be guarded and I'm unlikely to be sent anywhere else. My parents would like us to marry in Yorkshire so they can be there – but if we can't get a long enough leave, we can be married here. I'd like it to be soon, but that's up to you, Frances.' Frances felt all her doubts slip away. She had shaken off her fears and her bitterness had been gradually healing these past months. She felt free and ready to be happy again.

'Yes, as soon as possible,' she replied as he slipped the pretty diamond and sapphire three-stone ring on her left hand. Tears stung her eyes, but they were tears of happiness. She'd never believed that it would happen to her and she was overwhelmed by a feeling of love and gratitude, too. She was so lucky! 'Oh, Frank, I'm so happy. I can't wait for us to be married.'

'We shall be – and it will be forever. I shan't let you down, Frances. When the war is over, we'll find a nice home back in Yorkshire, where you'll be safe and can do whatever makes you happy.'

'It sounds wonderful,' she whispered, smiling through misty eyes. 'I'd like to continue to work for Mr Talbot as long as I can, though...'

'No reason why not if you're happy there,' Frank said and smiled. 'We'll work something out, love. Now let's go and celebrate your birthday *and* our engagement.'

* * *

Frances's thoughts were free of guilt and pain for the first time in years. She cuddled up in bed, remembering her happy day. How pleasant it had been in the restaurant of the quaint old pub that Frank had taken her to for lunch. They'd watched a swan family glide by, four cygnets paddling fast to keep up with their majestic parents. The sun had shone and everything had been perfect. She could hardly believe that she was engaged to be married, even though both Jeanie and Pam had told her they'd fully expected Frank to ask her.

He didn't hate her or despise her for letting herself be used the way she had; he'd understood that she had no choice. Frances felt free in a way that she hadn't done for years, even when Derek was kind to her. She realised now that she'd been grateful to Derek for his protective care, but she hadn't loved him as she loved Frank.

He'd talked about his parents, his home, and his ambition to be a vet, speaking enthusiastically of their life together in the peace and quiet of Yorkshire.

'We'll live in a nice village in the centre of the Dales,' he'd told her. 'My parents have a farm not far away, but you would find that too isolated. In a village, you can make friends.'

Frances had nodded, feeling too happy to question his dream of their future. She was happy enough living on the farm with the Talbot family but all she wanted was to be with Frank and have their own family.

'I'll arrange my leave and then speak to Mr Talbot about yours,' Frank had told her as he'd brought her home to the farm. 'I'm not sure how long I can wangle, but I'll try for a week – and I'll get a special licence so we can be married at my home.'

Frances had agreed to everything he suggested. She had no family and few friends. The Talbots were the closest she had to family, but if Frank wanted the wedding in Yorkshire, she would simply tell them on her return. She was sure they wouldn't mind.

Sighing, she snuggled down into the covers. If Mr Talbot succeeded in getting another land girl, Frances would have to look for a house to let so that she and Frank had somewhere of their own to be together when he was off duty. She'd been told by Jeanie that Arthur was ill, which had shocked her. He was a good man. It would be a tragedy if he died too soon.

An air of sadness lay over the Talbots of late, which was understandable when the head of the family was so ill. Frances was aware of it and saddened, because they were usually such a happy bunch. Would Tom and John get leave to see their father? she wondered. She prayed that Mr Talbot might get better news at the hospital when he went for his tests... It would just be too awful if he were to die while his sons were away fighting.

36

The staff car was open-topped and had seen better days, any suspension it had ever had, long gone to pot. It was hot and his skin crawled with sweat that trickled down his back. Tom wiped his forehead, glancing up at the unrelenting sun above. They had another hour or so to complete their run. It was the third they'd made to various groups with much-needed supplies, through desert terrain that reflected the heat and made your throat ache with the need for water. Their guide sat beside him, long legs stretched out, relaxed, eyes closed, now and again chewing gum.

'So where is this place then?' Tom asked, feeling irritated that the man could be so oblivious to the burning heat. 'How much longer?'

'About an hour, mebbe two,' Brigger replied and yawned. 'It is over there somewhere...' he pointed to a high range of sand dunes in the distance. 'No signposts out here, mate.' His voice had a faint Australian drawl that made him seem careless, but Tom knew he was the best guide. He'd been out here a long time and knew the desert well, which was why they'd assigned him to Tom's group.

'Is there fresh water anywhere near us?'

'Over there...' Brigger pointed to the same dunes. 'Providing it's still there and still drinkable.'

'What do you mean?' Tom frowned. 'Surely no one would contaminate it out here? It's madness when it's the only oasis for miles...'

'The desert people wouldn't, but it happens for various reasons. Calm down, mate. We've got plenty of water in the lorry behind.'

The water they were carrying tasted stale to Tom; it was perfectly drinkable but had the tang of the wooden barrels. 'Tastes disgusting...' he muttered and Brigger chuckled.

'You'll get used to it, mate.' He settled back and closed his eyes.

Tom felt like telling him to sit up and pay attention, but it was the attitude many of the men who had been out here a while had adopted. They were a tough breed, unheeding of rules, and he'd soon learned that few of them bothered to salute or acknowledge rank, unless sharply reminded. He could have ordered him to change places and drive but preferred to be at the wheel of his open-topped staff car himself.

Glancing over his shoulder, he saw the long line of heavily laden lorries following. The supplies they carried ranged from food and drink, clothing, post from home, to much-needed small ammunition. The groups they were supplying had been doing a lot of damage to enemy outposts, attacking in convoys of two or three vehicles and causing as much damage to planes, munition dumps and other strategic operations as they could. The Germans had had it their own way for too long, making advances despite all the beleaguered Allied troops could do to stop them, but these lightning attacks by maverick units, who came and went with no warning, had taken them by surprise and they were suffering setbacks, small perhaps but enough to make a difference.

The distant whine of an aeroplane engine made Tom look up, shading his eyes. He spotted the dark shadow coming out of the sun. Before he could say a word, Brigger was suddenly alert, scanning the sky with his powerful binoculars. He swore loudly.

'The bugger is coming straight for us...' Snatching up his machine gun, he snarled at Tom. 'Head for the dunes for all you're worth!'

A hail of gunfire was directed at the convoy, sand spurting up in showers as the plane fired its guns at them. Tom drove as fast as he could, but then, realising that the plane was a loner and going for the lorries, he swerved and took them back.

'Fire at the bastard...' he instructed Brigger.

One of the trucks had been hit, fortunately not the one carrying ammunition, which was at the tail end. Several of them had stopped and men were now shooting at the plane as it swooped overhead. Brigger was firing his gun for all his worth as the plane passed across their path after hitting yet another lorry. Because they had turned back, they were directly in the line of fire and both men ducked as they came under another hail of shots.

Tom swerved the car to one side and Brigger was thrown off balance but recovered before the pilot could turn and make another run at them. Brigger swivelled round and fired another round and then gave a yell of triumph as his shots shattered the glass screen at the side of the plane. It veered off course and they saw smoke coming from it as it descended rapidly and then crashed into the sand, where it exploded, flames and smoke flaring into the sky. He gave a grunt of satisfaction, but Tom had stopped the car and was out, running towards the vehicles that had been hit.

Several men were lying on the ground, where they had been thrown as an engine was hit and had exploded, bursting into flames. Three of them were injured and another was dead. Further down the line, the second truck to be hit had fared better and was undamaged, apart from blown tyres and some holes in the side.

Tom oversaw the transfer of the wounded men to the back of another truck, where they could be treated. The dead man was taken too. The orders out here decreed that you didn't stop to bury men killed in action, but Tom wasn't leaving one of his men to have his bones picked clean by the birds of prey that were already circling. Where did the damned things come from? There had been no sign of them until the attack had left men bleeding on the sand.

'We don't take the dead or the wounded if they slow us down,' Brigger observed as Tom returned to his staff car. He aimed a gob of spit at one of the birds. 'That pilot may not have been alone and the smoke will have been seen.'

'Bugger the smoke and bugger you,' Tom retorted. 'We'll move as fast as we can, but I'm not leaving them – any of them.' He ran an eye over the convoy. 'What have we lost?' He spoke to his sergeant who had been organising a transfer of goods from the lorry with the bullet-riddled tyres.

'Tents, various clothing – and the men's post, sir,' Sergeant Arnold said and Tom nodded. 'We're lucky he didn't get the ammunition.'

'We'll have to leave the truck with shot tyres here. One of you can return and finish unloading it and make a second journey, but we need to get the rest of the convoy over there...' He pointed to the dunes. 'We'd better increase the pace if we can.'

'Yes, sir!' Sergeant Arnold saluted. 'I'll get them moving again.'

Within minutes, the convoy was on its way. Tom walked back to his staff car and Brigger followed. 'How much longer once we get past the dunes?' he asked.

'There's an old fort or palace; ruins really, but shelter of a kind,' Brigger replied. 'You'll see it as soon as we've passed the dunes – an hour at most.'

Tom nodded. 'Good. I don't want to lose another lorry – or the men who have been injured. Is there a doctor with this group?' It wasn't always the case. These surprise attack units were basic and had to be able to move around fast, to abandon one base and find another if they were discovered.

'Yes, but he doesn't have much in the way of medical supplies.'

'I'm not expecting a hospital, Brigger, just some relief for my men. I'll patch them up myself if I must.'

Brigger looked at him for a moment and then nodded. 'Good for you, mate. Wake me in half an hour...' He leaned back and closed his eyes.

Tom suppressed the urge to hit him. Brigger had saved most of the convoy with his excellent shooting and they hadn't lost as much of their precious supplies as they might have. There was no point in imposing discipline out here; it was more important to keep a cool head under fire.

'You are an impertinent bugger, Brigger, and if we were back in England I'd have you on a charge,' he said in a conversational tone. 'But thank you.'

Brigger tipped his hat back and grinned at him. 'Thank you, sir, that was a nifty piece of driving back there...'

37

John was in the officers' mess that morning towards the end of May when he read the letter from Artie. His brother seldom wrote to him and he'd realised before he opened it that it must be important. He frowned over the few lines Artie had penned in his execrable scrawl. Their father was very ill. He'd been to the hospital recently and had the tests the doctor had recommended and it was as he'd feared.

> *I wouldn't have written if it wasn't certain. I know you're having a rotten time and must be tired, John, but try to get leave when you can and pop home, even if it is only for a few hours. Mum is dreadfully upset, though trying to hide it. There is no way I can contact Tom at the moment, though I've written – but I doubt he will get it. If he does, he probably won't be able to get leave. I was sure you would want to know. Sorry it's bad news. Come when you can.*
>
> *Regards, Artie*

John frowned over the letter for several minutes. He hadn't

had leave since he'd visited Lucy in Cambridge, nearly two months or more ago now. They had been flying constant missions and John hadn't asked for a pass, leaving that for the men with wives and children. His son was being well cared for and loved. John could do nothing for him yet, though one day, if God spared him, he would be there for Jonny. He took a few hours off to rest when he was so tired that he knew he wasn't fit to fly, but to go home he needed a couple of days at least. The news that his father was ill shocked him; it seemed impossible. His father always seemed just the same, indestructible. John had always expected life on the farm to just go on forever.

'Bad news, Talbot?' The voice of his commander broke into his thoughts.

'My father is very ill,' he replied. He still felt dazed by it, unable to really take it on board. 'My brother says I should go home for a visit – but—'

A firm hand descended on his shoulder. 'It's time you took a few days off,' Dave Carson told him. 'I've been meaning to speak to you about it, Talbot. We all need a break and you haven't taken one in months now. I'll arrange a special pass for you.'

John stared at him and then inclined his head. He'd been trying to push the news away in the hope that it would just disappear. His father couldn't be that ill! It hit him like a punch to his guts. It wasn't supposed to be like this – he was fighting to keep his family safe... but Faith's death and now his father's illness seemed to make a mockery of all he believed.

'Yes, I must go,' he managed at last. 'My mother is very upset – and my eldest brother is serving overseas.'

'Then go while you can,' Dave Carson told him. 'I'll be needing you for an important mission soon, Talbot. Take three days – it may be a long time before you get another home leave.'

'Yes, sir. Thank you.' John saluted. It was a relief to have the decision taken from him.

* * *

Pam was sitting at the kitchen table peeling potatoes in a bowl of water when John walked in. She looked up and saw him and burst into tears. John rushed to fold his arms around her, his heart catching. He'd never seen his mother cry before, even when they'd heard Tom was missing in action.

'Oh, John,' was all she said as she wept into his shoulder. 'What am I going to do without him?'

'Don't, Mum,' he said huskily. 'Don't think that way. He might go on for a long time – you know how stubborn he is...'

She gave a strangled laugh and drew back, accepting his large white handkerchief to dry her eyes. 'I'm sorry, love. I didn't mean to weep all over you. It's just... I've worried over you and Tom. I never even gave a thought to your father. I can't believe I didn't know...' Her eyes were filled with pain. 'I should have known, John. I should have seen it. I love him so much...'

'I don't suppose he wanted you to know,' John said. 'He would never want to worry you, Mum.'

'I know.' She lifted her head. 'Don't you tell him I burst into tears when I saw you.'

'I shan't,' he said and smiled at her. 'I'm sorry I shan't be around much to help for a while. I know I am responsible for Jonny, but I'm not sure what I can do – perhaps pay for a girl to help you?'

'Don't be daft!' Pam said sharply. 'Jonny is my pleasure, not a burden. I've got Lizzie, Jeanie and Frances to help me. Frances is a nice girl, John, much happier now than when she came to us.

She is engaged to that young man of hers and I think they mean to marry soon.'

'Let's hope she doesn't leave you in the lurch.'

'Oh, I don't think she will. Frank is fixed here for the time being and she enjoys her work, so there is no reason for her to leave.'

'You haven't seen any more of that devil who tried to hurt her?'

'No. I think you and Artie threw a scare into him,' Pam told him with a faint smile. 'I doubt he would come here again in a hurry.'

'Good...' John sat down at the table. 'Where is Dad?'

'He went out for a bit of a walk.' His mother reached for the kettle. 'I'll make us a cup of tea.'

'Yes. It's nice to have you to myself again for a while,' John told her. 'We usually have a houseful these days.'

'Yes, we do,' she agreed. 'Some of the airmen pop in now and then too. I always find something to give them.'

John smiled at her. 'Of course you do,' he said. 'How is George settling in? Has he broken anything recently?'

'No, of course not,' Pam said. 'Well, only one of my pudding bowls when he and Angela were fighting over who should lick it out when I'd been making a cake.' She looked at him, searching his face. 'What about you, John? You look very tired, love.'

'We've been working constantly,' he said. 'I expect you've read about it in the papers. I haven't had time to come home.'

'I thought perhaps it was too painful for you?'

'Yes, and no,' John replied thoughtfully. 'I love Jonny, but every time I see him, I think of her. She ought to be here, Mum.'

'Yes, I know,' Pam said sympathetically. 'When I think how little time you had together and how lucky I've been, it makes me want to rage at the world. It was a cruel thing, John.' She hesitated, then, 'I know you don't think so now – but it will ease in time. One day...' She left the rest unsaid as his eyes met hers. 'I won't say any more.'

'I know what you want to say, Mum...' John hesitated. 'There is a girl I met. She nursed me when I was in Addenbrooke's and we are friends. I know I will find a life again one day – but it won't be until the war is over. I don't feel that would be right.'

'Are you...' she hesitated, a little surprised. 'This girl...?'

'In love with Lucy? No, I'm not – but she is a nice girl, Mum, and Jonny will need a mother one day.'

'Don't marry just for that,' she said quickly. 'Take your time, John, please. I can look after your son for as long as you wish.'

'I know.' He met her gaze. 'Did you love Dad when you married him?'

'Not at first,' she said, catching her breath on a strangled sob. 'He knew I wasn't ready to love, but he loved me and wanted to protect me – but I was lucky. I soon came to realise what a wonderful man I'd married and I loved him – I still do...'

'The same as Tom's father?' John persisted.

His mother considered for a moment. 'Not the same – but after a while, I loved him even more. I think there are many kinds of love and you have to open your heart to them.'

John nodded. 'Faith was my ideal – so beautiful. Lucy isn't as stunning, but she is warm and genuine. Don't worry, Mum. I shan't make any decisions in a hurry.'

His mother was clearly considering her answer when the kitchen door opened and Arthur walked in, followed by Artie and Jeanie. The chance for such conversation was over in the flurry of greetings that followed.

John's mother soon had cups of tea and food for all of them and within a few minutes, Frances and Lizzie arrived, Frances carrying Archie in her arms and looking happy and relaxed.

'Is that Jonny I can hear?' Frances said, putting Archie back into his mother's arms. 'I'll fetch him down.' She looked at John. 'You'll be surprised at how much he has grown since you were last here.'

She went off up the stairs and the wails ceased as little Jonny was picked up and brought back down to the kitchen, where Frances first changed his nappy and then gave him his bottle.

'Come and have your docky, Frances,' Pam told her. 'Give the baby to John.'

Frances did as she was bid.

John cradled his son in his arms. He looked at his father across the kitchen and saw him smile and nod his head.

'He's starting to look more like you, lad,' Arthur said. 'I reckon he'll be a charmer when he grows up – have all the girls running after him.'

'He's beautiful,' John said. 'I think he has my nose – but his eyes are just like Faith's.'

He smiled down at his son. For perhaps the first time, it hadn't sent a dagger to his heart when he spoke Faith's name. This child in his arms was his, a living reminder of the girl he'd loved and lost. Here with most of his family, he knew he was home. It had been a long, long time since he'd felt this way and his throat closed with emotion. He wanted to ask his father how he was but knew he couldn't – not with everyone looking and listening. Perhaps later they could have a quiet moment alone...

38

'I was sorry to send bad news, John,' Artie said as they walked to the pub together that evening. 'But it's best that you have the chance to come home.'

'Have they said how long he's got?' John asked. 'He doesn't look ill – a bit tired and grey, but otherwise just the same.'

'As far as I know, they haven't mentioned anything like that,' Artie replied. 'Just told him to take it easy and rest; they gave him something for the pain, but I saw him behind the haystack the other day and he was clutching his chest and in a lot of pain until the drops helped. He puts them under his tongue.'

John nodded. 'He's stubborn. He won't give in – won't let us see he is suffering unless he can't control it.'

'I tried to help him once,' Artie said. 'He just told me to go away and leave him for a bit. I think he's had this longer than he lets on.'

John offered him a cigarette and Artie lit up. 'Are you going to be able to manage with just a couple of girls to help?'

'It won't be easy. I didn't realise how much Dad still did until this past week or two. Jeanie and Frances work hard, but there are things they can't be asked to do – heavy lifting and getting under machinery to free it – and it isn't easy to manage when something is clogging up, though the girls can drive the tractors.'

'I'd offer to help while I'm here, but I'm not sure I'd be much use.'

Artie smiled wryly. 'It doesn't work like that, John. It will be when it's raining, the ground is soggy and the tractor gets bogged down in muck and I have to unload a trailer filled with potatoes alone to free it... Sod's Law.'

'I've never liked farming,' John said and gave a harsh laugh. 'Give me a bucket of plaster and I'll work happily all day, but working in all weathers as you do...' He shook his head. 'You need Tom home. There is too much work for one man.'

'Pray God he gets back,' Artie replied. He drew heavily on his cigarette. 'If he doesn't—'

'Don't even think about it,' John suppressed a shudder. 'Mum couldn't take that – it would kill her to lose them both.'

'I know...' Artie stopped as they reached the pub. 'No good dwelling on it. Once the war is over, I'll find a man to help out... but God knows when that will be.'

'It's going to take a concerted effort,' John admitted. 'We weren't prepared for this war, Artie. I doubt anyone guessed how strong the Germans would be. We have to hope that now the Americans are in we can increase the pressure on them, make the enemy grind to a halt – but I think it will be some time yet.'

'Let's have a drink,' Artie said. 'I could do with a stiff whisky – if they have anything. They ran out of beer last week...' He swore softly and led the way inside.

* * *

John's leave went too quickly. Before he returned to his base, he spoke to his father, but apart from saying that he was fine and would see the war out, Arthur couldn't be brought to speak about himself.

'You take care of yourself, John,' his father told him. 'I know you're doing an important job – but don't be a hero. Your mother needs you home, and so do I, son – your boy, too.'

'I know – but I must do my duty, Dad. We have a big push coming up – something important. I haven't been told anything and I couldn't say if I had, but I know it is something special.'

'Well, do your best,' his father said and placed a hand on his shoulder. 'I know I wasn't best pleased when you didn't want to come on the land, John – but that doesn't mean I think any the less of you. I'm proud of what you're doing.'

John's throat was tight with emotion. He wanted to throw his arms around his father and hug him, but Arthur Talbot wasn't one for a show of affection.

'Artie is doing a good job,' he managed to say. 'He'll look after things on the land and so will Tom when he can. I'll always look after Mum.'

'I know that,' his father said. 'Don't fret, lad. I've had a good life and when my time comes, I'll go easy. I'm a simple man and I believe in God. So don't let your mother break her heart over me.'

'I'll try my best,' John promised, then, suddenly fierce. 'You fight it, Dad. Fight it for all you're worth.'

'Aye, I'll do that...'

* * *

Back at base camp, John listened to the briefing. They were going to attack Cologne in Germany. It would be a mass attack – the first RAF thousand-bomber raid. The destruction caused by such a mighty force would be devastating. Lying on his bunk thinking about it, John felt his guts turn. He'd been on some dangerous missions – but this was going to be harrowing.

Against the death and destruction he and his crew would be dealing out, the struggle of one man against illness was a small thing perhaps, but it was making his heart ache.

He got up and started to write some letters. The first was to his mother, to be delivered if he didn't return and the second was to Lucy. He considered for a moment and decided he would write to Tom, too, wondering where he was and what he was doing now. He would take a short leave next time he was free and visit Lucy. Perhaps they'd go to the cinema…

Artie stood looking out over the land, frowning as he thought of the work he must plan. These days he was so bone tired when he got to bed that he didn't always feel like making love to his wife. He hoped she understood. As if his thoughts had summoned her, she was there at his side, looking up at him, her eyes seeking his, understanding and loving.

'Don't worry so much, love,' she told him and squeezed his arm. 'It doesn't matter if we're a day late with the hoeing or whatever. Maybe you should let some of the fields lie fallow next year… or put the top field down to grass. We could have more stock grazing and cut down on the arable – make it a bit easier on yourself.' Stock was easier than all the work involved in planting and cropping, though still a daily chore.

'Dad has always liked to have these fields planted with wheat or root crops – they are some of his best land,' he objected. 'Tom gets good crops when he's here from the heavy land.'

'But you like the Fen best,' she said. 'We could rear more bullocks then – and have a few more cows. It is something Frances and I can do... and George too. He will help when he gets home from school. He is learning fast and Henriette loves him. She knows he likes her and gives her milk easily. He tells her she is a right pretty girl.' Jeanie laughed and hugged his arm. 'You are this farm's future,' Jeanie said, smiling up at him. 'You need to understand that and make your own decisions.'

'Yes, I know,' he said and put his arms about her, looking down at her beautiful face, her red hair aflame in the warm June sunshine. 'I know what I must do – and I can, because I've got you. Whatever problems we have, I know you will be there beside me.'

'Yes, I shall,' she promised, looking up at him with love. 'We'll do it together, Artie.'

He laughed, suddenly feeling gloriously free and happy. What a fool he'd been to hanker after a different life, one of excitement and danger. With Jeanie by his side, he'd already got everything he could ever want or need.

ABOUT THE AUTHOR

Rosie Clarke is a #1 bestselling saga writer whose most recent books include *The Mulberry Lane* series. She has written over 100 novels under different pseudonyms and is a RNA Award winner. She lives in Cambridgeshire.

Sign up to Rosie Clarke's mailing list for news, competitions and updates on future books.

Visit Rosie's website: https://www.rosieclarke.co.uk/

Follow Rosie on social media here:

 twitter.com/AnneHerries

ALSO BY ROSIE CLARKE

Welcome to Harpers Emporium Series

The Shop Girls of Harpers

Love and Marriage at Harpers

Rainy Days for the Harpers Girls

Harpers Heroes

Wartime Blues for the Harpers Girls

Victory Bells For The Harpers Girls

Changing Times at Harpers

The Mulberry Lane Series

A Reunion at Mulberry Lane

Stormy Days On Mulberry Lane

A New Dawn Over Mulberry Lane

Life and Love at Mulberry Lane

Blackberry Farm Series

War Clouds Over Blackberry Farm

Heartache at Blackberry Farm

Love and Duty at Blackberry Farm

Standalone's

Nellie's Heartbreak

A Mother's Shame

A Sister's Destiny

Boldwood

Boldwood Books is an award-winning fiction publishing company seeking out the best stories from around the world.

Find out more at www.boldwoodbooks.com

Join our reader community for brilliant books, competitions and offers!

Follow us
@BoldwoodBooks
@TheBoldBookClub

Sign up to our weekly
deals newsletter

https://bit.ly/BoldwoodBNewsletter

Sixpence Stories

Introducing Sixpence Stories!

Discover page-turning
historical novels from your
favourite authors, meet new
friends and be transported
back in time.

Join our book club
Facebook group

https://bit.ly/SixpenceGroup

Sign up to our
newsletter

https://bit.ly/SixpenceNews

Printed in Great Britain
by Amazon

37877449R00175